Moth Dust

BRIDGET BETH COLLINS

ISBN: 9798866293568

For little me

CONTENTS

"The desire of the moth for the star,
Of the night for the morrow,
The devotion to something afar
From the sphere of our sorrow,"
~Shelley

PROLOGUE

pectral clouds ripped across the sky, and lightning shattered the forest on the night the moths attacked. In the large, looming Nuthatch Estate, shadows crept out of their hidden places in menacing shapes. Little Henry Nuthatch imagined they were reaching for his secret.

"Why is this happening?!" Henry's mother screamed. Moths swarmed around her as she frantically grabbed dresses dripping in beads and jewels and threw them into her dark leather trunk. Moths tore at the curtains on her canopy bed and had already eaten most of her quilt.

"I didn't do anything!" Henry cried. He swatted at moths with his tiny hands. How could he have known that taking one cocoon from the forest would cause the moths to come to their home?

"They've eaten every last scrap of cloth in the mill," Henry's father said as he rushed into the room. "We're ruined." He went to his drawers, and grabbed a small sack, and handed it to Henry. "Take these to your room and hide." Henry looked inside the sack. It was full of mothballs. Their strong scent tickled his nose. He looked up, stunned, as his mother was playing tug-of-war with a battalion of fluttering wings. "No! No! NO! It's my favorite dress!" She pulled on a hem embroidered with pink roses and golden leaves, intricately sewn with metallic thread. The moths chewed at the collar and sleeves. When Henry's

mother finally wrestled it away, it was riddled with holes. She sank to the floor and sobbed.

"Go NOW!" His father barked.

Henry ran down the hallway to his room, chased by darting moths. He slipped in through his door and slammed it shut. He could hear tiny thuds against the door on the other side. He had to think quickly.

Henry's room was a haphazard menagerie of all his forest finds. Cages piled on top of each other were filled with animals who had been injured or abandoned. He quickly set about undoing all of their fasteners, setting them free. Tiny birds, lizards, a warty toad—his hands shook as he undid the last one. A chipmunk, snuggled up in a sawdust nest on his desk, stirred as he began rifling through his belongings. "Where did I put it? Where did I…" He ran to the jars lined up against the window. A cluster of snails eating lettuce escaped into their shells as he jostled their home.

A large, spindly purple and black spider lived in a brilliant web strung across his entire window. She was his favorite pet of all. She swung down on her string to get a better look at what he was up to. "The cocoon! Where is the cocoon!?" he pleaded.

The spider swung from her web like an acrobat and did an aerial flip onto the sill.

"Show off." Henry rolled his eyes. "Are you going to help me or not?" His stress showed in the tight wrinkles on his forehead.

She walked slowly and delicately, moving her abdomen-like hips from side to side. With a lazy point with one arm, she showed Henry what he was looking for. The cocoon was tucked between the snail jar and the window.

"Found it!" He said, as he picked it up.

The spider threw her arms up in a huff.

"Oh, Sorry," Henry picked her up, kissed her head, and placed her back in her web. "Thank you for helping me."

She puffed up her chest and stared at him with big, loving, mirrored eyes.

The golden cocoon practically glowed in the moonlight. "What's so special about you?" He turned it over and over in his hand.

Henry was going to run to the forest and put the cocoon back in the crevice where he'd found it. Or, better yet, hand it right to the moths and let them carry it off.

But he let curiosity get the better of him.

He held his breath and pulled the ends of the cocoon apart. The delicate silk tore.

"What in the…" Henry's face lit up at what he saw. His midnight brown eyes looked like galaxies, reflecting the shimmers that glowed up at him. He unfogged his glasses, furiously trying to unfog his mind as well. He lived in the real world; there was no magic or mystery about his daily life. Everything was practical and sensible. Scientific. But the fantastical thing he saw in the cocoon was real. Henry was so in shock that, like with most wondrous things we see in our youth, he would later wonder if he'd only imagined it, and then as he aged, he would forget about it entirely.

The thuds at the door got louder. Soon it was like the sound of popcorn, then what sounded like all the moths in unison banging against the door. But Henry did not hear them. He was so entranced by what he'd found in the cocoon that he did not see the moths swarming on the other side of his window, diving and hitting the glass.

But the spider saw. She licked her lips and sat perfectly still, watching and waiting.

All Henry could remember of that night was the door opening and the entire room becoming so thick with moths that he felt like he was moving through a cloud to get away. Eyes shut tight, he curled up on the floor and covered his head with his arms. He was so paralyzed with fear that he barely noticed as he was scooped up by his father's arms and carried to their carriage.

And the spider watched from her window, tears in her eyes, as they fled their estate with no plans to ever return.

1

DUST

Moths circle starlight and flutter at flames. They whisper sweet nothings into night flowers lit up by the silver moon. And deep in an ancient forest, still brimming with the old magic the world used to know, they are drawn to the light of a little girl…

Flora searched for cocoons in shafts of light piercing down through the forest canopy. Dust motes sparkled like gilded confetti all around her, lighting up strands of her hair and eyelashes. As she leaned over the gargantuan roots of a moss-laden tree, she spotted a gossamer fluff glinting in the shadows. She squealed, "Gotcha!" and snatched its silvery threads out of the bark. She held her acquisition up to the light to inspect it, making sure there was no caterpillar or moth still inside. This one was perfect.

"Like finding golden treasure," she said with a smirk.

Flora plopped the cocoon into the deep pockets of her lacy white dress and scaled up the rough bark of the tree with her bare feet. Little fronds of silken green curled around her toes, swollen from last night's rain. She breathed in deeply, smelling the earth's scent after a stormy night. Fresh, growing things met her nostrils. She always felt like it was the scent of the color green.

The gnarled trees of Silkwood Forest wove together like the patterns in her grandmother's weaving, and Flora knew them all

by heart. She stepped in the invisible footholds only her callused, padded feet knew. She held onto branches that had grown strong from her dangling through the years. Even as a toddler, she had tiptoed along their ridges, and as she'd grown, the trees still seemed to cradle her as she made her way through them. She climbed like a caterpillar into a mass of emerald leaves and poked her head up out of the canopy to let her freckles get a drink of sun. Twigs and moss stuck out from her tangle of wild brown hair. She pushed it out of her face and surveyed the treetops laid out before her like a tumbled quilt. Silkwood grew up from a leagues-long ravine that cut through the earth in a jagged slash. From where she was, she could see the giant weeping cherry tree in the center of the forest, the sparkling creek running past her cottage far in the distance, and closer than she'd realized, the smokestack of the Nuthatch textile mill loomed high above the tree line. A stream of smoke rose from its stones like a spirit escaping into the clouds.

That's strange, Flora thought. *Why would smoke be coming out of the stack?*

Years ago, moths destroyed most of what was inside the mill. They chewed up every last bit of its cloth in one night. The owner and his family had to shut down the business and move away. There were rumors that the moths had taken revenge for their cocoons being stolen for making silk. Most of the people who lived in the village of Silkwood were terrified of the moths in the forest because of it. They stayed away from the dark, thick chasm that was her home. The townsfolk thought moths were creepy, crawly, insidious little things that flew into your face at night when you walked near a light. But *they* didn't live among the trees like Flora did and never ventured near enough to really know the creatures inside.

"Those people are ridiculous," Flora said, rolling her eyes.

Flora *loved* the moths in her forest, flitting about like specks of sunlight on the wing, and she thought their caterpillars could weave magic. Flora's grandmother had taught her all about them and how they really had nothing to fear.

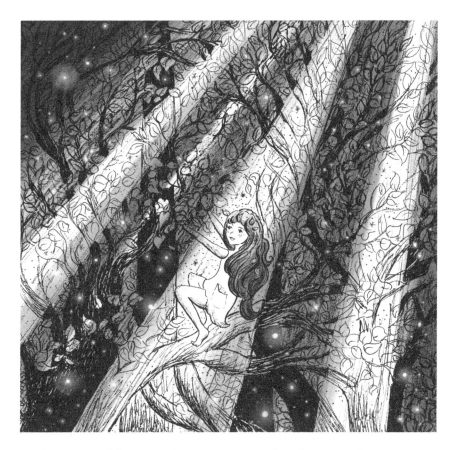

"How could anyone hate creatures that dance in the moonlight, and seek the stars, and make silk?" she said as she scanned the nearby branches for one of their tiny children, "that they weave into cocoons that grow them sparkly wings!" Moths were a marvel to her, and nobody could convince her otherwise.

Sometimes Flora felt like a moth herself…misunderstood by those outside her forest world, hiding inside the greenery and shadows so she could be who she wanted to be. Sometimes she even preferred the dark, as if she could see more clearly in contrast. She squinted her eyes, looking for a little friend who was doing just that. She zeroed in on a leaf lit up by the sun. There was a razor-sharp shadow of a caterpillar crawling on the back of it.

"I see you!" She laughed.

But someone else had seen the caterpillar too. A loud hiss came from across the canopy. Flora looked up and met eyes with one of Silkwood's fiercest predators: the barn owl. His white chest stood in ghostly contrast against the green foliage. He clicked his beak, ready to plunge for the tasty morsel.

"Oh no, please don't!" Flora pleaded. "Shouldn't you be in your hollow? It's not even nighttime!"

As if in defiant response, the barn owl flapped his speckled wings and hissed again.

"I won't let you have him!" Flora knew that large birds of prey were nothing to be trifled with. They could peck your eyes or haul small animals off into the sky and drop them to painful deaths. And *she* was very small.

She weighed the thought in her mind, but looked to the caterpillar and her heart twinged. She *had* to save it. She crawled as far as she could on her branch and held tight. She reached out her fingers and grazed the leaf the caterpillar was on.

The barn owl flew up into the sky and circled above her.

"For having a heart-shaped face, you have very little heart!" She grimaced, stretching her arm further. She furiously batted at the leaves nearby to try to shake the caterpillar away from sight.

But she couldn't reach, no matter how hard she tried. She would have to jump. She scaled back a little to get a better grip, then carefully stood like a tight rope walker on the branch. She took a deep breath.

"One, two…"

The owl shrieked. Then dove straight for her…

"Three!" She jumped.

She knew it was silly as she soared through the air. Within the seconds it took to get to the clump of leaves in the other tree, Flora thought, *whoops!* And then crashed into a mess of branches.

She held onto whatever her tiny hands could grasp and swung like a pendulum high above the forest floor.

In the distance, Flora heard laughing. It started with a giggle and then rolled into a stout barrel laugh. It sounded like a boy. She scanned the branches from where it had come. A glint of sunlight glimmered between the branches. Glass from a window reflected the sun. When she finally spotted the open window, she saw a head of auburn hair quickly duck out of sight. Flora squinted, wondering who it might be. Was he laughing at her? She did look a sight, dangling from the treetops like a silkworm. But she shrugged. She had more important things to worry about.

She scrambled her way up to where the caterpillar was and searched frantically. The owl had fluttered up out of range during the confusion, then landed in a nearby tree.

"Where did you go?" Flora huffed, then said, "Aha!" She plucked the fuzzy caterpillar out from under a leaf. He was black on both ends and orange in the middle.

"A woolly bear!" She said, delighted. She dangled him for the owl to see. "Better luck next time!"

The owl cocked its head and rolled its shoulders in an indifferent sort of shrug, then flew off toward his home.

"Maybe you'll find a big juicy rat tonight!" Flora laughed.

Flora let the caterpillar crawl up onto the tip of her finger. She counted the sections of his body that had orange fur. The woolly bear's orange segments told how many months of winter could be expected each year.

"Woolly bear, orange and black, winter's length is on his back," Flora recited. "Only two!? That will be a short winter. Good. I love an early spring!" She pulled a leather-bound book and a quill from her pocket. The pages in the book were filled with all her vivid drawings and descriptions of the moths and

caterpillars she found in Silkwood. There were pressed petals of the flowers they liked to drink from and the little poems she'd made about each moth. She found the page with the Woolly Bear Caterpillar and its orange moth, The Isabella Tiger. She wrote down *1907, two months of winter* in the margin, then she leafed through the pages to look at all her other finds.

Moths weren't just drab brown and grey. Many of the moths who landed in her hair and tickled her fingers in the forest were as shimmery as the light reflected on the creek. They came in all sorts of colors and patterns too: red polka dots, blue and black stripes, brilliant as a sunset, green with pink moons, dark ones with starry wings, tiny furry puff balls with feathery antennae… even ones that seemed ordinary sometimes had colorful underwings, like brightly colored slips under their skirts. Flora adored them all.

But there was one moth Flora was afraid of: The Black Witch Moth. Everyone knew the old warning,

"When the large dark wings of the Witch Moth fall,
A death or murder has come to call."

Flora had heard tales of the large black and purple wings, big as a bat, flying through people's doorways right before some dire thing happened. A bad flu, a pet dying, or a thunderstorm during market day. Any time there was some gossip about someone seeing a Witch Moth the whole town would lose their minds with worry. Sightings had become more and more frequent recently. Families would bundle up their elderly and sequester them in their beds when a Witch Moth was seen, praying death wouldn't come to their home that night. It made Flora nervous about the thing she feared the most: Gran dying. Her grandmother was the only family she had. It would shake up her whole world to lose her.

Just thinking about the Witch Moth gave Flora a chill on her neck and a creepy feeling that someone was watching her. She looked back toward the Nuthatch mill and shivered.

"Um…no, thank you…yech!" She bounded down her branch until its end began to bow and jumped onto the next tree's arm stretched out for her. Tree to tree, she ran down the high, mossy avenues of her forest. When she reached a clearing, she swung down over a gully with a vine. She lost her grip near the ground and swore, "Ragwort!" as she tumbled into a froth of flowers. (Her Gran always used the names of weeds to swear, and Flora had taken up the talent.)

Flora had landed in her favorite meadow. Tall purple foxgloves swayed in the cool air, buttercups glowed from the shadows of lacy bracken, and tiny blue forget-me-nots dotted the bases of the towering trees. She somersaulted and lay flat in a patch of white star flowers, the wind knocked out of her. When she could breathe again, she laughed, pretending to do the backstroke through a constellation.

The flowers she swam in had tiny shoots poking out of their backs, like the tail of a shooting star. Flora took one and bit off the end of the little tail and drank its nectar. It had the most delicious taste.

"It fills my whole body with light!" she sang. She lay there, drinking from the stars and letting sunlight pour over her as it peeked through the leaves and made patterns like rivulets of water through her closed eyelids. "This must be what magic feels like," she said, breathing it in.

At the end of the meadow stood the large, weeping cherry tree. In spring, its petals dropped down into the spring that bubbled right up out of the cherry tree's roots and flowed through the forest past her thatch roofed cottage like a line of pink ribbon. But in late summer, the tree was a green mass of leaves, dangling down to the ground like a large tent. Flora got up and waded through the flowers until she came to the tree. She smiled, knowing what was inside. She crawled up under the branches and lifted her face to see the magic within.

There were hundreds of moths fluttering around the trunk, swooping in and out of the weeping branches, and darting into holes. And caterpillars! All different sizes, some furry, some striped, and some with long spiky-looking horns. The cherry tree was Flora's favorite spot for finding cocoons. She bounded and splashed into the warm spring water to look in all the crags of the tree for her golden treasure.

"There must be fairy windows in the nooks of this tree," Flora said dreamily as she plucked cocoons from under mosses draped over the bark. She pulled another bit back and found a peculiar sight. The smallest little heart was carved in the tree, with the initials L and H inside. It was barely the size of her pinky fingernail.

"How on earth?" Flora looked in disbelief. She laughed and shrugged. "L and H. Hmmmm. Lucy and Horace." She scrunched up her nose. "Leonard and Hetty…no…Lilly and Harry!" She giggled. "Well, whoever they were, they had really tiny handwriting!" She lowered the curtain of moss and shrugged, thinking there were lots of strange things in her forest, and this was just another of them.

Flora continued her search for cocoons, only picking the ones she thought were prettiest. Each cocoon was as unique as the moths themselves; some were smooth and white, some looked like oval golden cages, some faintest green, some silvery, some brown and bundled up inside a leaf.

Flora never stopped to wonder if her spoils would be noticed. She only ever felt safe in her forest. Being hemmed in by its leaf-stained light was as real and comforting as love. That day, she found so many cocoons that she could barely hold them all. When it was time to return home, she streaked like a bright comet through the ferns, pockets filled to the brim with golden fluff and star flowers trailing from her hair.

2

FAIRIES

When the evening air cooled and the sky turned a violet haze of lost sun, Flora swung in her hammock over the stream next to her cottage. She'd hung it among strings of brightly colored paper lanterns and looked up into them as moths fluttered in and around them, attracted to their light. Watermelon vines and herby flowers from the vegetable patch nestled around her and brimmed over the stream.

Flora's grandmother Maja hobbled out of their home, a simple stone cottage with a thatched roof and a fat turret that looked like a witch's hat, and looked at the sight of her little granddaughter cuddled in her hammock. Her high cheeks wrinkled into shimmering creases as she smiled at her. She scooped up the cocoons Flora had found and kissed her on her forehead. "You found so many for me today, my little chenille." Flora always thought it was funny that her Gran called her that as a term of endearment. She had a chenille bedspread and it looked like a big birthday cake covered in puffy frosting lines. But nothing about her Gran was particularly normal.

Gran sat down at her spinning wheel next to the stream near Flora. She examined the cocoons with her big pink owl-eye glasses. She wore a billowy white nightgown covered in strands of fuzzy yarn and tufts of lace. It plumped up over her hunchback, and her white hair frizzed up into wisps like antennae. She reminded Flora of one of the large fuzzy white silk moths with big owl eye circles on their wings she'd find in the forest.

Gran had a fire going in the stones of the creek shore, and a large pot bubbled with water on top of it. She threw the cocoons into the water to soften them, and gently coaxed a shiny strand of silk from each one to pull into her spinning wheel. Each cocoon was made from one long strand of silk that could stretch across the whole forest.

Gran was almost always perched in the round stones of the stream bed to do her spinning or weaving. The spring that came from the cherry tree was filled with these round, unremarkable stones. But they had a secret inside. Flora picked a couple of them up from under her hammock and cracked them together as hard as she could. One of the stones broke open into two jagged halves. The insides were hollow and lined with crystals of the faintest purple color, like the sky above her. They glittered in the lantern light, reflecting pricks of light on Flora's face. "That never gets old," Flora sighed. "Why are they called geodes?"

"It means earth-like," Gran said, not looking up.

"Geo…Oh! Of course!" Flora whipped out her moth book and leafed through its pages. "Like the geometer moth!" She came to a page with a green moth and a tiny, matching green caterpillar. "Here it is…

"Inch worm, Inch worm,
How much you are worth,
inching across the leaves,
Measuring the earth."

"He inches his way across your finger by putting his head to his tail over and over." Flora snickered. "It looks like he's sniffing his butt."

21

"Flora…" Gran warned. But she stifled a giggle too.

Flora touched her drawing of the green moth. "Imagine having emerald wings," she murmured, laying back into her hammock. She looked up and saw the shadow of a moth in one of the paper lanterns nearby. She reached in and pulled it out.

They were always getting stuck inside, drawn to the flame. She gently touched its golden wing, and a trail of crystalline powder stuck to her fingertip. "They're as sparkly as geodes, too."

"Did you know that moth dust actually *is* crystals?" Gran asked.

"Really?" Flora grinned. "Do you think if I had a bunch of moth dust I could get it to grow on a string the way I can with sugar crystals?"

"I don't know where you would get enough moth dust for that," Gran chuckled, "but it does sound like a marvelous idea."

Flora looked out over the spring where the moonlight kissed it. Flecks of light glistened on the water, flickering on and off in a dance only they knew. Dark leaves from a bower of maple branches nearly brushed the surface, as if asking for a touch of the reflected light. Flora searched the shadows, yearning for a touch of magic just like the branches over the creek. She wished with all her heart that she could be as glimmering and lovely as the light reflected on the water. Oh, to have wings, a sparkling dress, or even a jeweled crown with such beauty. "I love shimmery things," she sighed. "The way the light dances off of the spring, and crystals…and cocoons! I wish I could make a dress just as sparkly."

Gran looked up and stopped her spinning. "Flora, you shine just like those shimmers."

Flora looked down quizzically at her reflection in the water. Two glimmering sapphires in a mass of matted shadows peered back at her. Her hair was a tangled nest of brown waves. A few wisps of honey streaks framed her face, unraveling down to golden tips that brushed nearly to her waist. She was a wild little thing…covered in green and brown smudges, sunburn, and scraped skin. Her shoulders and face freckled as a foxglove. A creature of the forest, through and through.

She tried to smooth down her wild hair. She scrunched up her face at herself.

"It's true," Gran said. "Beautiful, inside and out. But what really matters is being like one of those geodes in the spring. How you sparkle on the inside."

Flora smiled shyly.

Gran went back to her spinning, quietly humming strange words to her fabric. Gran would often weave into the night, her hunched back toiling over her work, and Flora would drift off to sleep, lulled by the sound of Gran's soft enchantments mixed with the shush shush of her loom shuttles. Flora had grown up knowing that her Gran used magic, but had never bothered to ask more about it. It was just a truth that was as normal as breathing. She'd never bothered to wonder why the twinkle in her Gran's eye looked so much like the stars winking in the evening light. Why that same twinkle could magically end up on one of the blankets she weaved.

"Gran… those words… what are they?"

Gran looked up sneakily. "Oh, I like to coax nature into helping me a little bit while I create my fabric."

Flora frowned. "But…how?"

Gran spoke softly, lyrically, "I just harness the light of the moon, the rivulets in water, the colors of the meadow."

Flora sat up, excited. "I've seen you do it with dye! The colors grow brighter in cloth when you're whispering to it."

Gran smiled. "True. But I have only a twinkling of the light that can be harnessed. I can make colors a little brighter, steal a little purple from a violet, the shimmer from a star… but it is nothing compared to what I think you could do."

"Me?"

"You're like a moth attracted to the light," Gran said. "You listen to the soft singing of mottled sunlight, you delight in the shimmer of silk. Sometimes I see a glow around you as you gather your star flowers."

"A glow?"

"Around those who have no love for living things, no respect for creatures small and meek, there is a haze of prickly darkness. Animals can see it. It looms around some humans' heads and leaks out of their fingertips. But those who are kind and gentle have a halo of light. Sometimes it's colorful, like a rainbow iris sparkling in the sun, and sometimes it's dazzling, like mica shimmering across a granite slab."

"Oh!" Flora was entranced by the idea of light coming off of herself and looked at her hands to see if she could see it too.

Gran looked at Flora with glimmering eyes. "If you were to try to harness those shimmers you love so much, I'm sure it would be the brightest Silkwood has ever seen."

Flora beamed. She thought of her love for all things sparkly. "Like a moth attracted to light..." she repeated. She looked up into the lanterns, watching moths get too close to the candles within. Frantic to find light, they would sometimes crisp their wings. It scared her a little, but at the same time, it enthralled her.

"Do you want to know why moths flutter up into the lanterns in search of light?" Gran looked at Flora over her pink glasses. She looked like she was trying to decide if she should tell her something.

"Why?"

Gran sighed, then leaned back in her chair and patted her lap. "Come here, and I will tell you."

Flora jumped out of the hammock. She loved snuggling up with Gran to hear her stories. She nuzzled into her soft night gown and held one of her papery, wrinkled hands in hers. She liked comparing their freckles. Flora's were like tiny pin pricks making constellations down her tan arms, and Gran's large freckles touched to form big reddish speckles across her porcelain skin, almost covering her entire weathered frame.

"Okay, I'm ready." Flora said. "Why do moths search for light?"

"Because they used to be fairies."

"Gran! Don't be ridiculous."

"It's true!" Gran snorted.

Flora raised her eyebrows, not quite believing, but wanting to.

"The ones in Silkwood were," She nodded. "There is an emerald spot, deep in the forest, where great big maple trees are draped in moss, a stream trickles with glittering mist, and tiny white mushrooms dot their way up trees to where hidden doorways wait."

Flora nestled in closer.

"And through those doors lived creatures with wings as sparkly as the moth wings you love so much."

"Oh! That would be so lovely!"

"They were a regal, powerful race called the Giltiri: The Golden Ones. And they had a special kind of magic that came from the dust on their wings. It made a light that let them weave the most beautiful silken cloth," she said, looking into the distance as if remembering.

"Like cocoons?" Flora asked.

"Yes, just like the silk from cocoons. And it was magical. With talismans of protection, cloaks of invisibility, sweaters with special runes, even magic carpets! They used to share their magic with the people who lived near the forest."

Flora's eyes widened. Gran made carpets and cloaks! "Did they share it with you?"

Gran smiled and raised one eyebrow.

Flora gave her a look that said she knew Gran was just telling her a fairy tale. But then, again, Gran seemed so sincere. Flora fiddled with the ring of diamonds on Gran's finger. "What happened to the moth fairies?"

"An evil spider caught them in her web and stole their magic."

"What? No!"

"She was so full of jealousy she could barely fit it all inside her tiny body. Magical, sparkling, miracle dust? She wanted it. She craved it so deeply that she shriveled at the pain. She caught the moth fairies in her web and took their wings. Then the spider spun herself a cocoon with spider silk and sprinkled the magic dust on herself so she could become a Moth Fairy."

Flora gasped.

"Can you guess which moth she became?"

Flora thought for a moment. What was the most frightening moth in Silkwood? One that could have once been a spider?

"The Witch Moth?!"

"Yes. And when she got her magic power, she turned the Giltiri into plain moths."

"That's terrible!" Flora bit her lip. "Why can't they just turn themselves back with their magic?"

"Their magic light was gone. Oh, they could use a little here and there, but it was nothing compared to what they had before. And they were so confused, being moths. So they are always looking in lanterns and in the stars, searching, searching for their lost light."

"Will they ever get it back?" Flora's eyes welled with tears.

"Don't worry, Flora," Gran whispered under an arched brow. She looked around, as if to see if anyone was listening. "They say ashes to ashes and dust to dust... But moth dust is not ruled by the normal laws of nature. Did you know that caterpillars actually die inside their cocoons and then come back to life completely remade?"

"Oooh! No!"

"A great sacrifice is required to create one of the most magical things in nature."

"Wings!" Flora said in awe.

"But before the Witch Moth turned the Giltiri into moths, one of them escaped. She was weak and without her full strength from the attack, but she had a secret that may be able to return their light."

"What was it?!"

Gran giggled, "If I told you that, it wouldn't be a secret!" She tickled Flora.

Flora scoffed and jumped off of Gran's lap with her hands on her hips. "Fine, don't tell me! Maybe I'll figure it out for myself!" She tried to keep a straight face but ended up giggling as she retreated to her hammock to swing. She gazed up into the forest, searching for any glimmer that might be the fairies' light. Gran was always such a good storyteller, weaving tales as beautifully as her cloth, but something about this story rang true for her. Some hidden force pulled her into it and tingled her imagination.

"There!" Gran said, "All finished." She hobbled over to Flora. Gran handed a large bundle of golden thread to her. "I made this for you with all the cocoons you've found in the forest this summer."

"SILK!" Flora brushed it against her face. Gran had made it nice and fuzzy, spinning the strands over and over to get the yarn much thicker than usual. Up close, she could see silver and white strands threading through the gold like stardust. "Oh, thank you, thank you!" she sang, grabbing Gran and hugging her frail body as tightly as she could.

Gran took Flora's face in her hands. "Flora, you are nonpareil, without equal." Then her face grew sad, and Flora could almost sense the hollow darkness inside Gran's chest as she uttered her next words. "There is great darkness in this world, Flora. Never let anyone take your light."

3

MARKET DAY

he next morning, Flora awoke with a heart exploding with excitement. It was market day. Flora could not wait to show off her latest concoction. She burst out of bed and threw on her new dress, which she had just finished making herself. It was a soft gray and brown cotton, ruffled thing with long white wisps of bunny fur coming out of the collar. She had caught the long-furred Angora bunnies in the forest and trimmed their long fur herself. It hadn't been hard. The bunnies always came right to her when she produced some parsnips from Gran's vegetable patch. She slipped on some light-as-air blue silk stockings Gran had dyed with indigo and squealed. She twirled, looking at herself in her round rose bramble carved mirror.

"Flora, you will be the talk of the town!" She said to herself with a wink.

She really *would* be the talk of the town. She knew that perhaps it wasn't what was in style at the moment, but she didn't care. She tried to take the double glances from strangers as curiosity and marvel more than confusion and surprise. She might feel a little strange once she was in front of other people, but alone in front of her mirror, she felt as lovely as a fluffy seed pod.

The forest came through in all of Flora's creations; a wispy knit sweater like a spider's web, a chunky scarf like a fox's tail, a geometric patterned dress sewn from various fabrics to look like a moth wing, or a whole meadow of silk ribbon flowers and embroidered fronds scattered up her tights.

Flora had figured out how to do all of the intricate knots and loops in her embroidery and knitting to create fantastic creations. Her grandmother had a book of riddles, and Flora felt like they were much the same. The butterfly stitch only looked like a bunch of lines at first, but if you could think ahead and get your loops in all the right places, it ended up with wings. Flora loved this kind of enigma: you never know what might be hidden inside of something ordinary.

Flora bound down the rickety steps of their cottage, led by the scent of toast. She ducked under the dried herbs and flowers strung from the rafters and practically fell into the breakfast nook lined with plush pillows. Gran had just made fresh gooseberry and honey juice and there were blue and speckled hard-boiled quail eggs to peel. Morning light poured in through the stained-glass windows, lighting up the steam rising from Gran's earl gray tea and casting colorful shadows across the table. Everything smelled delicious.

"I need you to help load the wagon with carpets and help set up the stall, then you can flitter off to your corners of the market. Okay, dear?" Gran dolloped her plate with cinnamon and mint cream and brandished a shiny persimmon. Flora snatched it out of her hand and took a juicy bite.

"Can I have some money?" she asked with her mouth full.

Gran's eyes twinkled as she pulled a coin purse from her pocket. "Don't spend it all on candy this time, Flora. The vendors give you enough for free as it is."

"I won't! I want to find some new treasure today. I won't know what it is until I find it!"

Gran's carpets and cloth were a kaleidoscope of color and pattern. Flora lay amidst them in the cart as it swayed with the tug and pull of her imagination. Her world was laced with the sparkling designs her grandmother weaved. Crescent moons, tree branches, delicate flowers in bright colored cloth—each was a detailed constellation of her Gran's artistry. Her weaving was an art so fine and detailed that the townsfolk said her patterns must have been created with some kind of magic. *Little did they know*, Flora thought. Many feared it, but that didn't keep Gran from carting it into town for the market. There were enough people who were willing to sneak a look, and most went away with something hidden inside brown paper packaging. "Wear one of her sweaters, and your back will no longer ache!" they'd whisper. She thought it was so silly how the townsfolk could think there was anything frightening about Gran. Life with her was as bright and delightful as a flame. It was the same with the moths. If they could just get to know them…

"Why are the townsfolk so afraid of everything?" Flora asked lazily.

"People are afraid of what they don't understand," Gran said.

"But your cloth…it's beautiful! Why would they hate beautiful things? Why would someone hate color?"

"Aaah," Gran said. "That's a strange mystery about the world. It's similar to how the spider hated the beautiful colors of the moths. There was one in particular I remember she shirked back from…an Emperor Moth with pink wings. They made her furious."

"What do you mean, you remember?" Flora asked.

"Oh I mean in the story…" Gran cleared her throat.

"Oh. You didn't tell me that part…But why? Why did the spider hate color so much? And pink! Who could hate pink?"

"Because it's beautiful. And she couldn't have it for herself." Gran grinned and wrinkled her nose. "Sometimes we begin to hate what we cannot have. That's the dark side of jealousy."

"What do you mean?"

"Well, like the people in the town. After the moth attack on the Nuthatch Mill, they were terrified of the moths. They would put up nets on their windows and keep flames at the edges of town. They put camphor and cotton balls in their drawers, and anything that so much as slightly reminded them of moths was shunned. Even silk!"

"But we have silk!"

"Yes, and I'm not the most welcome sight in town, my dear."

"But people still buy carpets from you."

"Yes, there will always be those who love beauty. Even if it has to be hidden. In fact, sometimes that makes it all the more desirable," She winked.

Flora thought this through. She loved moths because she'd never had any reason to fear them. Sometimes, when she was dancing through her meadow, they would rise up from the grasses and swirl around her. She felt sad for the people in the town—how little they knew about the forest. Then she thought of the spider.

"Spiders make beautiful webs, though," she said. "I've seen them glistening in the morning with hundreds of sparkly dew drops. They look like harps strung between the flowers."

"Aaah…" Gran sighed. "You see, that's the thing about jealousy. It's often born from not seeing one's own beauty. If we see ourselves clearly and accept ourselves for exactly who we are, we can more readily love others."

Flora looked down at her freckled arms. Gran was always telling her how special and beautiful she was. That was what grandmothers were supposed to do, though. Gran lifted Flora's little chin and made her look at her.

"You are beautiful, Flora, and you should know it's true."

"We've got a spot by the fountain!" Flora jumped off the cart and helped Gran set up their tent as quickly as possible. They'd barely put everything in place before she kissed Gran's withered face and was off.

The village of Silkwood was a smorgasbord of cobblestone streets and thatched-roofed buildings. On market day, it was

filled with stalls and tents of every color, with peddlers hawking their wares to the crowds. Every twist and turn through the labyrinth of streets brought on new smells that tickled Flora's nose and sights that would make the most stoic of individuals believe in sorcery. Flora would follow the rush and flow of the crowd and peek into stalls to look at wares and chat with shop owners. Her bright, whimsical musings put a grin on everyone's face. Flora whisked past a troupe of dancers jingling with silver bells, ducked under a table covered in mounds of iced confections, and found herself in a brightly colored candy stall.

Sweets and chocolates were sticking every which way from jars and displayed on golden trays lined with doilies. Cotton candy, gum drops, lollipops, clove syrup, French kisses, root beer extract, peppermint sticks... Flora peered through the glass case at a tray of tiny hard candies with flowers made of sugar inside. *How did they get them inside?* Flora wondered. She took out her coins. She didn't have enough to buy them.

The man behind the counter had an enormous mustache that curled at the ends and wore a brown and white striped apron. He was handling money and speaking with a stout elderly woman with a plain cotton dress and oversized straw hat who was buying cream puffs with chocolate frosting and tiny white pearls on top. Flora's eyes lit up. They looked delectable!

"One of my new favorites!" He said, "I got the idea from the new chef at the Nuthatch Estate. He showed me how to make these round sprinkles out of sugar; he calls them nonpareils. Your grandchildren will love them!"

Flora knew that word. Nonpareil. Her Gran had used it to describe her. *Without equal.*

"Well, they certainly are without equal!" The woman said, "But I can hardly believe the mill has started up again. It feels like yesterday that I was there, working for Mrs. Nuthatch. Though it's been, oh, 30 years."

"Such a tragedy what happened," the man said, putting his hand to his chest. "My father worked at the mill as well. He remembers the attack of the moths... Woke him up in the

servant's sleeping quarters. He says he'll never forget the
screams, people running, doors slamming."

"I was there that night too! I went to the mistress' room to
see what was happening, and there were those disgusting
creatures swarming all around her. It's no wonder she withered
away after it all happened."

Flora was skeptical. She thought of how the moths swirled
around her with delight in the forest, like little specks of light.
She spoke boldly, "That doesn't sound anything like the moths I
know!"

The man and woman turned to look at her. His eyes landed
on her wispy bunny fur collar, and his mustache twitched. The
woman scowled at Flora's wild hair and then took in her blue
tights. She covered a haughty laugh with her hand. Flora was
unfazed.

"Well, hello, Flora," the man said with a big barrel laugh. "I'm not surprised to hear you know some moths. What do they have to say about the attack on the mill?"

Flora shrugged. "Well, I don't actually *know* them… I just… I mean… Why *would* the moths attack the mill? Does anyone know why?"

"Well, I did hear Mrs. Nuthatch ask her little boy, Henry, what he had done. She thought it may have had something to do with the animals he kept, I guess. He was always bringing all manner of creatures into the house. Lord help his doting mother. He was a sight, swatting at moths with those tiny hands. His father gave him a sack of moth balls and told him to hide in his room. I watched him rush down the hallway, and those moths thudded against the door when he slammed it shut."

Flora gasped. "They must have been really angry about something to do that!"

"I always wondered," she said. "He seemed to have a secret, poor sweet boy. I've never seen a more worried, guilty little face. I was amazed when he returned years later."

"But he seems to have gone missing yet again," the man said with a sigh. "Such a mystery, the Nuthatch Estate is. Strange things seem to keep happening there."

"Well, at least it's being used for some good, now. The new head spinner is taking in all those children. Some people are upset about them having to work for her, but I suppose it's better than them being on the streets." She looked at Flora pointedly. "Speaking of which, where is your grandmother, dear?"

"She's selling her woven goods at our stall," Flora said. She twiddled a strand of hair with her fingers.

The woman stood tall and sniffed, "Ah. Of course. *Silk.*" She said the word with disgust. "Well… I suppose your wandering off can't be helped. But I do wish she'd keep a better eye on you, what with talk of the Witch Moth being sighted again. Your grandmother is getting frightfully old now, isn't she?"

"She takes perfectly good care of me!" Flora said, stomping her foot. "And I'm just fine all alone. She lets me roam the forest all day, foraging for her!"

The woman looked Flora over again. "That's obvious," she said.

Flora wanted to argue more, but the woman spoke curtly. "Take your fingers off the glass, dear. You're getting it dirty." She dipped her head to the candy man. "Good day, Horace." She strutted down the path to another stall.

Flora felt suddenly lonely and exposed.

The mustachioed Horace gave Flora a concerned look, then pointed to the flower candies. "Violet and rose flavored," He said.

Flora brightened. "They're beautiful."

Horace wrapped some of the sweets with a music sheet and tied it with string. "They bend the candy while it's hot to get the flower shapes, stretch them thin, and cut the ropes into these little bits. Then you can see the flowers inside, shrunk down." He handed the package to Flora. The music notes going every which way on the paper looked like a packaged song.

"For me?" She beamed.

He stifled a grin, trying to look stern. "Now run along before the other children take notice, and I get requests from all manner of urchins! Shoo!" Flora ran off quickly, but when she looked back at him, he was smiling and shaking his head in awe. She overheard him say to the next customer, "That girl is the silliest sight, but I can't help but adore her,"

Flora had heard that type of sentiment before from other shopkeepers, but she'd also heard just as many rude comments like the woman's. The paradox of opinions befuddled her.

"Oh, I have no intention of leaving, Maja." Flora heard her voice come closer. "Are your carpets as *useful* as they ever were?" The edge of the carpet Flora was wrapped in was lifted as the woman pinched its tassels and examined it. Flora didn't know what she had to fear, but her heart raced.

"That one isn't finished," Gran sniped.

"Ah, I see. I'm just so intrigued by your delightful patterns. This is the symbol for protection, isn't it?…or is it hiding? Don't they all mean something?"

"Not to you, they don't."

"Now, now. I am a weaver, too, am I not? Are you afraid I'll steal something?"

"You've proven yourself countless times on that account. Speaking of which, have you seen my daughter lately?"

Flora flinched.

The woman laughed a fake, breathy laugh. "I think I'd better be off. I've seen everything I needed to see. Thank you for letting me take a peek!" Her voice trailed off.

Flora was shocked. Gran never spoke of her mother. She kept her past hidden from Flora like a shroud of mist. Flora didn't know if her parents had abandoned her or if they were dead. She didn't even know their names. Every time Flora tried to speak of her parents, Gran's expression would turn to stone. Flora assumed there must be so much pain in her memories. She must have locked away so many secrets so she could live every day with her goofy grin and jovial songs. Part of her charm was in how happy she was, despite anything hard that came their way. Even when they were low on forest berries and winter grew cold, even when no one bought any of her wares, she still had open arms for Flora to snuggle and a silvery story to tell. Flora never wanted to shatter that happiness, so she lived with not knowing about her parents. But as she got older, questions burned inside her.

After a space of time, Gran lifted the carpet off of Flora. "Are you all right, little chenille?"

"Who was that?"

"Oh, just a fellow weaver who I don't care to share secrets with." Gran tried to smile, but ended up shaking her head.

Flora scrunched her eyebrows. She was nervous to ask, but she couldn't help it. "Gran, you spoke of your daughter...is my mother alive?"

Gran sighed and sat down on the carpets with Flora. Her ancient body creaked. Sometimes Flora forgot how old her Gran was, she seemed so young at heart. Gran hugged her and tangled her hand up in her hair as she held her head to her shoulder.

Flora looked up. A tear was rolling down Gran's cheek.

Gran spoke in a gentle, quivering voice, "I wanted to wait for as long as I could, but now..." She looked out into the crowd nervously. Flora could tell Gran was trying not to frighten her but was deeply worried about something. "The time has come that I will have to talk to you sooner than later. Let's finish up with the stall and get home. I'll tell you about your mother tonight, all right?"

Flora was elated. "Okay!"

It was getting late, and the drive back to the cottage was long, so Flora folded, swept, and loaded as quickly as she could. She sat in the back of the cart, nervous with excitement, as it rolled down the cobblestones toward the forest. Soon she would know about her mother! Her heart felt like wax melting against the flame of excitement. But as they meandered through feathery branches and over the reverberating road, Flora grew sleepy and lay down on the soft carpets. She looked up through the canopy

43

to the stars as her eyes drooped. There was a purplish star there that flashed. Flora tried to see it again, but the branches covered it. She settled in, and just before falling asleep, she saw a black winged creature flutter overhead.

She murmured in a sleepy stupor, "When the large dark wings of the Witch Moth fall, a death or a murder has come to call."

When they arrived at the cottage, Gran lifted Flora up out of the cart and, hobbling, carried her up the rickety stairs to her bedroom. Flora tried to keep her eyes open. "Gran…I want to know about my mother."

"There's time enough for that, little chenille," she said, tucking her under her covers. "We'll have a nice long chat while we forage tomorrow, okay?" Flora was already asleep.

That night, Flora dreamed of golden wings mixed with the silvery threads of her grandmother's weaving. Leaves and stars thread through each other, forming a swirling, brilliant night sky. She was flying with wings as sparkly as the shimmery ripples of light on the water. She laughed as she flew through flowers as large as trees. But suddenly she was falling. Though she tried, she couldn't catch a current of air. When she got near the ground, she plunged into a sticky elastic mesh that stretched down as it caught her and then buoyed her up into the air. But when she tried to get up…she was stuck.

Flora awoke suddenly. She opened her eyes and glimpsed something moving in the darkness out of her window. She bolted up and searched the shadows. Branches moved in liquid motion against silver clouds. The sugar crystals she'd grown on string glistened in her windowsill, tinkling against each other.

"It was just the breeze moving the branches," she said, trying to convince herself there was nothing to fear. She sunk back into her pillow and tried to smooth her racing mind.

Then abruptly, a large black moth swooped in through the window. Its wings were easily six inches wide and were covered in strange markings and purple chevrons that glinted as it circled over her bed. Flora screamed.

It was the Witch Moth!

4

THE WITCH MOTH

lora threw her blanket over herself as the Witch Moth dove at her head. "Ragwort!" She breathed. Could this be the same Witch Moth from Gran's story? She was certain now that the moth had been following her at the market. She had seen it in the alleyway, and again on their way home. All of her nerves stood on end.

She lay perfectly still until the air under her blanket grew stale, hoping the moth would fly back out the window. She was too terrified to move. All she could hear were the trees swooshing outside her window. Flora wondered how she could know if the moth was gone when moths don't make any sound. Several moments passed before she finally braved a peek.

Flora looked just in time to see the Witch Moth fly out her door and into the hallway… toward Gran's room. If the Witch Moth was there for a murder, Flora couldn't bear for it to be her Gran. Somehow she couldn't be brave for herself, but she *could* be for her.

"Oh no, you DON'T!" Flora punched her bed and fell to the floor in a mess of sheets. She grabbed her pillow so she could swat at the moth and scrambled into the hallway. She quickly wished she had a candle. There were dark wooden beams, jutting every which way, where a moth could easily hide. Flora inched her way down the hall, looking at the walls and ceiling as she went.

"I'm gonna pee if that thing jumps out at me." Flora nervously bit her lip. She could hear voices coming from Gran's room. It was very late for her to be awake, but it wasn't unusual for Gran to talk to herself. She was pretty kooky that way.

"Gran?" Flora knocked on her door. There was no sound. "Gran? Are you okay?" She opened the door slowly, then was startled when she saw a tall, sinuous woman in a deep purple dress with pointed puffed sleeves. Her long fingers were splayed above the fluffy sheets and blankets.

"What are you doing?" Flora asked. "And who *are* you?"

The woman whirled and straightened, her slick silver bun almost touching the ceiling of their tiny cottage. She had high, sharp cheekbones that jutted out beneath violet eyes. Her severe beauty startled Flora, but she found it sticky. It clung like a sweater that didn't fit. A striking necklace with a large amber stone wrapped in silver vines dangled from her neck. The kind with a mosquito or bug inside.

"Oh my dear, sweet girl," she crooned. "My name is Madame Cribellum, and I… I knew your mother." She looked at Flora as though she were a treat she was about to eat.

Flora didn't feel right. For some reason, she didn't trust this woman.

"But it looks as though you're here all alone," Madame Cribellum clicked her tongue and shook her head sadly. "A woman in town let me know about your sad state, so I thought I'd come check on you. Lucky for you, I happen to care for lost children. I will gladly take you with me." She slightly curved her long back in what Flora assumed was a strange curtsy.

Flora frowned. The woman at the candy stall must have blabbed about her. "No," she said firmly. "My grandmother lives here with me. Isn't she right there…?" She rushed over to Gran's pillow and stopped cold. Gran was gone. Flora searched the fluffy bed spread and sheets, but her hopes were dashed… There was nothing but a plump green caterpillar hiding in a little alcove under the pillow. It surprised Flora as it almost secretly crawled onto her hand and inched its way up her sleeve. Flora turned her back toward the woman so she couldn't see because the caterpillar held in its mouth a small piece of paper with words that looked like they had been scribbled by someone having to get away quickly.

To find the light, look for the mother

Flora was in such shock already, and this note confused her even more. *What is this supposed to mean?* She thought. What light? And Gran had never told her anything about her mother. She didn't even know her name. If only she'd been able to talk with Gran that night! But there was no time to think. Where, oh where, was Gran?

"Gran must be downstairs... or maybe she's still weaving by the spring. I'll go look for her..."

"Don't lie to me, girl." Madame Cribellum spit, her demeanor shifting to venom, "There isn't anyone in this house here with you. Come now, grab a few belongings, and we shall leave at once."

Flora panicked. She ran for the door as fast as she could, but cold fingers wrapped around her neck. Madame Cribellum breathed into Flora's ear, "Don't be afraid. Let all your fight drain away from you. That's it." Flora felt a numbness come over her, seeping in through the fingers at her neck.

"Get away from me!" She tried to kick Madame Cribellum, but her limbs felt so heavy. It felt like a magic spell was being put on her, and she was too weak to fight it. Too weak to even think.

"Yes, Madame," Flora said hollowly, in a trance, "I'll come with you. Just... let me go."

"That's a good girl," Madame Cribellum said with pursed lips. "Now hurry up and pack a bag of your things. Be quick about it."

Flora went to her room and grabbed her sewing bag. She threw in her book of moths, knitting needles, some candles, her chenille blanket, and the golden silk her Gran had given her the night she told her about the moth fairies. She put on a brown eyelet dress with deep pockets. Then she put a couple more in her bag like it, white and grey, some tights, and the pretty dress she'd worn to the market. She plucked one of the geodes off her shelf, brown and perfectly round. "To remember our cottage," she said to herself, dropping it into her dress pocket.

As she gathered her belongings, the spell began to wane. "What is going on?" she whispered dazedly to the little caterpillar as it crawled up her sleeve. "This is insane. I'm sure Gran is somewhere. I can't just leave..." She thought about escaping out of her window. But then she thought of the note. She read it again.

"To find the light, look for the mother."

If that woman did know her mother, she might be able to get some information from her. Should she try her luck? There was no time to think!

"I haven't got all night!" Madame Cribellum startled Flora from her bedroom doorway. Everything was happening too quickly. Flora fought back tears as she felt her body move without her brain catching up.

As Madame Cribellum marched Flora out the round front door of her cottage, she eyed Flora's sewing bag slung over her shoulder. "Aah, yes. I've seen this symbol on your grandmother's carpets," she said, eyeing the geometric star on the side of the bag. "The symbol for protection. I suppose her magic isn't as potent as it once was."

Flora suddenly recognized the woman's sweet, cloying voice. She had used almost the same words when she had listened to her that day...she was the woman from the market! Gran had *hidden* Flora from this woman. She couldn't go with her!

Madame Cribellum continued, "It will be good for the townsfolk to have woven goods that aren't tainted by this superstitious nonsense."

Superstitious nonsense? Flora fumed. Just as Madame Cribellum was about to grab her hand to help her into the carriage, Flora made a dash for it. Madame Cribellum tried to snatch her, but Flora was too fast. She ran as fast as she could up the path and dove down into the shadows around the side of the cottage. Keeping low, she scrambled through tall sunflowers and tangled tomatoes in Gran's vegetable patch and stumbled over the geodes on the shore.

"Now Flora," she heard Madame Cribellum say, her voice closer than she expected, "where do you think you're going? You can't live in the forest, and the townsfolk will want you safe and sound. I would hate to have to conduct a search for you..."

Flora knew she would make too much noise if she splashed through the creek, but there was a log tree that had fallen across to the other side she knew she could use as a bridge. Ferns whipped her cheeks as she ran as fast as she could through the underbrush. She only had a little way to go before she reached the log.

Flora thought frantically. She would escape into the deep parts of Silkwood and live off berries and mushrooms. She knew Gran would be back. All she had to do was wait for her. If she could get across the creek, she could climb a tree and use the branches in the canopy to escape. Nobody would be able to find her because nobody knew the woods like Flora did.

She made it to the log and slowed down. She would have to scale it carefully; it was slick with moss. She took off her shoes and dipped her toes into the plush green. She'd made this type of trek plenty of times, but if she fell in, she'd make a splash, and she didn't want the woman to hear. She walked slowly, glancing back. She was thankful for the darkness. There was no one following her. And there was no sound but the creek. She'd gotten away with it!

When she turned back, she walked into a clinging spider web that stretched across her face. She winced, letting out the slightest whimper. She spit and clawed the web off of her face and out of her hair. Usually she'd check her hair to find the spider, but there was no time, and she needed to tread carefully. She kept her gaze down at her feet. The creek swirled below her, but she was near the shore on the other side. Yellow water irises stood against the dark like candles aflame. She just had to get to their safety… A little further…Finally, she reached the end of the log and looked up.

Madame Cribellum stood there, ready for her.

"No!" Flora cried.

Madame Cribellum reached out, trying to grab her, but Flora jumped back. She turned and ran as fast as she could back down the log. She couldn't believe her balance as she plunged back into the ferns and raced through the sunflowers. "How did she move so fast?" Flora breathed. How did she even get over the creek without getting wet? Flora would have to try a new tack, rush past the cottage and into the forest behind. But when she came out on the other side of the vegetable patch Madame Cribellum was somehow there again. And this time, she was quicker. She snatched Flora, carried her by the back of her dress, and threw her into her black carriage.

"Too late, my dear!" She cackled, and they were off. Flora hugged her belongings and watched her cottage disappear into the darkness.

She was caught.

5

THE GOLDEN SWEATER

et me out!" Flora screamed. The creaky carriage crawled through the night. Flora yanked on the door handle, but it was locked.

"There, there," Madame Cribellum crooned. She put her finger to Flora's forehead, and Flora felt that same reassuring drain of care from her mind she'd felt before. She slumped back into her seat. "Never you mind, my dear." She grasped Flora's hand, and Flora felt her cold fingers sucking warmth from her own. Flora shook her head, trying to remember what she was so upset about.

Flora knew where they were going when she saw the large smokestack looming toward them, then the large building it was attached to, stretched out like a tarantula hugging the forest.

"The Nuthatch textile mill?" Flora asked.

"Why, yes. It has recently come under new management. I am the head spinner now."

"Didn't moths destroy all the fabric?"

Madame Cribellum snapped her neck toward her. "Don't speak of those wretched creatures!"

Flora shut her mouth. She had never seen the looming mansion up close. She stared, wide-eyed, at the unkempt vines growing up over the sandstone walls. They curled around the rooftop conservatory.

The only Nuthatch to ever come back was little Henry when he had grown. But he had sealed himself up in the mansion and hardly ever came into town. As far as anyone knew, he had become insane and withered away. No one had seen him for almost ten years.

Flora imagined him lying still on the floor of the conservatory, covered by the exotic vines he'd planted. She

shivered. But then she saw a light, ever so faint, reflect across the panes of glass. Someone was in there!

The carriage stopped at the end of a long drive lined with topiaries shaped like all manner of birds. Swans, owls, eagles, hummingbirds, peacocks, and what Flora assumed were nuthatches. Flora figured it had to do with the Nuthatch name—a tiny type of woodpecker with a black and white striped head, blue-gray wings, and red belly. The topiaries were a stark contrast to the haphazard growth on the estate. Flora wondered who kept them clipped.

As if reading her mind, Madame Cribellum said, "I've hired a groundskeeper to tackle some of the main parts of the estate. It's been very slow going, as it's been many years of disrepair. But things are starting to look as they used to." She unlocked the carriage door and opened it for Flora to exit onto the circular drive next to a fountain shaped like a large seashell, with water pouring from a spout in its center.

The mill glowed with hundreds of panes of leaded glass arched windows and was topped with sloping mansard roofs and towering turrets. An ornate grey stone crest loomed above the giant door. A nuthatch and an N were intricately carved into it with leaves and berries. "Don't nuthatches look like little badgers with those two black stripes on their heads?" Flora asked, forgetting her fear. Madame Cribellum ignored her. She took Flora's hand with cold fingers. "Come now; I'll show you to your room."

The wood doors of the estate creaked and then boomed wide open. Flora's heart pounded.

Madame Cribellum led Flora into the main hall. It was more ornate than anything Flora had ever seen, though it was worn with neglect. There was a giant crystal chandelier covered in cobwebs, windows adorned with tattered deep red drapes, and a marble floor that must have once been shiny. But Flora ignored the dust and took in the dark mahogany-paneled walls, burgundy velvet settees, and gleaming oil paintings. It was like stepping into a ruby. She looked up to find the sky painted on the round ceiling. A woman was lounging in the clouds, a wreath of flowers in her hair.

Madame Cribellum saw Flora looking and said, "The Goddess of spring. Painted for Henry Nuthatch's mother." She winced. "I have plans to restore all of this," she said, waving around.

Flora still gazed up at the painted woman as she trudged behind Madame Cribellum. She was the woman who had lost everything when the moths attacked.

She was led up one of the two mahogany staircases winding up to a landing with a marble bust of a man with a monocle.

"Clifden Nuthatch. Henry Nuthatch's late father. This was his home, his mill. These were his offices." She pointed to the doors along the landing. "Mine now. You are forbidden to enter them unless asked to do so by me or the current spinner in charge." She pushed Flora up another set of steps much narrower than the grand staircase. "The servants' quarters are this way."

Flora scrunched her nose at the smell of damp as they walked down a hallway with peeling wallpaper lined with doors, some of which were open. She looked in and saw other children sleeping. In one room, there was a boy sitting up in bed with auburn hair sticking every which way. He leaned so he could watch her pass. That hair…Flora thought she recognized it from her day in the forest…the boy who had laughed at her when she fell from the tree!

Madame Cribellum grabbed her arm and yanked her forward. "Ermine should have locked these doors by now. I'll have to speak with her later. The other children sleep in the dormitories, but until I get to know you better, I think it would be best to keep you isolated. We have order here and extreme vigilance for decorum. You, I am afraid," she said, looking at Flora's mass of wavy curls, scuffed black boots, and snaggy gray tights. "are a mess."

Flora crossed her arms and breathed out sharply. She had to hold in her anger. She thought, *This isn't like the market where I can just escape back to Gran after I stick out my tongue at someone for being mean. I have to play nice…because as soon as this lady isn't looking, I'm getting out of here.*

"But we'll soon have you in good shape," Madame Cribellum grinned.

Flora lost track of the twists and turns they took until she was led up a rickety spiral staircase to the top of a tower and then shoved into a sweltering hot room of stone walls.

"This room is built into the wall of the smokestack. It should be nice and warm for you," Madame Cribellum smiled hollowly. The room was so hot, Flora could feel beads of sweat building on her forehead. "Now, get plenty of sleep. Work starts early in the morning."

"Work?"

"Of course. I've been told you have a gift for weaving; is that right?"

"My Gran did, but I've learned quite a bit from her, and I've always had lots of ideas for fabric…"

"Well, then. We'll put those little fingers of yours to good use." She turned to leave.

"Wait! Can you tell me about my mother?"

Madame Cribellum laughed that hollow, breathy laugh. "I think the important question is, what do *you* know about your mother?"

Flora gulped. "Nothing."

Madame Cribellum swiveled closer to Flora. "You mean to tell me you know nothing? Nothing at all?"

"No."

Madame Cribellum grinned. "What about your father?"

"Nothing. Please, can you tell me anything?"

"Oh my dear. I haven't spoken to your mother in years…I'm afraid you'll be here a very *very* long time, Flora." She slammed the door and the sound of a key scraped inside the lock.

There was nothing in Flora's room except for a large, round hole cut into the stones with a view of the stars and the forest below. It had no glass, and no frame. Flora crept over to it and looked down. She was high above the ground; the tree branches were just a few feet away, but not close enough to grasp and climb to freedom.

"Pigweed!"

There was an eerie fog swirling at the base of the smokestack. Bushes jutted out of it like tiny islands in a sea of white. Flora's heart lurched at the thought of falling. She really was stuck here.

Finally, Flora was able to cry. The tears came from deep within. Her chest heaved in spurts. She took her geode out of her pocket and held it close to her heart. She was finally alone to think about all that had happened. It seemed only moments ago that she had been wrapped up in Gran's warm arms, and now she was a world away, frightened and alone with nothing but a rock to remember her by. It had all been so sudden! Maybe Gran was just out foraging glowing mushrooms and would come home to find her missing… Maybe she would come find her tomorrow and rescue her. Flora would believe it except there was that strange note. Gran had left it as if she knew she'd go missing…

Light, and her mother? It still made no sense to Flora. It was almost as if Gran's story about the moth fairies losing their light had something to do with her mother. But how was she supposed to find her if she was trapped in a mill? She felt like, at any moment, she would awaken from a nightmare. But she did not wake.

Flora's sobs were startled by a movement on her sleeve. The white caterpillar Flora had found in Gran's bed was still there.

"Oh, hello, little friend." Flora smiled and wiped her eyes. "Will you watch over me tonight?"

The caterpillar bobbed its head as if to say yes. Flora watched as it crawled up the stones to the top of the round window, then dropped down on a strand of silk until it was hanging over her. The silk glittered in the starlight.

"Silk!" Flora cried. She had forgotten about the beautiful golden silk Gran had given her. She pulled it out of her bag, and it fell into her arms in a river of light. She cradled it against her chest. Then she looked up at the caterpillar. If it could shimmy down a rope of silk, perhaps she could too!

Flora unraveled the silk and dropped one end over the edge of the window, as far as it would go. It dangled down about halfway to the ground. Not far enough.

"Maybe I could swing out to the branches?" She tied the other end of the silk to the doorknob. It was the only thing in the room to tie it to. But when she came back to the window, she realized the silk was even farther away from the ground. It would be a long fall to any branches that could hold her weight, and she wasn't sure she'd make it. She held tight to the silk. It was thicker than normal silk, but still very thin and delicate. She straddled the window and tried putting some of her weight on the string. It pulled taut. Flora dropped her other leg over the sill, and her legs dangled out into oblivion, but her chest was still held by the stones. She eased herself out.

The many layered strands of silk began breaking. She could feel the tug and pop of each one. She scrambled to grab the edge of the stone sill and balance herself before the silk broke clean from the doorknob, and in a quick motion, she clutched the edge with both hands. The silk still dangled beneath her, and she pulled it up with her onto the ledge, her heart racing.

"Ok, so that's not going to work." She caught her breath and bundled the silk back up into her arms, defeated.

"For now, I'll just have to make the most of this."

She wearily unloaded her bag of belongings and lit her candles. "There. That's a bit brighter," she whispered. Then she curled up in the curve of the round window, covered in her chenille blanket. She dipped her toes in the mortar like she did with tree bark when she napped in the forest.

She looked up at the caterpillar again. "Lucky you, you can just make more silk if yours breaks." She dropped her head against the stones. "And you'll be able to make a cocoon and just fly away once you grow wings…"

Flora brightened. "Maybe that's just what I'll do!" Determined, she pulled out her knitting needles and began knitting the soft strands of her silk.

Flora knew she couldn't really grow wings, but the idea made her feel better. The stars overhead pricked at her senses as her needles clicked together. Nobody could help her; she was all alone, so she would just have to help herself. Flora felt the rhythm of her knots woven over, and under, and through… through her insides like a warm flicker. She cried at the memory of Gran's clicking needles and the soft shawls and sweaters she had made. Flora's tears were hot on her cheeks, and she saw out of the corner of her eyes that they were glowing in the light of the candles like tiny mirrors. She wiped her wet skin, and to her surprise, her fingers held what looked like liquid light.

"Did that come from *me*?" She whispered.

She didn't know if it was from the stars watching over her, or the memory of Gran, or the act of creating… *Probably all of it combined*, she thought. *Well, I can't stop now…who knows when this will happen again?* She rubbed the molten tears onto her silk thread and kept making her sweater cocoon. She thought of her Gran's nature magic, and tried to soak up the starlight twinkling down on her, gathering it in her mind like folds of shimmering fabric. As she absorbed the light, the strands in her hands began to glow. It started where her knitting needles were and continued on until all of her creation was almost pulsing with a warm light. *I should probably be singing or saying some spell*, Flora thought. But she couldn't through her tears and startled senses. Just the memory of Gran, and the thought of flying away was enough. She would find a way out of the mill. She would find a way to the stars if she could!

She knitted late into the night, and the caterpillar kept watch.

The next morning, Flora awoke to the light of a pastel-colored sunrise stretching out from the treetops, and long drips of wax hardened across her windowsill. She was snuggled in the curve of her window, wearing the fruits of her late-night knitting. It was a fuzzy, golden sweater that reached down to her knees. It was so oval and plush that it looked like she was wearing a cocoon. Flora felt the soft patterns she'd created with starlight. Moons, flowers, vines—all the memories she had from the forest.

"I won't take it off until I fly away from this place," she promised.

6

THE MILL

here was a knock on Flora's door.

"Yeees?" She said slowly. She looked down at her sweater and then back up at the doorknob. If it was Madame Cribellum she didn't know how she would react to Flora creating something from silk. But her sweater was so bulbous and bright, there would be no way to hide it.

When the door creaked open, it was not Madame Cribellum. It was a tall girl with brown skin and black hair tied into two braids. She wore a simple white dress with black polka-dots. With a very professional face, she said, "Good morning. Madame Cribellum asked us to come wake you up and show you what is expected of you."

"Good morning." Flora said, getting up off the windowsill and putting out her hand. "I'm Flora."

The girl took it and gave it a formal shake. "I'm Ermine. And this is…" She turned around. There was nobody with her. "Maple!"

A plump little face with yellow ringlets peeked out from the door frame. Her cheeks turned a bright rose pink. "Hi," she said shyly and grinned.

"Nice to meet you," Flora said, and put her hand out for her, too.

"Oh!" The girl named Maple rushed into the room and gave Flora a big hug. "I'm so sorry about your Gran. We heard that you were orphaned like us, and it must be so horrible for you… and it's so horrible that you have to be *here*!"

Flora, surprised, hugged the girl back. It was the first kind words she'd received since the night before. She looked down at

Maple's faded pink dress with a yellow Peter Pan collar.
Something about this little girl both warmed her inside and made
her feel very deeply. Tears welled in her eyes. "Thank you," was
all she could get out.

Ermine's lip quivered. She stood by with her arms behind her back, shifting foot to foot. She gave Flora a small smile. Flora didn't quite know what to make of her, but she thought she was probably a nice girl, just a little bit formal.

Maple stood back and looked up at Flora. "I like your sweater!" she said. There was so much exuberance in her little body, Flora felt it rippling through her.

"Thank you. I made it from some silk my Gran made for me."

"It's so shiny!" Maple squealed, touching the designs. "And fuzzy!"

"I wanted it to look like a cocoon."

"It is really well crafted," Ermine said, coming forward and touching a small moon on Flora's sleeve. She looked enamored, but then said solemnly, "But don't expect to be sprouting wings any time soon. Come on. We'd better get started." She gracefully swept from the room and started down the stairs.

"Oh no, you're wrong about that," Flora called to her. "Now that we've met I feel a little bit bad about this, but I'm sorry, I have to say goodbye." Flora shrugged to Maple and began gathering her things.

"Excuse me?" Ermine scoffed.

"I don't belong here. No offense, but I'm not really an orphan like you girls. My grandmother is probably just in the woods looking for crystals or something…." Even Flora wasn't sure of the words coming out of her mouth, but she didn't want to listen to her gut or anyone else. She wanted to get. out.

"But you can't leave!" Maple squeaked.

Flora whirled on them. "Why not? You've just unlocked my door, and I didn't see any guards or anything…it shouldn't be too hard to sneak into the woods. I know the way back from here."

The girls stared at her, mouths agape.

"What?"

"But it's too dangerous!" Maple croaked.

Flora rolled her eyes and heaved a sigh. She'd forgotten how frightened the townsfolk were of moths. "I'll be careful; don't

67

worry. I know the forest like the back of my hand. And honestly, there's nothing to be afraid of. I've been catching moths and collecting cocoons in Silkwood my whole life! They're actually really beautiful creatures once you get to know them." She whisked past the girls and shuffled into the hallway. "Let's see…I just go down these stairs and…" she'd already forgotten all the twists and turns she'd taken the night before. "Oh ragwort, I'll have to figure it out once I'm down there." She began tiptoeing down the steps, though they creaked at the slightest touch, her bundle of belongings slung on her back.

"Are you crazy?" Maple stuttered. "I don't mean the moths… Madame Cribellum will catch you! And even if she doesn't, you'll get caught in her web."

Flora stopped and turned around slowly. "What do you mean by that?"

"Maple!" Ermine gave her a pointed look.

"I mean…" Maple looked nervously at Ermine and then back to Flora.

Ermine laughed nervously and pushed Maple aside. "She means it's *like* Madame Cribellum has created a large web around the mill. No matter where you go, it's like she's always there. Every door out is locked, and no window will budge."

"And Madame Cribellum has brainwashed most of the kids here into thinking she can control them. You've probably experienced it yourself," Maple said.

"That's ridiculous, Maple." Ermine took a few steps down to Flora.

Flora thought about the night before. Madame Cribellum had practically sedated her with just a finger. She had also used such soothing, manipulative words. She was so shocked by her grandmother's disappearance and the Witch Moth coming through her window. Was it her grief speaking? Or something else. "She did make me come with her when I didn't want to. It was almost like I was put under a spell. But maybe it was just my imagination."

The girls looked at each other with knowing faces, then at Flora sadly.

"A long time ago, someone did try to leave," Ermine said flatly, "and…" her voice broke, "…and they were punished."

Flora's determination waned. She saw the darkness in Ermine's eyes, and it had nothing to do with how deep brown they were.

"And believe me, Flora," Maple said solemnly, "you do not want to be on Madame Cribellum's bad side."

Flora heaved a deep sigh. She wasn't sure how to get out. She wasn't even sure how to get back to the front door. And there was the nagging suspicion that Madame Cribellum knew something about her mother. She sauntered back to her room and plopped her bag on the floor. "I guess I could wait and see the rest of the mill." She grinned and squinted her eyes mischievously… "See what I'm up against and search out weaknesses."

Maple jumped up and down and clapped. "Oh I hope you do stay!"

Ermine sniffed. "I wouldn't hope that for anyone."

"Oh I don't mean it that way…" Maple sidled up to Flora and put her arm in her arm. "I just mean I like you! And it'll be nice to have someone new here to talk to," she whispered loudly. "Ermine is pretty boring these days."

"When you do the same thing every day, there isn't much to say," Ermine said dryly.

Flora laughed. "Well, we'll see how it goes. My grandmother will probably show up to find me here. I'll give it a day. Maybe two."

"I would put escaping out of your head entirely," Ermine said, straightening. "It's not worth it. If you're good Madame Cribellum won't notice you as much. If I were you, I'd try to blend in. Now let's go. We're already late!"

Ermine bounded down the steps two at a time.

"You don't have to be so grim!" Maple called after her. She grabbed Flora's hand, and they followed.

Ermine waved above her and said, "This is the outer wall of the smokestack. I don't know why she's put you up here, but I can only imagine it's to keep you from escaping. It's a long way down to the ground."

"I did think about trying to shimmy my way out the window…but my silk is too fragile," Flora said.

"Oooh! I wouldn't even try!" Maple said, "I can't believe you don't even have any glass in your window! I'm terrified of heights."

"Terrified of everything," Ermine snorted.

They passed a few landings and several stairs. "It's easy to find your way because all these doors are locked. Who knows where they lead?" Ermine shrugged. "I only have a key to the dormitories, (because Madame Cribellum trusts me to keep curfew), to some of the offices, and the work rooms. Anyway… Just follow the stairs down to the bottom of the building."

"Do we have to do a lot of work?" Flora asked.

"Yes," Ermine sighed. "It takes all day and sometimes nights to get Madame Cribellum's orders finished."

"She keeps us locked up in the dormitories and only lets us out for meals and work," Maple said.

"That's awful!' Flora exclaimed.

"But we have some fun when she's not looking!" Maple said. "Evenings after dinner when she retires to her room. And sometimes we even play hide-and-seek when she's on a business errand. Thorn knows how to pick locks, and someone always keeps a look-out!"

"That's about once a month," Ermine said, rolling her eyes. "And last time Cloud got stuck behind one of the cotton bales, and Madame Cribellum made us all skip dinner."

"And breakfast!"

Flora was listening intently. Sneaking around and playing hide-and-seek did sound like fun. But even better was that this

Thorn person knew how to pick locks. He would be the one who could help her escape.

They came to a large banquet room with long curtains with gold flowers shrouding the view onto the garden. There were three long tables dotted with children sitting in silence. Their sallow faces stared into the distance. Any cheerfulness or light the children had brought with them into that dark place was hidden deep inside their tiny bodies. Bowls of a sticky white goo were set before them. Madame Cribellum sat at her own table, without any food, surveying the group. She nodded to Ermine when she came in, and Ermine nodded back.

"Come sit down quickly!" Maple said, rushing to an empty space on a long bench. Flora took a seat in the middle and was flanked by her new…friends? She hoped they were. She wasn't entirely sure about Ermine, but Maple seemed like just the sort of girl she'd like to be able to spend time with. So much joy, even in such a dismal place. Flora loved her already. It would be hard to leave her when she did eventually escape. Which she was still determined to do. *Maybe I could take her with me*, she thought.

Madame Cribellum stood and walked slowly down the aisle between the tables. "You may eat now," she said. "The work bell rings in ten minutes."

"Ten minutes!" Flora scoffed.

Every head in the room turned toward her.

Madame Cribellum's eyes fixed on her. "Now you only have five." She whirled, her cape flitting against the back of the chairs, and walked out of the room.

Everyone groaned. A large boy at the end of Flora's table pounded a fist on the table. "Way to go, dummy. You have to wait until she leaves before you say anything!"

"Give her a break, Atlas. She didn't know!" Ermine snapped back at him.

"Sorry, Ermine," Atlas said. He shut his mouth and looked down.

"Everybody get eating!" she said. "We don't have very much time."

Flora was astounded that Ermine stood up for her. The other children obviously looked up to her. She seemed like she was the oldest. Probably around twelve or thirteen.

"Thank you," Flora said.

Ermine glared at her.

Welp. That camaraderie didn't last long, Flora thought. She took a spoonful of the…what was it? Porridge?… "yeeeelk," she said, putting it into her mouth. It was worse than it looked. She looked around at all the kids eating furiously. *How could they?* She thought. Then she looked up at the face across from her.

Laughing amber eyes stared back at her. It was the boy with auburn hair! Up close she could see the splotch of freckles on the bridge of his nose and the dimples in his chiseled cheeks. He was grinning ear to ear.

"Not your favorite?" He asked.

Flora felt suddenly mute. This boy…he looked like a crumpled-up autumn leaf. She could almost feel the crisp air and smell the apple woodsmoke of fall just looking at him. Even his brown fair-isle sweater reminded her of the cozy warmth of sitting by the fire and drinking hot spiced tea. He cocked his head in a questioning manner.

Just then, a loud bell rang.

"Time for work!" Ermine spoke with finality. She looked down at Flora's bowl. "Flora! You should have eaten more! Hurry and take a few more bites. You'll be starving by lunch time."

Flora looked down at the mush, and her stomach turned.

"Sometimes if you plug your nose you can't taste it," Maple said, "But don't worry. You'll get used to it. We don't get very much to eat so everything starts to taste good eventually."

As they shuffled out of the room, Flora looked for the boy with tousled reddish hair in the sea of children.

"His name is Thorn," Ermine said. She nudged Flora and raised an eyebrow. Flora felt herself flush.

"Oh…I don't even know him! I just…um..I just…" She didn't know what to say.

"Everybody gets a little crush on Thorn, Flora. But we've all gotten over it," she laughed. "His little pranks eventually get old." They walked down the hall toward two large, booming doors. Ermine seemed to come to life, a spring in her step. "Time to get spinning!" She said as she practically danced toward the room.

"She seems to enjoy the thought of work," Flora said to Maple as they shuffled slowly.

"She's the best spinner," Maple said. "You should see her… it's like she was made for it. And I am the *worst*." She laughed.

Spinning made Flora think of her Gran, sitting at her loom, creating magic. She knew the weaving here would be nothing compared to hers. She suddenly felt claustrophobic, being herded like cattle through the hall. If she was constantly being watched, working, and locked up, how would she ever be able to do as her grandmother's note asked?

"Hey!" Flora caught up to Maple and asked, "What was the name of the kid who could pick locks?"

"Thorn?" Maple asked. "He was the one sitting across from you this morning."

Flora flinched. She had to unlock her door. She had to find her mysteriously missing mother. And she had to figure out how to get past the strange secret magic web the girls had talked about. But worst of all…she'd have to drum up the courage to talk to a cute boy!

She yelped as she was smooshed between the other children through the impending doom of the giant spinning room doors.

There was work to be done.

7

STARS

n the middle of a dark, sweltering room, where big machines whirred and cotton dust fluffed through the air, Flora secretly embroidered stars.

She sat at a loom in between Maple and Ermine. The two had shown her how to work the enormous contraption, covered with metal wheels and cogs, and strung with so much yarn it looked like a giant cobweb. Flora learned quickly. She had seen her Gran work at her smaller wooden loom, and it didn't take her long to get the hang of it.

But making the same old, drab fabric had begun to bore Flora. She'd made an endless bolt of dark gray that day, and her creative heart wanted to make something unique and special. Something magical. Her fingers worked delicately with her needle and thread as she placed constellations on the fabric. She had snuck some of her own thread from her sewing kit to make them. She used gold thread for tiny stars, silver thread for larger ones, and white thread for tiny sparkles around each one. Her work was intricate and detailed. When she finished each star, she touched it lightly with her fingertips, smiling to herself. It was like holding a piece of the night sky.

Life was a trance of spinning, and twisting, and spooling for the children. Flora woke up in the dark hours of the morning to begin work, and at the end of long, tedious hours, she came back to her grimy room to mope and sleep before the next day would begin again. There hadn't been any time at all for Flora to try to escape like she'd hoped. She'd been at the mill for what seemed like ages, though she knew it hadn't really been that long. She was beginning to feel the fog of Madame Cribellum's strange magic over them. The monotony of her life there made it hard to tell if it had been days or weeks.

The only hint at change was the trees outside her smokestack room. They had slowly turned their vermillion and ruby shades. Flora longed to touch them, to play in their brilliant hues, but would only get small touches of their beauty when a stray leaf would fly up into her window and alight on the stones or stick in her hair. Autumn came and went without her so much as setting foot in the crunch of the forest floor. Her heart ached at the loss of it.

Flora looked at the windows along the walls of the spinning room. They were already laced with frost. She wished she could be among the snowy trees instead of in the stuffy heat of the mill. A large fire crackled in a stone fireplace at the end of the room, close to where she worked.

"Why don't you take off that sweater, Flora? It's so hot!" Ermine cooed like a mother hen.

"She'll never take it off!" Maple squeaked. "Remember, it's from the cocoons in her forest! Ugh! I hate it when my yarn snags!" Maple stomped her foot. She had lost track of her weaving when she looked up to speak.

Ermine heaved a sigh and got up to help.

"It's not my fault!" Maple whined. She jiggled her curls and smiled over at Ermine with her big, wet eyes and coy mouth.

Ermine shook her head and laughed. "Here, let me." She skipped past Flora and quickly unraveled Maple's knot. "Done!"

"How do you do it so quickly!?"

"I just don't think about it!" Ermine laughed. She gave her a hug, and Maple collapsed in her arms. Ermine was the best weaver in the mill. It always seemed like she was finished with

her work and helping others to get theirs done before the bell rang. "Come on girls, we have to finish up our quota for the day!" she said as she brushed past Flora. Then she tripped, looked down, and saw the starry fabric trailing on the ground under Flora's stool. Flora quickly gathered it into her lap.

Ermine looked over her shoulder. "What are you up to?"

"I'm embroidering stars," Flora whispered and showed Maple and Ermine her glittery silk pattern on the cloth. "I'm sick of the same old boring fabric, day in and day out."

"They're so sparkly!" Maple crooned.

Ermine's eyes lit up. She ran her fingers over the stars, then pulled them back quickly, like they had bitten her. "Static shock," she laughed nervously. "They're beautiful, Flora, but I don't think Madame Cribellum will like you doing it." She shook her head.

Flora hid her embroidery under another piece of brown fabric. "So don't tell her!" She giggled.

Ermine gave Flora a shrug and a look that said, *You'll regret it*, then went back to her own loom.

Flora knew why Ermine felt a shock when she touched her stars. She had been practicing using the same magic she'd discovered when she made her sweater. She figured if looking at stars could make her tears turn to light, she could probably find other ways to create light too. She took a sneaky peek at the room around her to see if anyone was looking, then took her fabric out again. She looked up at the icy windows. Tendrils of frost were cluttered in the corners. Where they reflected the cool light, sparkles danced across the pane. Flora let it resonate toward her, filling her. She closed her eyes and imagined glittery frost creeping through her. Her ribs tickled with splintered ice, and her lungs reverberated…Then she blew gently on the new stars she had created. They lit up like embers, then sputtered out. What was left was an iridescent sheen that made them glimmer when she moved the fabric in and out of the light. She'd been trying out her frost technique all morning.

That was probably the shock Ermine felt, she thought. *Interesting.* She knew she should hide her light, but it was too irresistible to not make her stars shine.

A shadow in the shape of a tall, thin woman crept across Flora's fabric.

Flora froze.

Madame Cribellum angled her body around Flora and stuck her nose in her face. "What do you think you're doing?" She yanked the needle and thread out of Flora's hand.

"Making stars," Flora said in a small voice.

Madame Cribellum stared at her. "Excuse me?"

"To give some light," Flora said. She scrunched her face up, anticipating Madame Cribellum's anger.

Madame Cribellum yelled in her face, "RUINED! A whole ream destroyed by your ugly little marks!"

"I'm sorry, I…"

"I don't care if your hunch of a grandmother taught you to embroider the entire night sky. You will keep weaving with the others, or I will suck every last drop of creativity from those fingers of yours by having you break cotton bales! Am I clear?"

Flora nodded.

Madame Cribellum straightened and her face softened. Then she looked Flora over and grinned. "Hmm, It looks like you're beginning to take after your grandmother in more ways than one."

Flora smiled, confused. Was Madame Cribellum paying her a compliment? "Do you mean my embroidery?" She asked meekly, "I wish I could make stars as lovely as hers, but she's much better than I am…"

"No, my dear. I don't mean your embroidery," she laughed. "You've spent so much time hunched over, I think you're growing a lump on your back! Sit up straight, girl!"

Flora felt her back and shuddered. It was true! She *was* growing a lump. It wasn't very large, but it was definitely there. She sank even lower into her seat and looked around to see if anyone noticed.

Madame Cribellum snipped her fabric with a pair of golden scissors and put it into her pocket. "I don't want to see another wasteful embellishment from you. Do I make myself clear?"

"Yes, Madame." Flora nodded quickly.

As Madame Cribellum's heels clicked away, she screamed, "THORN! Come mount some more yarn on this creel!"

Thorn came skipping in his brown corduroy pants and suspenders. He jumped up onto Flora's loom with ease and began fiddling with the bronze dials. His presence flustered Flora like wind rustling through autumn leaves. She still hadn't talked to him. She was always getting tongue-tied and embarrassed whenever he came near her. Asking him about picking locks was out of the question. But he was the bright spot in her dark days. She always secretly hoped he would have an errand to run in her area.

Then Flora thought of the lump growing on her back and gulped. She hunched down and tried to make her hair fluff over it.

Her maneuvering made Thorn look down at her. "Woah!" he exclaimed.

Flora looked up at him with wide eyes, thinking he was disgusted by her hunchback. But he was looking at her fabric.

"I like it." He said, with a sure nod.

"Oh!" Flora smiled shyly.

Thorn climbed up the loom almost to the ceiling to thread the yarn up and over a giant spool, then jumped down with the end.

Like a caterpillar, Flora thought.

Ermine came over to Flora and gave her a little squeeze. "See? I told you you'd get in trouble." She said, "I keep telling you, as long as you keep your head down and do your work until the whistle blows, she won't bother you."

Flora hung her head, embarrassed and humiliated.

"Here," Ermine said, "I'll help you get your loom started up again. I'll be the one who'll be blamed if we don't meet our quota." Her hands worked quickly and smoothly. "Thorn, hand me that bobbin, will you?"

Thorn tossed Ermine the bobbin and then leaned up against Maple's loom, where she was furiously tying knots. "Having trouble with your yarn breaking again, maple?"

"I don't know why she keeps putting me with the weavers!" Maple cried. "I can't weave to save my life. I would be much better as a doffer with you, Thorn. I can hand things to people no problem, but all this yarn going every which way makes me feel crazy!"

Madame Cribellum screamed from somewhere on the floor, "THORN!"

Thorn sighed. "Bye, girls." As he ran off, he gave them a wink.

Maple blushed, and Ermine rolled her eyes.

Flora bit her lip as she maneuvered the thread through her loom shuttle. She pondered Ermine's advice. Keep her head down? How long would she have to do that for? She wanted to fill the whole room with sparkling designs. She missed finding cocoons, and moths, and all the shining things in her forest. She missed swishing her skirts through waves of flowers and dangling from mossy tree branches. She couldn't imagine never doing it again. If she stayed cocooned in the suffocating world of the mill, would she forget that world? Would she become like the droning, working children who barely ever smiled?

"How long have you been here?" She asked Ermine.

"Forever."

"But I thought the mill opened back up recently."

Ermine shrugged. "It feels like it's been forever. Nobody can remember ever not being here."

"But that's impossible. You have to remember something. Not all of you could have come when you were babies. How old are you?"

"I don't know."

"What?! How can you not know? Haven't you ever had a birthday?"

Ermine blinked.

Apparently not, Flora thought. "What about you, Maple?"

"I don't know either. But I've seemed the same age for a very, *very* long time."

"Is Madame Cribellum drugging you all?" Flora laughed, but inside she was frightened. This place was so very strange.

"Madame Cribellum keeps us all under her trance so we will forget," Maple said dramatically.

Ermine laughed and tugged Maple's arm sharply. "It does *seem* like she's using magic some days."

"She does!" Maple cried. "I swear we're in some sort of pern-a-ment stasis."

"Permanent." Ermine corrected her.

Flora cringed. "I don't want to forget anything about where I came from."

Maple scrunched up her face. "I hate to tell you this, Flora. But you'll feel like you've been here forever soon too. You see, there's a sort of spell..."

"Can't stop chattering away, can we?" Madame Cribellum's sharp voice was right behind them. The girls jumped. "Flora, tomorrow you will be dipping yarn in hot wax and oil and drying it on the steam drums."

Flora's heart sank knowing she would be nursing burned fingers for the next few days. "Yes, Ma'am."

Maple took a deep, brave breath. "Madame, may I work with the doffers next week?"

Madame Cribellum's head turned slowly toward her. "No, Maple. You may work with the spoolers, repairing breaks and snags."

"But that's harder than weaving!" Maple whined. She covered her mouth as soon as she let it out.

Madame Cribellum fixed Maple with an icy stare. She crept over to her, and her hand flicked out. She produced one long, bony finger and touched Maple's cheek with it. The pink in her cheek drained to white, and her eyes glazed over. Maple shook her head and said, "Yes, madame. I'm sorry for arguing. I will work with the spoolers tomorrow."

"Thank you, my dear." Madame Cribellum pursed her lips into a simper. "And would you mind doing a double shift today? We need someone to work through the night."

"Yes, Ma'am," Maple said hollowly.

Flora twitched in anger.

When Madame Cribellum was gone, Flora leaned over to Maple and asked, "How are you going to spool, Maple? You can hardly fix one snag!"

"Can't I?" Maple stared through Flora. She began working again, her small hands beginning to blister as they rubbed against the yarn.

At dinner, Flora sat with Ermine and Maple in the dining hall as usual. Cold, mushy beets had been slopped onto their plates.

Flora's mouth watered as she thought of her Gran's nasturtium honeycomb salad and mulberry meadowsweet cordial. She'd give anything for one taste of the nectar from one of her meadow flowers. Even one tiny pansy or sprig of thyme… or ooooh! Sugared pinecones!

Tasteless food went into her mouth and left her full, but still hungry.

Maple whined with every bite.

Flora shoved her plate forward. "I wish I'd never come here. I wish I'd found a way to run into the woods when my Gran disappeared. I wish I'd kicked and screamed and…I miss home."

The girls stared at her. "It's amazing you still have fight in you, Flora," Ermine whispered.

Flora pulled her book of moths out of her sweater pocket and leafed through the pages. They reminded her of her favorite meadow. Of the green light shifting through the forest. Of nights in the hammock under the moon.

Ermine looked over and winced. "You'd better not let Madame Cribellum catch you with a book of moths, Flora. She *hates* them."

"Everybody seems to hate moths," she said, rolling her eyes. "It's so silly."

Maple shuddered. "But Madame Cribellum especially. One time the whole entire forest of moths came and ate all the fabric in the mill! I think she's afraid they might come back."

Flora still couldn't imagine her sweet moths doing anything so treacherous. "Maybe they had a reason," she said matter-of-factly.

"Who, the moths?" Ermine snorted.

Flora furrowed her brow. "Sure, why not? Animals have feelings too."

"But insects?" Ermine raised an eyebrow.

"Henry Nuthatch was a little boy when it happened," Maple said. "They say he was playing in the woods and took one of their cocoons. It made them angry."

Flora was surprised. "But I've taken plenty of cocoons from the forest!"

"Oh! Do you think the moths will come after you, too?" Maple asked nervously.

"Hmm. All of mine were empty," Flora said. "Gran always made sure I checked. The cocoon Henry took must have had a moth still inside. Funny, my Gran once told me a story about a race of moth fairies in the forest. Maybe they were the ones who destroyed the mill…"

Flora suddenly dropped her fork onto her plate with a loud clang.

What if it was actually true? What if they *did* have something to do with the moths destroying the mill? Her mind swirled with images of golden silk and sparkling webs, wings and lost light….

Ermine laughed at Flora's sudden seriousness. "You goof! It's just a story."

Ermine is probably right, Flora thought. She was just imagining things.

Maple giggled nervously. Her rosy cheeks turned a deeper shade of pink.

Flora looked Maple over…her bright pink cheeks, her yellow hair…it reminded her of something. She opened her moth book to a page with a fuzzy, plump moth with a yellow head and pink and yellow wings. It was as tiny as her fingertip. She'd drawn it grasping her nail.

"Maple, I have to show you something." She showed her the picture. "You remind me of this moth!"

Maple looked into the book and grinned, "Cuuuute!! Look at its big yellow antennae!"

"I have a poem for it," Flora said. She turned the page. "The Rosy Maple Moth," Flora read, stunned. "It even has your name!" She recited the poem she'd written for it.

"Darling Rosy Maple
wears a yellow mink,
Drinks all the maple sugar,
Then she blushes pink!"

Maple gasped. "And pink is my favorite color!"

"It definitely suits you!" Flora touched the faded pink frills on Maple's puffed sleeve.

"Oh this…" Maple looked down at her dress sheepishly. "Madame Cribellum made me bleach the color out. It still has a little pink, but it used to be a lot brighter."

"Why would she do that?!" Flora balked.

"She got angry and said it was a fril-oh-vus color. We don't even have any pink dye!"

"Frivolous," Ermine corrected her.

"I bet we could make some pink dye." Flora's eyes glittered. "Gran and I would make it from berries or pink flowers all the time!"

Maple's face sunk. "We'll never have berries or flowers here."

Flora grabbed Maple's hand and gave it a squeeze. "I'll think of something. I promise."

Maple's curls bounced as she shook her head. "Thanks anyway," she sighed.

"Gonna eat those beets?" Thorn startled the girls. He was sauntering past with his plate.

Flora quickly put her hair down to hide her hunch, hoping Thorn couldn't see it through her thick hair.

"I'm done!" Maple sat back in disgust.

Thorn sat down, crowding between Flora and Maple, and dumped Maple's beets onto his plate. Their red juice splattered onto the table and nearly got on Maple's dress. She squealed, "Thorn!"

"Whoops! Sorry, Mapes." he smirked and tugged one of her ringlets gently. She blushed as red as the offending beets.

Flora looked down at the beet juice. She breathed in sharply and smiled. *Red!* She thought. "I'm going to keep mine, thanks!" She said this as she leapt up and took her plate of beets with her.

"Hey, where are you going?" Thorn called after her. Was that disappointment on his face?

"I'm going to bed early. See you all tomorrow morning!"

"You can't take your plate with you…" Ermine's voice trailed after her.

But Flora was already bounding up her smokestack stairs, two steps at a time.

8

THE ROSE

Flora sat in the center of her smokestack room, smashing beets on her plate. Images of Gran foraging in the forest for dye specimens flooded into her memory like the last bit of pink sunlight flooding in through her round window. She smiled at the thought of Gran covered in mud from finding Indigofera tintoria along the banks of the hot spring. There were many plants that only grew in the tropics that could grow quite easily in Silkwood because of the spring. Even during the winter their roots stayed warm. Gran would bring home baskets full of leafy twigs, sometimes with their pink flowers still on. She would braid their stems, then soak them in water. The leaves were just a normal green, but overnight the water would miraculously turn blue! It was just like magic. Then it was only a matter of adding some lime, a beating and mixing process, and then fermenting. Flora loved watching as her grandmother's strong hands worked the bowls of frothy mixture. The color would turn from a dirty green to a vivid midnight blue over time.

Flora loved every color, but thinking of that indigo dye filling her Gran's wrinkles, smudged on her apron, and splattered up onto her face gave Flora a special twinge of joy. Flora, of course, tried to help and made more of a mess of things than was worth it. She would splash and drip and create a pool of peacock blue at her feet. But Gran never seemed to mind. She'd let her be by her side, humming a ditty and wiping froth from Flora's dress.

After they were done with their work, they looked like a couple of frazzled stars fallen from a cerulean sky.

Maybe it isn't so terrible having a hunch like Gran, Flora thought. She felt her back. She seemed much too young to have one. *Maybe it won't grow any bigger.* She tried not to worry. If Gran had lived with one, she could too. She tried hard to swallow a sob. She missed her Gran so dearly. A bright tear from Flora's eyes landed on the plate of mushy beets.

"I need to pull myself together if I'm ever going to finish this!" Flora said. "I need to get blue out of my mind. Because I'm making *pink*!" Flora rummaged in her sewing bag and pulled out a white silk ribbon. She didn't have any water to dilute the beet juice, so she smooshed the ribbon into the juice on the plate. Slowly but surely, she was able to get the ribbon to a light shade of pink. When she was done, she carefully held it up to a candle to dry, whispering the same type of magic words Gran used to when she'd imbibe a fabric with a little extra spell for the wearer. *It should have the spirit of the sunset,* Flora thought. She would keep

her light a secret, like Gran had always told her to, but there was no harm in using it every once in a while if nobody was looking... She smiled as she looked out at the pink sky and made up some words.

"Spirit of the blush sky,
Essence of the red blood beet,
Hidden under the earth in darkness,
But now sugary and sweet."

Flora thought about how the beet had been uprooted from its home. How it bled to make something beautiful. *She* had been uprooted. *She* had been drained of joy and life. But she, too, could still make something beautiful. As she spoke her spell, the ribbon lit up. It was hard to tell where the candlelight ended and the flicker of light in the ribbon started. They seemed to meld together. Flora gently rubbed the ribbon between two fingers, and the dim pink flame stuck to her fingertips. She held it up to her face and smiled. It was a bright, gleaming, *perfect* pink.

When the ribbon was dry, Flora folded and sewed it in a special way and hid it in her bag until the next day. She fell asleep dreaming of a brilliant, dye-splattered sky and Gran's honeyed songs.

The next morning, Flora found Maple in the servant's hall, trudging her way in a tired daze after working her double shift all night.

"I have something for you, Maple!" She grabbed her hand and put a perfect silk ribbon rose inside it.

Maple's eyes went wide. "It's PINK! Oh Flora! How did you...?"

"I used the beets from dinner for the dye!"

"It's beautiful!" Maple held the rose to her face, and her rosy cheeks radiated with glee.

"Here, let me pin it in your hair." Flora attached it to Maple's yellow curls.

Maple did a twirl and sighed. "Oh, thank you, thank you!"

As the other children came into the hall, they crowded around her in awe. They hadn't seen something so shiny and new in so long. Maple beamed with pride. They asked Flora how she'd made it, where she'd gotten the dye, and if she could make flowers for them as well. Flora's stomach did a flip as she noticed Thorn was among them, watching intently.

Flora heard more heeled footsteps down the corridor but thought it was only more children coming to ogle. She was explaining the stitches and the way she'd folded the ribbon as all the children got quiet. Maple nudged her, and one boy said, "Ssshh!"

But Flora kept talking… "you just take a ribbon and turn it around itself like this…"

A familiar voice cleared her throat from above the children.

Flora realized with horror why the children had hushed. Madame Cribellum was there! She ripped the flower from Maple's hair and inspected it. "I don't have a stitch of pink in the mill! Where did you get the dye?"

Flora was silent.

Madame Cribellum seethed. "I HATE PINK!"

Maple gasped.

Flora was stunned. Madame Cribellum really *did* hate pink. She reminded her of Gran's story about the spider jealous of the pink moth wings. But how could a woman dripping with every desire be jealous of a small child? How could she treat sweet little Maple so horribly? She brimmed with anger, and a spark of light inside her ignited.

"You spider!" She yelled, stomping her foot.

Madame Cribellum took a step back, eyes wide. Flora thought she could almost see fear in her.

Then Madame Cribellum's eyes squinted, and she took out her sewing scissors. She spread the ribbon flower with her long, spindly fingers. Then she held the flower up high, and all the children held their breath. Maple let out a tiny, strangled squeak as Madame Cribellum snipped the flower in half.

Flora balled her hands into fists and scoffed, "You witch!"

Madame Cribellum grabbed Flora by her thick hair. She spoke with hot breath into her ear, "That's enough out of you, you little worm!" She lifted a hand high above her head, ready to strike Flora.

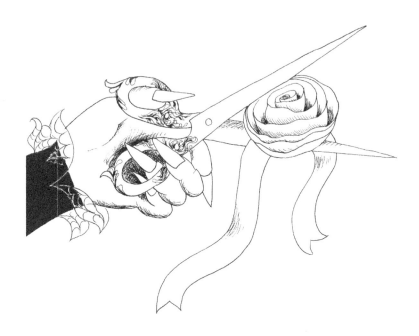

All the children gasped. Some hid their faces with their hands. Flora flinched in fear, ready for the hit, but then Maple cried out.

"No, pleaaaase!" She whined and pulled at Madame Cribellum's skirt. Maple had turned a particularly bright shade of rose. Madame Cribellum looked down at her and blinked. Maple puffed out her cheeks and stuck out her bottom lip. Her eyes gleamed in what was one of the cutest little pouts. *Nobody could resist that face*, Flora thought. *Well, nobody normal. But Madame Cribellum is not normal…or is she?*

To Flora's dismay, Madame Cribellum's face flushed pink too. Then she let go of Flora's hair and shook her head as if she were trying to get rid of the blush on her face.

Flora looked at Maple. Had she used some kind of magic? She'd felt it the first time she'd met Maple, too. It was as if her blush rubbed off on her, and it was seeming to have the same effect on Madame Cribellum. She looked befuddled and confused…as if trying to free herself from a sudden fog in her memory.

Maple beamed, then looked at Flora shyly, like she'd just gotten away with something. She *did* know the power she had over people! Flora could hardly believe it.

Madame Cribellum looked as though she might cry. "You're just like your mother, Flora. So…So…" She held her head and swooned.

The cogs inside Flora's head spun so fast, she could barely keep up. Did Madame Cribellum still know her parents? Maybe she had some information about them in her office. An address, a name? How could she get it?

After collecting herself, Madame Cribellum smiled her fake, too-sweet smile. "We have an enormous order that needs to be filled by the end of the month. An entourage from Paris is coming, and my fabric will sell for a very pretty price when their order is ready! Everything must be absolutely perfect. Understood? "

"Yes, Madame," the children chimed. There were excited whispers all about. "And I don't want to see any embellishments, understand? Only sensible, useful fabric. Stick to the instructions and orders!" She let the bits of pink rose fall to the floor. "I have to go into town for a short while to make arrangements for our guests. While I am gone, Ermine is in charge." She smiled at Ermine like she was her pet. "Now everyone, to work!"

Maple huffed and picked up the bits of flower. The cut had gone across all of Flora's folds and left it in pieces. "I wish I'd hidden the flower," she said to Flora. "I'm so sorry."

"No, Maple. Beauty is meant to be seen and worn. You didn't do anything wrong." She picked up another piece. "Besides, now you have petals! Just imagine you're climbing a cherry tree and they're falling all around you!"

Maple wiped her eyes and tried to smile. "What's a cherry tree?"

Flora's heart skipped a beat. "Oh Maple! It's the most beautiful tree in the forest. It has blossoms that look like tiny pink clouds. You would love it."

"I hope I get to see one someday," Maple said. She put the petals in her pocket and headed to the weaving room, head down.

Flora was being brave for Maple, but inside she was fuming. Why was Madame Cribellum so mean? Flora had only done something kind and created something beautiful for her friend. It was as if Madame Cribellum didn't like beauty itself, and wanted to punish those who did. And the fact that Maple had never even seen a cherry tree? It broke her heart. Flora's face darkened as the sparks inside her finally cooled. She looked in the direction Madame Cribellum had gone with slitted eyes. She would teach her a lesson somehow. She *had* to.

As the children shuffled toward the spinning room, Flora caught sight of Thorn. She'd have to talk to him, even if, at the moment, it seemed even scarier than facing Madame Cribellum. He was Flora's only hope to find some way out.

Taking a deep breath and shoving her nerves into a deep pocket of her chest. She wove through the other children, grabbed Thorn's hand, and shoved him into an alcove.

9

MARIPOSA

ell hello there," Thorn said, dimples nearly bursting through his cheeks. He had a startled, yet oddly pleased, look on his face.

Flora felt entirely flustered but had no time. She shoved down the rising burst of glee filling her insides.

"I heard you know how to pick locks," she said.

Thorn smiled devilishly, the dim light of the alcoves' sconces burnishing his eyes to gold. "Did you, now?"

"Have you ever broken into Madame Cribellum's office?"

"Shhh!" Thorn's eyes darted up and down the hall.

"Does she have information on our parents?"

"Quiet!" Thorn frantically pulled Flora further into the alcove and covered her mouth. "We don't have any parents, Flora."

Flora ripped his hands off. "Why is everyone so forgetful in this place? Everyone has parents, silly!"

Thorn sighed. "Not any that care about us."

That stung. Flora's shoulders drooped. In all of her worrying and determination to escape, she hadn't thought of that. What if her mother didn't care?

Thorn cringed. "Sorry. I guess I don't know about yours. Maybe they do care…they just aren't able to. Or something." He shrugged.

Flora looked up, determined. "I have a grandmother. And she didn't die. She disappeared. Madame Cribellum was already at my house before anyone could have told her I was alone.

There's something really weird going on here. There has to be some way for her to keep us here without our parents knowing."

Thorn looked unimpressed. But he looked down the hallway, pondering.

"Please. Please help me!" Flora bit her lip.

"Okay, fine. Madame Cribellum usually takes a while in town. We have some time." He gave her his arm and ushered her down the hallway.

Flora's heart leapt. She might find something out about her parents! And she was talking to Thorn. Alone. All her nerves were aflame.

When they came to the main entrance, he stopped and hid behind one of the grand red curtains, pulling her in behind him. They peered between the creases, up one of the cherry staircases, toward the offices. Flora was so close to Thorn, his hair brushed her cheek. She got a faint whiff of the leaves that smell like brown sugar in the fall, sunlight warming them as she crunched through a pile with her boots. She closed her eyes and leaned closer to him, then was startled when he spoke.

"There won't be anything in the two little offices," he said. "There's just packing information, receipts, lists for orders, stuff like that. But there might be something in her main office."

"What about her bedroom? Does she have a lounge? A study?"

Thorn looked at her incredulously. "You're brave, aren't you?"

"What?"

"I would never go into her actual living quarters. She might have something there, but she would know for sure you'd been in there. Ermine and I have to go into her offices all the time, so it's not such a big deal for us to sneak in."

Flora clicked her tongue. "Well, what are we waiting for?"

"For her to leave. She's probably up there preening. Hold on…"

There was a clatter from above, and Madame Cribellum whooshed out of the landing and down the staircase. She wore a black cape and a fanciful black hat with intricate decorations jutting every which way as she walked.

"For someone who wants us to make such boring fabric, she certainly wears elaborate things." Flora whispered.

Thorn snorted, then nudged her to be quiet.

When Madame Cribellum had slammed the front doors and locked them, Thorn and Flora tiptoed across the marble floor and ran up the stairs as quietly as they could. Flora stopped at the top.

"Wait…Can you pick those locks?" Flora pointed at the grand front doors.

Thorn shook his head tersely. "Even if I could, there's no way we'd be able to leave."

"Why not?"

Thorn looked like he wanted to say something but held back. "It's better if you just don't try it, Flora. Trust me."

What did that mean? Flora cocked her head in confusion, and was about to say more, but Thorn was already dipping into Madame Cribellum's office. Madame Cribellum hadn't even bothered to lock it.

Thorn was right. There was absolutely nothing of use to Flora in the office. She rifled through papers, and bound notebooks, and long lists and found nothing.

"Told you," Thorn said, leaning up against the wall with crossed arms.

Flora slapped down some papers and looked up at him. Hanging next to him on the wall was a black-and-white photograph of a young man in a smart suit, glasses, and dark hair parted down the middle, standing next to a young, long-lashed Madame Cribellum. They were cutting a ribbon in front of the estate with giant scissors.

"She really loves using those scissors," Flora said dryly, thinking of Madame Cribellum cutting Maple's ribbon rose.

Thorn turned to look at the picture and breathed a short laugh. "That's Henry Nuthatch with her. He went missing years ago. None of us ever met him."

"So Madame Cribellum helped him open the mill back up after the moths destroyed everything." It was strange to see this version of her. She had a big smile on her face. Her hair was done up more loosely, and she was wearing a dress that must have required a tight corset. She looked like the images of starlets Flora had seen on post cards and catalogues at the market. She was waving to the crowd. "She looks so happy."

"He doesn't," Thorn said. Henry looked stern, as if opening the mill wasn't his idea.

Flora laughed. Then she pursed her lips. "What about her room?"

Thorn shook his head. "You're insane."

"Please?" Flora gave him her very best pout.

"Fine. But we have to be quick. And you have to leave everything exactly how you found it."

"I promise."

They left the office and crept down the hall in the other direction from the dormitories. Here, the wallpaper wasn't peeling, and ornate crystal sconces lined the wall. They came to a door with elaborate millwork. "Is that a spiderweb?" Flora touched it.

"Ssshh!" Thorn got out some sharp utensils and began picking the lock until it clicked. He turned the crystal doorknob.

When the door opened, Flora felt the same creepy feeling she got when she felt like she was being followed by the Witch Moth. A strange buzz started between her shoulder blades and trickled down her spine. They stepped into a room with an ornate purple chaise lounge, a bulbous velvet settee, and a large black rug with deep purple designs. A chandelier of dark iron and amber drops was hanging from the ceiling. It looked like a spider dripping with tree sap.

They could see Madame Cribellum's bed through an archway. There was a large, curved window behind it overlooking the front lawn with spider-webbing millwork. Flora felt safer knowing Madame Cribellum's window looked out the opposite direction from her own room's forest view.

There was a shiny black lacquered vanity with ornate golden knobs under a large silver Art Deco mirror. On top were various makeup bottles and tubes and a large jar filled with a shimmery powder. Flora dipped her fingers into its soft contents and sparkles stuck to her skin. She rubbed them onto her palm. They

reminded her of something. Something from the forest, but she couldn't think of what.

She looked up, saw her reflection in the mirror, and turned to see if the lump on her back was showing. It was plumping up her sweater under her neck. There wasn't really anything she could do about it, but she could still stand up straight. She tried to run her fingers through her hair and gave up when she was met with tangles.

"You have really bright eyes," Thorn said, looking at her reflection in the mirror.

Flora looked at her sapphire eyes with a small smile. She loved her eyes. But Thorn had said bright, not pretty, so she tried to hide her smile by changing the subject, and went for the cabinet. "Maybe there's something in here."

"Careful!" Thorn said, "Don't leave any smudges."

Flora pulled the golden knob carefully without touching the shiny wood and looked inside.

"Newspaper clippings?" Flora lifted them up and looked through them. "They're all about Henry Nuthatch."

Thorn came to look over her shoulder and read some of the titles.

"Textile Tycoon's Family Devastated over Destruction of Mill, Moves To City. Flora Nuthatch, Beloved Wife and Mother, Dies of Sorrow Over Lost Home. Henry Nuthatch Treks Through Jungle to Find Illusive Tiger. Henry Nuthatch Vows to Destroy Moths that Plagued Father's Mill. Naturalist Canoes Through Canyon to Glimpse Pack of Wolves."

"Somebody's obsessed," Thorn said.

Flora read from the article about moths. There was a picture of Henry in a safari hat and khakis holding up a large Atlas moth in the jungle…

"Estranged heir Henry Nuthatch has traveled the world since being forced from his home as a child. His love of animals has led him to some daring adventures and alarming discoveries. But, he says, "Those fluttering moth wings of my youth have always seemed to find me, whispering my past through the trees and beckoning me back to Silkwood." Silkwood, his childhood home, was overrun by moths, forming a phobia in the otherwise lover of nature. To conquer his fear, Nuthatch has learned of ways to kill them. Spurred on by his mother's fatal fever, the young naturalist has sworn to return to the forest filled with moths to examine them with his new scientific knowledge, and to find the right plague, his own fever…to pay them back."

"Dramatic," Thorn said.

Flora dumped the articles back into the drawer and opened the next one. A pungent herbal smell rose up to her nostrils. There were several amber glass bottles with corked stoppers. She lifted one up and uncorked it. "Camphor," she said. "It's used to repel insects."

"Like moths?"

"Yes."

She corked the bottle again and placed it back among its peers. In the final drawer, there was nothing but an envelope with quickly scrawled calligraphy written across its top:

Mariposa

"Is that Madame Cribellum's first name?"

Thorn shrugged. "Yeah, I think so."

Flora prodded her fingers into the envelope and brought out a letter. "It's from Henry Nuthatch." She skimmed the contents. "He's thanking her for helping him so much with the mill, couldn't imagine a better spinner, her friendship means so much to him, her economic mind..."

"Uh oh...sounds like he wasn't interested in her," Thorn said.

"What do you mean?"

"Keep reading..."

"He says he has to leave before the weaving can start..."

"See?"

"There's nothing in here about our parents." She shoved the letter back inside the envelope and slammed the drawer shut. "This is so infuriating! I thought I would at least find *something*!"

Thorn took his sleeve and rubbed the marks Flora had made on the drawer. "I'm sorry," he said. "At least you're still trying. We all gave up a long time ago."

"I have to try. My grandmother told me to find my mother. Actually, she wrote me a note that said to look for *the* mother." She pulled her book of moths out of her pocket and found the note tucked inside a page with a few pressed wild flowers. "To find the light, Look for the mother," she said.

Thorn read the note, then looked up at Flora with curiosity in his eyes. Flora's own eyes narrowed. He knew something!

Footsteps sounded in the hall.

Flora's eyes went wide as Thorn grabbed her quickly and then pushed her through the archway. "Hide!" He mouthed. He rushed for the bed and dove underneath. Flora followed as quickly as she could.

They smooshed up next to each other, as still as possible. Their hearts skittered like two bunnies in the grass as a fox approached. Their faces could easily be seen if anyone knew where to look. They listened as the door to the bedroom opened and footsteps moved across the room.

Madame Cribellum quickly dragged her lanky body in and collapsed onto the purple tuffet in front of her vanity. She adjusted her enormously floofy hat in front of the mirror and looked at herself with disgust. She fondled her amber necklace and stared at it with a sorrowful, sour expression.

"Henry, look what you've left me with. These meetings get harder and harder. I want your success to live on…I want…"

She sighed heavily and grabbed a large makeup brush. She dipped it into the jar of sparkly powder and brushed it across her face. Her haggard face seemed to pull taut at the dust's touch. She flicked more dust onto the top of her head. Then she rubbed it into her skin and hair, and it seemed to absorb into the follicles and pores. She closed her eyes and relaxed. When she opened her eyes, she grinned at her reflection. She batted her eyes and looked up at Henry's portrait on the wall.

"Everything I've done has been for you, my love. Why couldn't you see that?"

For some reason, Flora's nose chose that moment to tickle. All the powder Madame Cribellum had brushed into the air found its way to her nostrils. She felt a strong desire to sneeze, and she twitched. She pinched her nose and looked at Thorn with watery eyes. He looked back in helpless fright, shaking his head.

Madame Cribellum bristled and slowly turned toward them.

Thorn jolted in fear.

"Madame Cribellum!" came Ermine's voice from downstairs. "The wool shipment has arrived!"

Madame Cribellum stood up abruptly, grabbed her hat, and waltzed back out of the room.

   The children waited under the bed in silence for a good five minutes before moving. Thorn rolled out, and Flora crawled after him. They stood up and shook dust bunnies off their clothes. In a grand swoop, Flora's sneeze finally came.

   "That was close," Thorn breathed.

Flora nodded enthusiastically. "How will we get back without her noticing?"

"Come on, I know some short cuts."

They walked through the archway and...

"Ahem?!"

Flora gasped.

But it was only Ermine. She stood in the doorway, hands on her hips. "Do you know how much trouble you'd be in if she caught you in here? Get back to work, you two! What were you thinking?"

"Sheesh, Ermine, you scared us to death!" Thorn said, and he and Flora rushed past her into the hall.

"Please don't tell her!" Flora pleaded.

"Are you kidding? She won't tell. She'll be in even worse trouble than we would be." Thorn laughed as they ran down the hall.

Ermine stopped them at the top of the stairs and yanked Flora's arm. "Why were you in her room?"

Thorn shrugged and looked to Flora.

Flora sighed. "I was looking for information about my parents."

Ermine gave her a sad look and shook her head. She knew Flora hadn't found anything. "You need to give up on this, Flora. You're just going to end up disappointed. Or hurt." Ermine nervously rubbed her leg and bit her lip.

Flora couldn't understand Ermine. Why wouldn't she want Flora to find something if she could?

"Now hurry! Madame Cribellum is doing her rounds next." She turned and began gliding down the stairs.

For someone so stoic, Ermine was as graceful as a deer. As Flora stumbled after her she looked down at Ermine's pointed toes. Everything about her was a perfect dance. Her polka-dotted dress swished like a ballerina. But as she bounced, Flora noticed that there were scars on the backs of her legs. She hadn't seen Ermine without her black tights on before. She wondered how she'd gotten them.

The children scrambled through passageways and doors in a roundabout way to get back to the spinning room.

As Flora shuffled back to her loom, her hand caught the light of the fire and Madame Cribellum's powder glimmered on her fingers. She sat, curious, thinking back to another time when she had been near a similar golden glow.

Lanterns strung through the hollows of her mind. Moths flit from thought to thought. She was back in her hammock, by her river. Then she remembered the little golden moth who'd gone too close to the flame. She plucked it from her memory and touched its wings.

Flora knew what Madame Cribellum had in that jar…

Moth dust.

10

THE GEODE

he children got back to work at their looms, falling into their usual rhythm. Maple sulked and worked slowly, but Ermine was her usual best.

"Cheer up!" She said, "When the Parisians come, Madame Cribellum usually has the chef bake something special to impress them! We usually get to eat all the samples while he's testing out recipes!"

It didn't matter how tired or bored everyone else was; Ermine was quick and light on her feet. Her fingers worked so quickly, you could barely see what she was doing before she had a whole bolt finished.

"You have the energy of a webworm, Ermine!" Flora laughed.

"Excuse me?" Ermine stopped and stared at Flora.

"What's a webworm?" Thorn tried not to laugh.

"They can weave webs over whole trees in the forest!" She pulled her moth book out of her pocket and flipped through the pages. She found the webworm page and gasped. She'd forgotten what they turned into.

"What is it?" Maple peaked over at the page.

"They turn into Ermine moths!" Flora yelped. She showed Maple the image.

"And they have spots!" Maple squealed, "Just like Ermine's dress!"

Flora read the poem.

"Ermine spun a giant marquee,
To house all her friends
For the webworm party,
She'll look so ravishing
When she comes to the ball,
Wearing her favorite
Spotted fur shawl."

"What's a marquee?"

"A tent," Flora said. "They're also called tent caterpillars."

"Ugh..Flora, don't be silly. Cribellum will hear you!" Ermine glanced over, then did a double take. "What? That's really strange."

"Right?!" Flora shook her head in disbelief. "It's just like how the Rosy Maple Moth looked like Maple. How is that possible? I wonder if…" Flora turned a few pages to a moth that looked like a crumpled maroon leaf with tiny crescent moons on its wings.

"Look! There's a Purple Thorn moth, too. It looks just like Thorn!" She leapt into the air.

Thorn knit his brows when he saw the moth with his name. "What in the world?" He cocked his head. "That's crazy." He read the poem for his moth.

"Mr. Thorn
Is a perfect thief,
He steals all my roses
Disguised as a leaf."

Thorn laughed. "Hey, I like that one."

Flora turned more pages, and the children recognized other names from the mill. Emerald, Tiger, Satin, Cloud, Alcides, Gypsy, Ruby…

"What about that one?" Maple pointed to a giant moth with purple and black chevrons.

"Oh that's The Black Witch Moth," Flora whispered. "There's a legend that she's really a spider who stole magic dust from the moth fairies to give herself power, then turned them all into plain moths. She uses their magic, just like a spider sucking blood." The children crowded around Flora to hear better.

"When the large dark wings of the Witch Moth fall, a death or murder has come to call."Ermine read. "That's creepy."

"Mariposa de la Muerte." Maple read slowly. "What does that mean?"

Flora wracked her brain. "Ummm…Butterfly of death, I think."

"Shhhh!" Ermine looked at Flora with pleading eyes. The rest of the children in the room were looking at Flora. Their machines stopped.

Flora's heart sank as she realized there must be something or someone behind her. "Deadnettle! Not again!" she cursed, rolling her eyes. "This lady is everywhere!" She whispered to the others. They snickered. But then Flora became serious. She couldn't let Madame Cribellum see her moth journal!

"WHAT is going on in here?" Madame Cribellum's loud heels rapped across the floor toward them, her spindly fingers splayed. "Give me that book!"

Flora fell into a blind panic. She would lose all the memories from her beloved forest if Madame Cribellum took it! It would be a thousand times worse than losing the pink rose. It was the only thing she had to remember her beautiful moths. She yelled "No!" and tried to rush away.

Madame Cribellum grabbed Flora by her sweater, and she bounced back toward her. She yanked the book out of her hand and leafed through the images, disgust creeping across her face. "Moths!"

"My grandmother taught me all about them," Flora said, "and I've studied the moths in the forest my whole life!" She thought of Madame Cribellum's drawer full of camphor. "They're not evil like you think! They have magic!"

Madame Cribellum froze. "Is that so?"

"Well, I think they're magical," Flora said. "They can camouflage, knit cocoons, and the inch worm can even measure!"

Madame Cribellum pursed her lips, and she began to shake with anger as she leafed through Flora's book. "We have far too much work to do," she finally said. "And especially no time for telling fairytales about moths while we ought to be filling our quotas for the day." Her eyes pierced down at Flora like violet flint. "There's only one place these creatures belong…" She slammed the book shut and walked, determined, over to the fire.

Flora's eyes welled with tears. Her precious book! All her poems, all her drawings, all her memories of her forest… She knew she shouldn't speak; it would only make Madame Cribellum more angry, but she couldn't help it. "You hate stars, you hate pink, and you hate *moths*!? Madame, I used to think the whole world was filled with nothing but beautiful things, but now I see that you are the exception!"

Madame Cribellum glared at Flora, chin upheld, and dangled her book over the flames. The corners of her mouth curled into an evil grin.

"Please don't!" Flora pleaded.

Madame Cribellum's fingers began to open.

Then, without thinking, Flora angrily grabbed her geode out of her pocket and threw it at Madame Cribellum as hard as she could. The stone missed and crashed against the brick of the fireplace. It shattered, and to everyone's shock, the stone released a flash of bright, glittering light that filled the whole room. Jagged crystals shone up from the pieces. Madame Cribellum cowered back, dropping the book to cover her eyes. She was blinded!

"Light!" Flora gasped. She wondered how many more of the geodes in the spring had magic inside. Or perhaps she had just never been in such a dark place to notice. Flora felt a glimmer of hope inside but then began regretting her decision as Madame Cribellum regained composure. She shot forward and touched Flora's forehead. The color drained from Flora's face, and she could barely feel her own body. In a haze she moved as Madame Cribellum pushed her out of the weaving room and up the stairs toward her room. She walked in a trance to her door, and Madame Cribellum shoved her inside.

"I had a feeling you'd be just as entitled as your mother was, Flora. But I had no idea you'd be so vicious." I think it would be best if you stayed in here for the rest of the day so you can learn your lesson. You'll be missing meals. And you can forget about the cream puffs I was having the chef test for the Parisians!"

High up above the forested world, Flora cried in gasping bursts. Her book! Her book she'd spent so many summers filling with drawings in her meadow, pondering poems with wings flickering in the sunlight. It had been her last fleeting string that still tied her to home. Her heart was broken, just like her geode. She snuggled up inside her sweater and pretended it was a soft hug from her grandmother. "Oh Gran…where are you!?"

Flora was so homesick, she didn't care about finding her mother anymore. She was probably dead anyway. Sometimes that was easier to imagine than Flora being abandoned. She didn't even know her name. How was she supposed to find her? It was hopeless. There would never be anyone to watch over her anymore.

Except for the caterpillar. She looked up to find it and saw that it had built a cocoon in the mortar of the stone window. She touched the brown and gold threads carefully.

"Why did you have to go and do that? Now who's going to keep me company?" Flora sulked. "Sorry. I'm just in a rotten mood. Honestly, I wish I could escape in there with you."

The minutes ticked by. Flora was so hungry, she felt a little delirious. She stared into the tree-filled distance for a long time, then laid down and looked up at the sky. Every once in a while, a cloud in the shape of an animal would pop its head out…A tail, a fin, a wing…and then they would disappear into the froth. But soon all Flora could see in the clouds were puffs of pastry, tufts of whipped cream, and chocolate swirls. The smell of sweet, buttery cream puffs came wafting up from the mill kitchen. It wasn't fair. She'd wanted to try them ever since she saw them at the candy stall at the market. They never ever got to have anything so delicious. Nothing but gruel, stale bread, the occasional gloopy casserole, dry chicken…It was the one time the Parisians would be there, and she'd get to try the chef's trials…

Then she could hear the children laughing. Laughter! Out loud and not hushed. She wished she could be down in the dining hall to experience it.

Flora's stomach growled. She tried to close her eyes and fall asleep, trying to block out the thought of food. But she was startled by a scraping sound at her door. Flora got up to inspect the noise. It was coming from the lock in her door. She whispered, "Hello?"

11

THE MOTH HOUSE

he doorknob turned, and the door creaked open.

"Hi." It was Thorn wearing a big grin on his face.

Flora couldn't contain her happiness. And confusion…"What are you doing here…?"

He slowly brought something out from behind his back. "Ta da!"

"My BOOK!" Flora grabbed it and jumped up and down, tears in her eyes.

"Cribby dropped it when you threw the rock at her. I picked it up and hid it under some fabric."

"Thorn!" She gave him a hug, then quickly pulled away and blushed.

She dazedly opened her book and leafed through its pages with tender fingers. She kissed the front page that had an inscription from her Gran, her handwriting so familiar. She put it in her sweater pocket and made sure it was hidden.

Thorn watched her patiently, then said, "There's something I want to show you." Suddenly, he was grabbing her hand and whisking her down the stairs. "Come with me!"

Flora's heart lurched.

He led her down a few passages and then back up another set of stairs. The occasional window showed that they were on the top floor, in a wing of the mansion that overlooked the garden. Snow dusted the manicured box hedges of the small ornate parterre.

Thorn stopped in front of a large brass door carved with leaves and vines. Its handle swirled up out of the vines into the shape of an art nouveau flower.

"Won't Madame Cribellum catch us?"

"Oh, she's busy taste-testing the chef's creations. That should take some time. Which reminds me…" He paused and pulled something else out from behind his back. "Snagged you one."

"A cream puff!" She held it as if it were the dearest thing she'd ever received. "You've no idea how long I've been wanting to try one!" She closed her eyes, and then, as if making a wish… she took a bite. It was a dream. Puffy pastry on the outside and

sweet cream on the inside. And it was drizzled with chocolate icing sprinkled with pearlescent little orbs.

"Nonpareils!" She squealed.

"What does that mean?" Thorn said taking out some utensils to pick the lock in the door.

"It means *without equal*." And Flora agreed. She couldn't help stuffing her face. Each little ball of sugar crunched in her mouth like a sweet burst of joy. She finished her treat by the time Thorn had picked the lock in the door. But the true treasure was what was on the other side.

"It's the conservatory on the roof of the mill!" Thorn said. "I started coming here a few weeks ago." The children stepped into a room made entirely of glass. It towered above them into a round pinnacle, panes of glass held together with a skeleton of iron. Flora felt like she was under a large cake plate. And growing all along the path that guided them through the room were plants. Some were familiar to Flora, ones she had grown to know well from her forest. Others were exotic. Giant leaves larger than herself plumed out of spiny trunks, spindly vines crawled up the walls, and flowers draped over the walkway. Tall palms and tree ferns reached up and splayed close to the glass. The air was thick and warm.

Flora was entranced. She looked at Thorn with excited eyes.

"Thought you'd like it," Thorn smirked.

"It's amazing!" She touched a leaf to her cheek, then put her nose to it to breathe in its scent. "I'd seen it from the outside, but could never have imagined how beautiful it is inside! This is the best gift I could ever ask for."

Thorn beamed. "The Nuthatches grew plants in here to make dye," he said. "I thought you could find some way to make colors from these plants. The way you did for Maple's rose."

Flora could hardly contain her excitement. There were little plaques by each of the plants.

"Pomegranate," Flora read one of them. "Dry, crush and boil rind for yellow dye."

"Take some!" Thorn nudged her. "Nobody will notice."

"I don't know, are you sure? Madame Cribellum seems to notice everything." But without hesitating, she began walking through the plants, reading their plaques. She took leaves and buds, bark and roots, here and there, and put them gingerly into her deep dress pockets. Thorn helped her gather some berries from a high branch.

"Elderberries!" Flora hopped in excitement.

She almost felt as if she were back in her forest again. "How does it stay so humid in here?"

"There's a vent over by the door and a wheel to open a valve. Steam comes out of it. I think it comes from a hot spring."

"That makes sense! A lot of the same plants grow by our spring because it's warm. Maybe whoever made this uses the same one! Or there could be another spring nearby. Either way, it's such a good idea. It's like a magic garden bubble." Flora smiled dreamily, then frowned. "Does Madame Cribellum like it?"

"Don't worry. I've never seen Cribby come in here."

Flora felt reassured. She sat down on a stone bench next to a spray of orchids and took everything in. Then she sat up abruptly. She noticed something twinkling through the leaves.

"Look!" She bounded for a stack of shelves in the wall by the vent. "Crystals!" There were dozens of specimens lined up, mostly white quartz. There were a few especially sparkly druzy pieces and some purple-tinted points. One was dark black with brown edges. "Ooooh. This one is smoky quartz."

"Ok...you have to tell me. What was inside that rock you threw at Cribellum? Was it like one of these?"

Flora liked having a secret. She smiled mischievously. "Kind of. It was a geode. It looks like an ordinary rock on the outside but has crystals like this on the inside." She picked up one of the druzy pieces, and it scattered light across the shelf. "They're really sparkly, but I've never seen the crystals give off light like that geode when it broke."

"Madame Cribellum was scared to death of it! I think she'll think twice before bothering you again after today," he nudged her with an elbow. "Dooo you have any more of them?" He grinned.

"I wish I did!" Flora sighed. "I got that one from the stream I used to live next to. It comes from a spring under a cherry tree in the forest. It's full of geodes!"

"Too bad we can't go there and collect a hundred of them. I'd like to start a war with old Cribby. Can you imagine the look on her face if we all started throwing exploding, blinding light rocks at her?" He imitated Madame Cribellum's shriek.

Flora rolled her eyes and stifled a laugh.

"Here, this way. I want to show you something. It's the real reason I brought you here." They walked through thick vines at the end of the room, where the glass ended and the stone exterior of the building jutted out. It was dark from years of leaves swirling up toward the top of the conservatory and finding no way out. Flora pushed back mounds of thick foliage curtains and came across something she didn't expect. "Moths!" She ran toward a large, framed stretch of fabric hung on the wall. It was at least ten feet high and spanned from the ground all the way to where vines covered the top. It was covered with pinned moths and scientific notes on Lepidoptera.

"They're Henry Nuthatch's. Remember the article in Cribellum's office saying that after his parents went into ruin, he became obsessed with moths. He must have collected them and made this conservatory to study them. It looks like he ended up liking them."

"It's a butterfly house!" Flora exclaimed. "Only better. Moths are so much more magical. A moth house!"

Thorn laughed. "I've been wondering about that. Why do you think moths are so much better than butterflies?"

Flora looked at Thorn quizzically. "Because they make silk!" She looked at the moths on the fabric and sighed. "And because there's something so enchanting about creatures of the night. They search for the stars and fly by the light of the moon. And they're furry, like little bunnies! And have you ever seen a pink butterfly? No. But there are heaps of pink moths…"

"All right, all right…I get it. You love moths!" Thorn laughed.

"I miss going out into the forest and seeing them in the shadows. They were like spirits of starlight flitting past." She stared off into space, remembering her meadow evenings. Thorn watched her curiously. Then she sighed heavily and brought herself back to reality. "So. Henry Nuthatch was a naturalist. He loved animals. He collected crystals and moths."

"Yeah, it's strange. They say that he started out with a vendetta to destroy all the moths in Silkwood, but this looks like he ended up fascinated by them instead. That's what I wanted to tell you about. I know this may be hard for you to hear because you're so set on finding your mother. But I realized something… Someone who collects moths is called a *Mother*." He said the word with a short "o" and a harder "th" like cloth, broth, or moth.

Flora's mouth was agape. "How do you spell Mother?"

"M. O. T. H. E. R."

"The same as mother?" She said the word with a longer "o" and softer "th" like smother, other, or brother.

Thorn nodded. "Sometimes there's a hyphen. See here…" he pointed to a scrap of paper on the moth frame. It had a small note with a date for a "moth-er lecture".

Flora grasped Thorn and grinned. "That's it! Oh, I could kiss you!"

Thorn raised an eyebrow.

Flora began pacing. "To find the light, look for the Mother. She must have meant the MOTHer! Pigweed, Gran, why couldn't you have used a hyphen?!" She looked to the heavens and shook her fist. Then she turned to Thorn. "I saw a light on in here the night I first came to the mill…maybe Henry as been here recently! Maybe he's close!"

Thorn's face fell. "That was probably me. I found the conservatory around that time. I would come in here at night sometimes. Actually, yeah. That night I'd made it back to my room just in time. I was lying on my bed when you walked past."

Flora's excitement left her like a deflated balloon. She slumped down onto the ground next to the moths.

"I'm sorry, Flora. He went missing years ago. Nobody knows what happened to him."

"We already searched Madame Cribellum's room. There wasn't anything in his letter about where he was going." She said. "It's another dead end."

Thorn sat down and put his arm around her, fluttering the moths on the frame.

Flora felt flutters in her stomach, too.

"Maybe there's something here that could help you?" He pointed to the moths.

She looked up at all the beautiful colors displayed on the moth canvas. She pointed to a moth with black and white stripes on its upper wings and orange underwings with black spots. "This one is a Garden Tiger moth," she said, "and this is a sunset

moth. See how the orange and red and blue look like a sunset?"
The sunset moth was the brightest on the whole board. Its colors
shimmered like jewels on black velvet. "It's also called a King
Moth."

"Beautiful," Thorn said. He looked at Flora and smiled.

They sat together, admiring all the different moths for a
while. Flora told Thorn all she knew about each one, reciting
some of the poems she could remember making, and he seemed
genuinely wrapped up in her explanations. "And see
here….these are underwings. They're special because they look
like ordinary brown and gold moths when they're resting, but

when they fly their underwings are bright colors like orange and pink and red." She recited,

"The underwing is a marvelous bloke,
With secret colors under his cloak."

Thorn laughed. "But why don't they have color on their upper wings?"

"Because when they're shut, they can blend in with the bark of a tree. And then when they open they scare all the things that would eat them. See how they flash like bright eyes when they open?"

"Oh yeah…they do!" He looked carefully at the underwing moths and the corner of his mouth lifted into a smile. "I like it when something's true colors are hidden underneath like that," he said. "It's like when you don't realize someone's beauty until you get to know them."

Flora smoothed her thick hair over her hump nervously. She couldn't help but compare herself to the underwings. "They're not as beautiful as the sunset moth though. At least not when they're closed."

Thorn cocked his head. "They're already beautiful. See how they're all sparkly when they catch the light? Their squiggly lines look like gold and silver."

"I guess you're right."

"They need a better poem...something that makes them sound prettier." He looked up, thinking. "How about..."

"Like a twinkling star,
On a moonless night,
The underwing flashes
Her hidden light."

Flora brightened. "That's really good, Thorn! Much better." She looked at the underwings with a gleam in her eyes. There were still new ways to admire moths.

Then Flora bit her lip and scrunched up her face. She knew there had to be something more to Henry that her Gran wanted her to find. "Hey...this is all Henry Nuthatch's stuff, right? If I'm going to find the light my grandmother was talking about, I could start with his things...maybe it has to do with his crystals...or there might be something on the back of this frame. Gran always writes things on the back of pictures. Information about who's in them, the year... " They pulled the giant frame from the wall together. It was much lighter than Flora expected. But when they looked on the back, they were disappointed.

"Ragwort! Nothing."

"Look!"

Flora's entire body was engulfed in the frame, so she had to pivot to see what Thorn was pointing at.

There was a small secret door behind the frame! It blended with the stone perfectly. The only way to know it was there was a small crystal latch.

Flora set the frame down against the wall and rushed to open it. Surprisingly, it was unlocked.

"That's a first," Thorn said.

"Madame Cribellum must not know about it!"

They entered onto a tight spiral staircase made of white alabaster.

"It's like the inside of a moonsnail!" Flora said. It rose up into a small room with low walls with tiny round windows. They were inside one of the sloped roofs of the estate. There was a desk made of dark mahogany wood covered in papers, paints, brushes and pens. A detailed aqua and green globe gleamed on a golden stand. There were a couple of plush leather chairs, and lined against the low walls were bookshelves covered in what looked like a world traveler's hoard. Taxidermy, jars of scientific-looking specimens, exotic art, photographs of distant places…

Thorn lit a lamp on the desk as Flora poked and shuffled through the shelves and looked at the walls, delighted by what she saw: a handsome picture of a teenage Henry Nuthatch in a jungle with a baby tiger, a notebook filled with drawings of rare animals, a snakeskin in a basket that kept unraveling into oblivion when Flora lifted one end.

"This must have been his mother." Thorn lifted a black-and-white photograph from the desk. It showed a tiny Henry encased in his mother's arms, dark curls brushed to the side. He was holding his hand up to the camera to show something special. Flora scrunched up her face. It was a large, spindly spider.

"He certainly loved animals," she said. She took the frame. "I wonder how old he was." She turned the frame over and popped open the back. There was a note inside written in prim penmanship. "Looks like his mother wrote something."

Henry has the most incredible attachment to animals. He brings home all manner of beasts who are injured or sick and keeps them in his room. Sometimes he keeps them as pets if they want to stay, but mostly they return to the forest, all the better for his sweet nature. I can't say no to him; he loves them so. Even the other day, he found a big black and purple striped spider in a puddle in my garden and announced he could nurse it back to life. Most children would be scared, but not my Henry. She was nearly dead, but for a few small twitches in her legs. He bound her legs and warmed her in the sunlight of his windowsill. Now the two are inseparable! She weaves the most brilliant iridescent webs and does delicate tight rope walking shows for him. It's almost as if Henry can understand her, and she him!

"Yeeelk. I do not like spiders," Flora said. "But it is really sweet that he helped it. And that his mother let him care for creepy crawly things. You can tell she really loved him."

Thorn nodded, then continued rifling through the pictures. "Ha! Look at this one!" He lifted a picture of Henry older, perhaps 20, looking dapper in a suit and fedora. His solemn face looked all the more funny because of the exotic birds on his shoulders and hat. Their feathered tails nearly went down to his knees. Flora giggled at the sight.

"Here's something!" Flora blew dust off a large book filled with writing. "It looks like a diary. I bet I could get lots of information about him from this."

As she lifted it, an envelope fell from the pages. It had Henry Nuthatch written in gold ink across it.

Thorn took it.

"Should we see what's inside?"

"We might as well…he's missing, so it might be a way to find him. Maybe he'll be grateful in the end."

Inside the envelope, they found a letter. It was written in the same lovely, bright gold ink as his name on the envelope. It read,

My darling Henry,

Forgive me for not coming in person, but the most wonderful thing has kept me from the more dangerous shadows of the forest. I cannot wait to tell you! Please come and be with me. I don't want to keep our love a secret any longer. My parents will have to accept you once they know how much I love you. Mother may be the emperor, but her family comes first. I am counting the seconds until you return!

All my love,
Luna

"Who is Luna?" Flora asked

"No idea. I wonder what the surprise was."

"And an emperor? Emperor of what?" Flora read the letter over again in her head. Why did Luna paired with Henry seem so familiar? A memory formed in her mind, like water filling a dry sponge. "L and H!" Her face beamed. "I SAW Henry and Luna's initials on the cherry tree in the forest! Carved inside a heart!"

"Huh." Thorn said.

"But that's not all of it…The letters were tiny. Like minuscule tiny. I don't even know how I was able to see them myself." Flora knew they had to have been carved by someone who was tiny herself…could it be?

"That's strange," Thorn said. "Why do you think…"

"THORN!" came a bellowing yell from down the stairs.

The children didn't notice the sky was growing dimmer. In their excitement, they forgot that tea had come and gone, and the work bell had rung. "Oh no! Will you be in trouble?" Flora winced.

"No, I'll just tell her I needed to use the bathroom or something. I'm always doing different jobs throughout the mill, so I have reason to be in all different places anyway. But if she knows I'm gone, then she's not preoccupied anymore, and she might want to check on you."

"Quackgrass!" Flora whispered loudly. "I have to get back to my room!"

"Just leave everything here. You'll be able to sneak back again. Don't worry."

The two crept back out of the secret study and rushed through the plants of the conservatory.

"I'll leave the door unlocked. There are so many doors; there's no way she'll check." Thorn squeezed her hand. "I hope you find something useful."

They snuck out the door and quickly went their separate ways. Flora clutched her book of moths to her chest, and her insides squeezed with delight. Thorn had turned one of the worst days of her life into one of the very best. When she was a flight of stairs above him, she whispered loudly down to him, "Thorn!"

He slid to a stop and looked up.

She held up the book and said, "Thank you!"

He gave her a genuine smile. Not the smirking, winking kind he gave all the girls. A knowing, kind smile. She wouldn't trade that look for all the cream puffs in the world.

12

FRIENDS

"Come on, come on! I have a surprise for you!" Flora held onto Maple and Ermine's hands as Ermine reluctantly went up the stairs, and Maple walked on her tiptoes in excitement.

"Eeee! What is it, what is it?!" Maple squeaked.

"Flora, what are you up to?" Ermine said, "You're already in so much trouble from the stars, and the rose, and the MOTHS! I don't want to get dragged into whatever you've cooked up next."

"Would you stop worrying? We're not going to get in trouble," Flora rolled her eyes. *Sometimes I wish Ermine would just loosen up,* she thought. *Well, hopefully this surprise will help!* It was after a particularly gruesome morning working their fingers to the bone, but Madame Cribellum was so preoccupied with preparations for the Parisians arrival that there was no doubt in Flora's mind they wouldn't get caught. They had a whole hour during lunch. "Ok, close your eyes."

Flora opened the door to the conservatory and pushed her two friends in. She led them down the path, with a few grunts and nervous whimpers from the girls, and into a clearing directly under the finial top. "Ok, open them!"

The girls gasped.

Flora had set up a table with a tablecloth, candles, and plates full of herbs, berries, seeds, and nuts she'd found in the conservatory. She had created a feast out of what she recognized and could find from the garden. She'd found an old section of herbs and vegetables. Even fruit trees! Henry Nuthatch had

loved to garden. She'd made lemon cordial and drizzled it over verbena salad. There were bright orange little kumquats and…

"Strawberries!" Maple cried.

"Where did you find all of this?" Ermine smiled, despite herself.

"In here! Thorn showed it to me yesterday. I snuck around and found some things. Look! I made elderberry syrup!"

"Are these pink mushrooms?!" Maple sat down on one of the plump cushions around the table.

"They are!" Flora sat on another.

"When on earth did you find time to do this?" Ermine asked, "And where did you get these cushions?" She sat down with a skeptical look on her face.

"Thorn let me out of my room yesterday. I snuck around all evening and into the night!" Flora was wide-eyed with glee. "And the cushions I found in a linen closet down one of the staff corridors! I was looking for something for a tablecloth. I ended up using an old lace bed spread, but these were in there too! I had to patch them up a little."

"A little? There are patches everywhere!" Ermine picked at a brightly colored floral one. "I could have helped you mend them."

"There wasn't much left to mend. I think the moths got to them. I found old sheets with holes in them too. That's what I used for the patches!"

"Who cares where she got patches?" Maple scolded, "Let's eat!"

"The girls oohed and aaahed their way through every bite." It was much better than the bland gruel they'd had for breakfast.

Ermine finally said, "I haven't had anything this delicious since…since…"

"Since never!" Maple said. "I don't even know how I know what a strawberry *is*!"

The girls laughed.

"I have something else for you!" Flora went down a path and came back with three flower crowns she'd made with ferns, peach-colored orchids, tiny white strawberry flowers, and black elderberries. She adorned her friends, and they giggled with delight.

"I've never had a flower crown before!" Maple said. "I love the colors you chose."

"You have to show me how you braided these vines for the base," Ermine said. "I want to try making one, too."

"It's nowhere near as intricate as the braids you are able to do with your hair, but there's a little trick to getting the stems to fit

together," Flora said, showing her the basic method. Ermine watched patiently, then took the flowers and began braiding with even more embellishments. Maple and Flora smiled at each other knowingly as if to say, *of course Ermine would excel at weaving flowers together.*

Flora took the girls hands and leaned in. "Hey, I think we should make this place into our own secret hide-out. With Thorn too, of course, since he was the one who found it. We could make it a place where we can say all the things we want to say during our work but can't because Cribby is watching."

"Like when Madame Cribellum tripped over the yarn spread across the aisle today. Didn't she look like a feathery pheasant getting its head chopped off?! I nearly died not being able to laugh!" Maple covered her mouth as she giggled.

"Yes! Oh my gosh, I swear feathers went in every direction," Flora laughed.

"What was she doing even wearing a feather boa?" Ermine wheezed.

"Coming up with ideas to impress the Parisians, I guess?" Maple said, "I like feather boas, but on her it looked like a stick bug wearing a ream of unraveled toilet paper."

The girls howled with laughter.

"Shhhh! We'll get caught before the fun even starts if we can't keep it down!" Ermine tried to stifle her own fit of giggles.

Suddenly, the girls heard someone loudly clearing their throat. They all jumped in surprise and instantly fell silent. They looked all around but couldn't find who was there.

"What are you girls up to?" Thorn seemed to appear out of nowhere.

How did he come in so unnoticed? Flora thought.

"You left the door open, silly." He nudged Flora as he grabbed a strawberry, threw it into the air and caught it in his mouth. The girls stared.

"Ok, what are you gossiping about? Did you see Cribby fall today? She looked like a cockatoo split in half."

The girls laughed nervously, and Flora sighed, "You scared us to death!"

"I almost peed my pants." Maple said solemnly.

They all began laughing again.

"Stop making me laugh so hard, or I may actually do it!" Maple squealed.

After their nervous laughter subsided and they'd eaten the rest of Flora's spread, Flora looked up at Ermine. She seemed to be in a good mood. Maybe she could get her to talk... She asked, "Ermine, do you know anything else about what happened to Henry Nuthatch? Did Madame Cribellum have something to do with it, do you think?"

Ermine frowned. "All I know about Henry Nuthatch is that Madame Cribellum was in love with him, and he didn't love her."

"What? How could you keep that from us? Really?" Flora stared at her, eyes wide.

"It's never come up," Ermine said flatly.

"I knew it!" Thorn said.

"How do you know?" Maple asked.

"I've heard her talking to herself about it late at night while I've locked the dormitories. She's obsessed with him. Always talking about how she was the one who deserved him. How she didn't think it was fair."

"No wonder she's such an old crank," Thorn said.

Flora was deep in thought. "I don't get it. Why would he give Madame Cribellum the mill then?"

"Maybe they were friends?" Maple said, wiping strawberry juice from her mouth. "Childhood friends, maybe?"

"Who knows?" Ermine said. "Anyway, everyone says Henry Nuthatch fell in love with his work instead."

"The mill?" Maple asked.

"No, his moths!" she said.

"Another reason for Cribby to hate moths so much!" Thorn joked. The others laughed.

"No, that's true!" Ermine said without any humor. "She hated how much he loved the moths. She says it under her breath all the time."

Flora thought about the note she and Thorn had found from the mysterious Luna. He wasn't just in love with the moths. He was in love with another woman. "Jealousy," Flora whispered to herself. *Jealousy makes people hateful*, she thought. She pictured the spider who was jealous of colorful, magical wings.

"Why would he start loving moths, though?" Maple asked. "Didn't moths destroy the mill?"

She had a good point. Why did he start loving moths after everything that had happened to the mill and his family?

"Maybe there's something in his journal about it," Thorn said. Flora glared at him.

"What journal?" Ermine's face was especially stern. Her good mood was evidently gone.

Flora sighed. "We found a secret doorway. It leads to Henry Nuthatch's study. Come on, I'll show you."

Maple beamed at the little study, and even Ermine seemed impressed.

"So many books!" Maple squeaked.

Flora found Henry's journal and clutched it in her arms. "If you say we can't be in here, at least let me keep this. I need to figure out what happened to Henry. So far, I've been reading through his explorations in the jungle. A really tragic section about his mother's death. It's kind of hard to read his handwriting, and he goes on and on about specimens, but the pictures are really detailed, and he talks about everything that happens to him. I think I'll find something about his disappearance if I keep reading. Maybe it had something to do with the moths."

"We'll get in so much trouble if Madame Cribellum finds out," Ermine said, pulling away some cobwebs from a shelf. "I don't need to remind you of…is that an ermine?" She reached out and pet the fluffy tail of the little white taxidermied beast. It was the creature the fuzzy ermine moth was named for. It looked so real, as though it might crawl up her arm. She suppressed a smile.

"And look at this!" Flora handed Ermine a dusty leather tome with a golden figure with a tutu on the cover.

"A book on ballet!" Ermine squealed as she began leafing through the pages of detailed movements and intricate dance costumes.

"And there's lots on exploration!" Thorn spun a globe nestled near a stack of maps.

Maple was finding her own gems. "This book is filled with paintings of iced cakes! They're *dripping* with chocolates. I'm drooling just looking at the pictures! Con…fect…What does this say, Ermine?"

"Confections," Ermine said. She furrowed her brow. "It wouldn't hurt to use this place to help Maple learn to read better…"

"That's a wonderful idea!" Flora squealed. "So we can keep it?"

Ermine put her hands on her hips. "Fine."

"Oh, thank you! Thank you!" Maple and Flora chimed.

"But we have to be careful!" Ermine said grimly.

13

THE COCOON

ver the next few days, the children made the conservatory their own special hideout. They knew that as long as they were perfect during their work hours, Madame Cribellum would never need to come up to the landing the conservatory was on. They could be wild and silly and tell stories and play games all they wanted in what Flora had called their "Magic garden bubble" but they were hardworking, silent, drones on the outside.

One Saturday afternoon, while Madame Cribellum was out, they were playing a game of chess with a board and pieces Thorn had found in Henry's study, along with a deck of cards and an old wooden puzzle. They were playing two-on-two when Thorn and Ermine knocked down Maple and Flora's king.

"No fair!" Maple whined.

Thorn laughed. "How is that not fair? We said checkmate!"

Maple's big eyes filled with tears.

"It's just a game, Maple!" Ermine chided.

"You know what, Maple?" Flora tried to distract her. "There's a cacao plant in here. It has instructions on how to make chocolate on its plaque." Flora got up to show her. "Look at this pod! It's huge!" She lifted the brown specimen up with both hands.

Maple wiped her tears.

"How do you get chocolate from that?" Ermine asked.

"There are beans inside the pod. You dry them, peel them, heat them up, then you smash them and mix them with sugar!"

"Oh is that all?" Ermine rolled her eyes.

"There's some other ingredients to make chocolate, but I think if we just put it in water, we could make hot chocolate!"

"Hot chocolate!" Maple clapped. "But how are you going to heat it without anyone noticing?"

"And where are you going to get sugar?" Ermine put her chin in her palm.

"I think if we use the valve that heats the conservatory, we should be able to heat it up."

"Oh! Good idea!" Thorn said.

"And I think we could probably steal some sugar, a pot, and some cups from the kitchen."

"No way. That's out of the question." Ermine said.

"I think if Maple comes with me, it'll be a piece of cake," Flora said, grabbing Maple's arm.

"Me!?" Maple squeaked.

"Come on! I know you can get whatever you want with that little pout of yours." Flora could just picture her blushing cheeks and cocked yellow ringlets as she buttered up the chef.

And she wasn't wrong. When Flora and Maple snuck down to the kitchen, Maple beaming her blush as brightly as she could, the boisterous, plump chef was beside himself and only too happy to give them something other than gruel or boring root vegetables. His poofy chef's hat teetered with delight as he rummaged through the crockery.

"Don't tell your mistress," he said. "She would be furious with me if she knew."

Flora thought perhaps his skills were being wasted on the mill since Madame Cribellum wouldn't let him cook anything special unless there were important guests.

Not only did he give them a pot and some sugar, he let them have four teacups rimmed with gold and painted with flowers.

"Thank you so much!" Maple squeaked and blew him a kiss. They left him sitting among his copper pots, smiling and waving with bright pink cheeks. Maple's charms had worked their magic.

Flora was beside herself as they carried everything back. "Maple I swear...your cheeks turned the color of a flamingo! The chef didn't stand a chance."

The girls carefully set the teacups down on their table in the conservatory. They'd concentrated so hard to make sure they didn't drop them, so when they looked up they were surprised...

"Ermine!...It's so pretty!" Flora gasped.

While they were gone, Ermine had brought oodles of shimmery ribbons and hung them through the trees around their table in intricate festoons and brilliant displays. They swirled in and out of branches like magical vines.

"There were a bunch of extra ribbons in the storage closet," she said nonchalantly. Flora was puzzled. How did Ermine get them up there? They hadn't been gone all that long. And some of the acrobatics through the trees would have been impossible, even for Flora during her foraging days. "How were you able to get them intertwined so perfectly without a ladder?" she asked.

"She's like an Ermine moth, remember?" Maple laughed. "They decorate whole trees with their silk, right?"

Flora laughed, but then she scrutinized Ermine with squinted eyes.

Ermine shrugged, then she twirled, and the ribbons in her hands swirled around her.

"Look what we have!" Maple brandished the teacups.

"Those are darling!" Ermine grabbed a light green one with white polka dots. "I want the one with spots!"

"You and spots…" Thorn said, rolling his eyes.

"I get the one with pink roses!" Maple squealed.

That left one with sprays of blue poppies and one covered in golden filigree.

"Here, take this one. It matches your eyes." Thorn handed Flora the one with blue poppies. Flora took it shyly, then turned away so he couldn't see her smile.

"Well, I guess I'd better get to work on the cacao beans! In the meantime, let's put this sugar somewhere safe." Flora put the small sack of sugar in the pot and carried it to the shelves of crystals. *Huh*, she thought. The pot, the sugar, the crystals…They reminded her of how she used to make sugar crystals and hang them in the window. *I wonder…* She held one of the crystals up to the sunlight pouring through the conservatory glass. She smiled as she could see colors in the light.

"Look, you guys, it's a prism!" She went over to the others. "Light goes in through one side and a rainbow comes out the other. See?" She pointed to the ground where a rainbow fell.

"That's amazing!" Maple leapt over to the pile of crystals and grabbed a handful. "Let's make more!"

"I used to make crystals out of sugar and hang them in the windows of my grandmother's cottage," Flora said softly, turning the crystal over in her hands.

"Well, we can do that here," Ermine said, pulling a ball of string out of her pocket. Ermine always seemed to have a ball of string on hand. She tied a little bow around one of the crystals and held it up to the wall. Little rainbows and pricks of light glittered from its shining facets.

They all worked together to tie crystals to string and attach them to the ribbons Ermine had hung.

"It looks like a party in here!" Flora said.

The room seemed to flutter and jangle with rainbows in every direction. Maple swirled her skirts, catching their colors in her petticoat, as Ermine nudged the crystals, making the rainbows dance. Thorn stretched out on the ground to look up at the display.

"None of you know your birthdays, so we can just have one every day!" Flora laughed.

Through a few trials and errors, Flora finally figured out how to make hot chocolate. The children had all found a quiet place to relax in the conservatory to read and sip the velvety mixture.

Flora read Henry's journal intently. She'd gotten through his return to the mill and his interest in the moths. His quest began with pins and shadowboxes, but he had to wait for the moths to die to examine them, and he wanted to see them alive. He built the conservatory on top of the mill with the goal of capturing one of every kind of moth in the forest. Flora read a long section about the conservatory, its use of vents from the hot spring, and plans for the leaded glass. He shipped the pieces from Venice.

Then she read how he'd slowly begun admiring the moths, astonished by how many of them didn't belong in Silkwood, with colors so rare he should not have found them. Flora never knew the moths in Silkwood were rare, but she made a knowing grin when he talked about their colors and how impressive they were. "Tell me something I don't know!" Flora sighed.

She read Henry's words:

"While I set out to destroy these vermin, I found each day a new warm edge to the frill of hatred in my heart. These wings have filled my nightmares since childhood, and yet now, up close, they are more beautiful and intricate than my wildest dreams: blue tiger stripes, bright green with moons, sugary as marzipan, huge brown bat-like sails, spiky as sea urchins. Each new specimen I found tingled that warm edge until one day my heart burst into flame... when I remembered her."

Flora turned the page, and she was shocked to find a drawing that made her spit her hot chocolate back into its blue poppy cup.

"Hey everyone, look at this!"

The others came to her side and stared in astonishment. It was a picture of a ripped open-cocoon in a little boy's hands. Inside lay a tiny girl with green wings.

"A fairy!" Ermine whispered.

"With pink hair!" Maple gasped.

"Those are luna moth wings," Flora pointed. "This must be what Henry Nuthatch did to make the moths attack! He stole one of their cocoons! And it wasn't just moths—it was moth *fairies*! The Giltiri."

"Glittery?" Maple asked.

"No, GILTiri," Flora corrected. "Gilt. like the thin layer of gold on a frame or fabric. My Gran also called them The Golden Ones."

Ermine raised an eyebrow. "How do you know this isn't just a pretend thing he drew? How do you know it's real?"

"It's all right here," Flora pointed and read,

I finally remember. I never told a single soul my secret, and I kept it for so long that I began to think I had made the whole thing up. Memories are swirling in my mind like sediment in dirty water. As I sift through them, flecks of gold begin to make their way to the surface...

When I opened the cocoon on that fateful night of the moth attack, I found something I never could have imagined. First, I gently tore the end off. Just a peek. That was all I wanted. But there inside...were feet! Tiny feet! I probably should have left the tiny person alone, but I was just a young boy. I ripped the cocoon open all the way, and there was a tiny girl snuggled up inside! The cocoon had been wrapped around her like a blanket. She had hair the color of an old French rose and light brown skin. And from her back unfurled the softest, pale green wings with two tiny pink gibbous moons. Their ribbony ends faded to pink, and were wrapped around her feet. She sleepily turned over and winked up at me with her bright emerald eyes. She shimmered with faint light; all the dust on her wings, and skin, and hair glimmered up at me. I had never seen anything so beautiful. Of all the treasures I'd found in the forest, this was by far the best. She raised one eyebrow, and the corner of her mouth curled into a confused yet intrigued expression.

But the moths were quick to claim the girl from my hands. A giant moth with dazzling, colorful wings shot out of the swarm. It was in stark contrast to the muddle of mostly brown and white moths. I watched as the moth slowly morphed into a fairy. But he was fiercer than any sweet childhood story. I was terrified, even though he was small. He stood tall on the windowsill, his chest puffed out. A circlet of gold rested on his head of long black hair. His wings were outspread, resplendent with brilliant aqua, orange, bright pink, purple and black patterns. (I know now that it was the Sunset Moth, also known as the King Moth.) Before I could realize what was happening, the fairy threw a tiny spear with a crystal tip at my face. It pinged against my glasses and left a small chip.

"You will pay dearly for what you have stolen!" The sunset moth shouted as he took the girl from my open hands. It was clear from their resemblance that he was her father.

"Watch out for the web!" Another moth cried. She came to the sunset moth's side, and with a pop and brilliant sparks burst into fairy form as well. She quickly slashed the spider web with a dagger from her boot.

My spider seethed.

"There's a picture of his spider in his office," Thorn said.

The female moth's wings were a light speckled brown, a speckled Emperor Moth, I now know, and when she saw my spider, she flashed enormous black spots circled with dark pink and red rings on her underwings. They looked like owl eyes. My spider flinched back and shuddered with fear.

Flora realized there was something so familiar about this story. The spider who was frightened by pink wings. Her Gran had told her that part...but how had Gran known?

"Oh Ripheus, he's only a child!" She had haphazard red hair under a thin circlet of diamonds. She took the tiny girl from the Sunset Moth and held her close. "Was it surprising to wake up to a stranger, my dear?"

"It doesn't matter!" Ripheus barked, "They've been here stealing silk from our forest for long enough!" And at his words, the moths began to swarm...

"The rest of this page is his description of running away with his parents." Flora scanned the page.

"Do you think it's true?" Maple asked.

"If he was just a small child, it would have been hard to remember. And everyone says he went crazy." Thorn said.

"Ummm... I think I would remember a fairy in a cocoon," Flora said. "But wait, there's more..."

But years have passed, and I had forgotten what I saw—until I saw her again. I was in my garden when I saw her in the sunlight on the edge of the forest. She was picking blackberries. She was human-size, and much older, but I recognized her. Her long rose hair, her thick lashes, and that luminous, almost glowing skin—like a Tahitian pearl. I wondered why she was so

familiar... Like a fool I picked a handful of garden flowers and
walked toward her.

"I was wondering when you'd come back," she said without
looking at me.

"You…you were?"

She turned and smiled with those emerald eyes. Then I knew it was her, for sure.

"But you're…"

"Human?" She pulled back her long cloak to reveal soft green wings. They unfurled and swished around her ankles. "I'm not. Giltiri can change." She walked toward me. "That's our magic—metamorphosis. I could even change you, if you wish." She took some of the dust from her wing and held it up to her lips. She blew it into my face in a sparkly puff. Before I could say no, the world was growing larger, and I fell swiftly to the ground. But her delicate hand was there to catch me. Then she shimmered into a small size as well. We were standing together among prickly blackberry vines as big as tree trunks. The flowers I had been holding floated to the ground all around us.

"I'm Luna," she said.

"Henry."

She fluttered up into the air, then hovered close to the ground and grabbed my hand. "Come on…there's so much I want to show you!"

I looked back toward the mill, at everything I knew. How the world shifts when you have a new perspective.

I finally understand why the moths attacked, and it is a balm to my soul to know that my mother's death and the ruination of my home were not in vain. I would have done anything to find my little one, too. I would have scoured the earth and destroyed anything in my path to protect her. It's strange. I think I am in love. I think I have been since the moment I first saw her, all those years ago. Is it penance for what I did as a child? It doesn't matter now. I will do anything now to be with her, too.

It's been many weeks now, and Luna has told me the most marvelous news. I've made a decision. I want to be one of the Giltiri. Metamorphosis! I want to join her in the forest forever. Dash the mill! I shall have to make arrangements.

"He really was crazy," Ermine said.

Flora frowned. "You don't believe it?"

Ermine shrugged. "Having to leave home and his mother dying was probably really traumatic. He could have hallucinated...or I don't know. Made something up to make himself feel better. Maybe he met this Luna person, and he imagined that she was a fairy as a romantic notion. He has a lot of fairy tales in his book collection." Ermine shrugged.

"He's a man of science, though!" Flora pounded her fist on a cushion. "Everything I've read in this journal is true. Why wouldn't this be?"

"There's no such thing as magic, Flora," Ermine said.

Flora fumed. Why was Ermine always trying to snuff her light out? "Whatever." She slammed the journal shut in a huff, tucked it under her arm, and brushed through the foliage to the door.

"I believe it, Flora!" Maple called after her.

14

THE WEB

he next evening, when the four had sauntered into the conservatory after a long day's work and plopped down onto the patchwork cushions, Maple whined, "I am sooo tired of spinning. I feel like my whole body is going to turn to fluff!"

Even Ermine had a frown on her face. "At least you don't have to spin it. Usually I'm not one to complain, but that was a LOT of wool that came in today. We usually don't get that much done in an entire week!"

"Cribby's trying to break us, I think. Ever since Flora came, I swear the work has been ten times harder." Thorn threw a hazel nut at her.

Flora looked down. She was exhausted, too. She didn't know what the work was like before, but she did have to admit that it was a ridiculous amount. Her fingers had grown calluses where the thread had rubbed against her skin. Her neck and back ached from being hunched over for so long. And she probably *was* the reason Madame Cribellum was going so hard on them.

"Don't blame *Flora*!" Maple said, "Maybe Madame Cribellum is just worked up over the big order due. The Parisians are coming in a couple days, right?"

"Maybe once it's done, she'll go on holiday and give us all a break," Flora said.

"Not even this place is making me happy," Ermine gestured to the glass dome around them. "I'm just so tired. I think I'll go to bed."

"I guess I should too," Maple agreed.

Thorn yawned, got up, and put his hand out to help Flora off her cushion. But she crossed her arms and pouted.

"What's with you?" he asked.

"This is the third time this week you guys have gone to bed early!"

"We're tired, Flora!" Maple leaned on Ermine.

"I'm sick of her defeating our spirits like this! Are we really just going to go to bed early and not enjoy this beautiful night? Look outside! See the snow falling? We get to be all huddled up in here with the flowers and get to watch snowflakes without getting cold! Let's enjoy it, please? Madame Cribellum already went to bed. We can stay for at least another hour."

The other three looked up at the snowflakes lighting on the conservatory and melting against the warm glass. It *was* lovely. But Maple sighed. "I'm just...too tired to care anymore."

Flora stood up, determined. "What about some hot chocolate? It won't take long to make. I have a powder ready to go..."

"She shouldn't have it so late at night. It makes her wired," Ermine said.

Ugh! Ermine was always so sensible. It drove Flora crazy. "Ermine, stop telling us what to do!"

Ermine looked at her in shock, then narrowed her eyes. "Flora, you're just tired. Let's get to bed."

"There you go again!" Flora said. "Always being so practical. So boring! You're such a spoilsport!"

Ermine looked like she was going to say something back, but then her eyes welled with tears.

"Flora, stop it," Maple whispered. She put her hand in Ermine's.

Flora felt a twinge of guilt, but she was too angry. "You know what? I'm sick of this. I'm going to get the heck out of here. I'm tired of you trying to stop me. I can't believe I went this long without even trying! It can't be that hard to shimmy out of one of these panes of glass. I bet I could slide down the roof here..." She didn't think of what would happen next. She began frantically pushing against several panes of glass and found one that nudged loose from the iron. "Aha!"

"Flora no!" Ermine shrieked. The sound shocked Flora. Nothing remotely loud ever came from perfect, calm Ermine. But it only made Flora feel more rebellious.

"Stop telling me what to do! What are you so afraid of?!" She pushed up against the glass, and it fell forward.

Ermine gasped, and Maple covered her face, ready for the crash.

Flora caught the top of it in time before it crashed to the rooftop below. She giggled. "That was close!"

There was a collective sigh from the other children.

"Careful!" Maple said.

"Flora stop..." Ermine came forward and took the glass from Flora and set it against a pot gingerly. Before she was able to grab her, Flora was already scooting out of the conservatory.

"See you later!" Flora stepped onto the rooftop and ducked out into the open. Snow flurried all around her. She breathed in the crisp air. It was white, cold, delicious freedom. She looked back. The other children had rushed to the open glass, their faces framed by the iron pane. But instead of being delighted like Flora thought they would be, their faces were covered with terror.

"What?" Flora asked, suddenly unsure of herself. "See, all we have to do is climb down!" She could see some branches near the end of the rooftop. She carefully stepped out over the snow.

"I wouldn't do that, Flora," Thorn said. Flora turned around but kept walking backward.

"Even *you*, Thorn? I can't believe you've never thought to do this!"

"I have, Flora. We all have. But Ermine is the only one who's tried…and she got caught and…"

Suddenly, Flora was frozen. Not from the cold, not from shock. She was stuck in something invisible. As if she'd backed into thousands of invisible sticky strings. And they burned like the coldest ice. She could feel her skin searing against the lines. She tried to move her arms forward, and her whole body jangled with the movement. She was stuck in the web Maple had spoken of on the first day. She had thought it was just a metaphor, but it was real! But how? She couldn't see anything. It was like… like…

"Magic," she whispered.

"We have to leave!" Maple squealed. "She'll come soon. And when she finds out Flora knows about her powers… she'll do something terrible. She said she'd kill whoever told you about it. I tried to tell you…but Ermine stopped me. She tried to warn you without actually telling you."

Flora thought about the scars on Ermine's legs. The cold burning got stronger against her skin. She winced at the pain.

"We have to get her off of there," Thorn said.

Ermine looked at him and shook her head. "We'll never get her off. It's too powerful."

"We have to try." Maple said, "If she comes here to find her, she'll find out about the conservatory. We'll never get it back!"

"Is that all you care about?" Ermine huffed. "Flora will be punished!" She grabbed Maple and held her to her. "Maple, you at least go to bed. We'll deal with this."

"No, it'll take all of us to pull her off. I want to help!"

160

Flora felt horrible. She'd endangered all of them with her stupid antics. "You should all go. I'm so sorry. I didn't know…I mean, how could I? But still…I don't want you to get into trouble." She was still grappling with the idea of Madame Cribellum truly having magic. Of course she did. It was always so obvious now that she thought about it. But for some reason, it was hard to believe when it was in small doses. It always snuck up on her, and then she thought she'd imagined it. The way the children couldn't remember their pasts, the way Madame Cribellum could get them to do anything she wanted, even though there were far more of them than her. And there was an eternal supply of thread. Flora gasped. "If Madame Cribellum can make a web... do you think she makes the thread we use for the mill??"

The children looked back in disgust.

"Ew, GROSS!" Maple said.

"Like she's some kind of big spider?" Thorn gagged.

Ermine stepped out onto the roof. "That's disgusting. Yuck, I never thought about it. Maybe? Let's talk about it later. First, let's get you off of here." Thorn was quickly by her side, and they both took one of Flora's arms each. They were about to pull when...

"Wait!" Flora yelped. "The way a spider knows something is in its web is when it moves and the web vibrates!" She thanked her grandmother silently for telling her this detail when she'd plunged into an orb weaver's web on one of their forest hikes. At the time it had made her laugh, but now she was terrified.

They all stood perfectly still.

"You've already moved the web, though," Maple said.

"But maybe not enough," Flora said. "Maybe she hasn't noticed yet."

"So what are you supposed to do? Stay there until spring?" Thorn said, "I think she'll eventually notice."

Flora thought hard. She balled her hands into fists, closed her eyes, and took a deep breath. Her Gran told her not to let anyone take her light...but she couldn't help it. She had to try to use it to unfreeze herself.

"Listen. I'm going to show you three something. But you have to promise not to tell anyone."

They looked at her with quizzical faces.

Flora closed her eyes and searched within herself for the flame she'd been carefully stoking inside herself all day. She hardly had enough power for what she wanted to do, but she had to try. She imagined her blood was like oil from a lamp. She let the light inside her slowly dip and whir into the oil and speed through her veins. She felt herself heat up ever so slowly.

The web jangled involuntarily, and Flora's eyes popped open.

"Oh no!" Maple whispered, "She's coming!"

"Quick…were you going to show us something?" Thorn asked.

"Shhh! I have to concentrate!" Flora bit back. She closed her eyes again, trying to shut out the vibration in the web. She was already warming up her body with magic. Not actual heat, but light. She could feel it pulsing through her. She started up again and let the light radiate out until she could feel it in her fingertips.

"Flora! Your fingers!" Ermine gasped.

"And your hair!" Maple squeaked.

Flora's light was leaking out in tendrils from her. She was thankful she hadn't tried to use her magic for anything on the sly that day. She'd stored enough up for this moment. When she could feel her magic reach her toes, she opened her eyes. "Ok. Now try to pull me off!"

Maple and Thorn looked hesitantly at Flora's glowing body.

"Oh, come on!" Ermine said, yanking on Flora's leg. It came undone. Flora's light got brighter at her excitement.

Thorn and Maple grabbed Flora's arms and pulled. Like a piece of bark stuck to a magnolia tree, Flora was peeled off the web. Her hair was last; she had to tug at the unruly strands like she was playing tug-o-war. She finally fell back onto the roof with her friends in a heap.

"I'm sorry, Ermine. I'm so sorry," she panted. The sting of the web still ached on her body. Flora imagined the agony Ermine must have felt being punished by Madame Cribellum. She finally understood fully why Ermine was trying to steer her away from escaping. She never wanted to feel that pain again. "I know you're always just trying to protect us. You're not boring. I didn't mean it."

Ermine pet Flora's head and hugged her. "It's okay, Flora. You didn't know. Maybe I should have told you…"

"Please forgive me. I was being stupid." Flora buried her face in Ermine's sleeve.

"Come on, let's go!" Thorn said. "Madame Cribellum will be here any minute!" He leapt for the open pane of glass and ducked inside the conservatory. The others followed. They hid in the shadows and under large leaves, waiting.

Flora was completely drained. She'd never felt so exhausted. She peeked through the foliage out to the snowy night air where she knew the web was. Suddenly, where nothing had been, thousands of gossamer threads lit up in iridescent splendor. Where the snow touched it, it glittered.

"Look! You can see the web!" Maple pointed.

"Shhhh!" The others stifled her excitement.

Flora hated to admit it, but she marveled at the web's beauty. Such intricate patterns in a myriad of woven lines. Then it began to vibrate, and with each movement, it made silvery harp sounds. Then, as if in a sugarplum-themed winter circus, Madame Cribellum came tight rope walking along the top strands in a tiny white lace negligee. She had a long, fluttery silver night robe lined with fur over her shoulders, but her spindly legs and feet were bare. Her silvery hair hung loose. Somehow, though Flora couldn't believe she thought it, Madame Cribellum was strikingly beautiful.

Except for the tight grimace on her face. Her eyes roved over the web, searching for what had been snagged in it. Finally, she took a deep breath.

"It must have been that dratted owl." She said to no one.

Then she looked right at Flora.

Flora blinked. Could she see her through the glass?

"It's not fair," Madame Cribellum said, looking up over the entire conservatory.

Flora breathed. She hadn't seen her; only glanced her way. She silently thanked the shadows for hiding her.

Madame Cribellum gingerly slid down onto a strand of web and dangled her lanky legs into the air. She sighed heavily. "Why did he choose her? Why? When I was his favorite pet. He was *mine*. And she…they…took everything from him. I watched them terrorize him, stopping at nothing to get their child back. Was it worth destroying his life?"

She stared into the distance with a glassy expression and fidgeted with her amber necklace. A tear fell down her cheek. "When he came back, he begged me to destroy them. I know he was drunk when he finally stumbled home, muttering curses in his grief. All his animal cages were empty, they all had left…but I had stayed, waiting in his windowsill after all those years…and I heard his heart's intent! …I know he couldn't hear me, but I promised to help him."

She clutched her amber necklace, knuckles white. "I wasn't fooled when your heart was taken. Those wings you adored, horrible creatures framed in gold. I thought I had you in my web…that we would be together forever. All those traitorous excuses and goodnights…disappearing into the forest into the arms of the moth girl with the green wings..." She spat the words like a curse.

"I remembered my promise. I told you I would do anything for you. Anything." She shook her head. "Maybe I shouldn't have stolen the children...maybe..."

Then she squinted her eyes and hardened her expression again.

"It's not my fault they're a bunch of ugly little ungrateful worms! They deserve this life! At least I saved them. They don't have to live as those disgusting creatures! " And with that, she took one end of spider silk and catapulted down from the web in one fell swoop, like an acrobat, and flew away out of sight behind the roof.

The web went out like a light.

Flora looked over at the others. They were shaking.

"You KNEW about this?!"

Ermine had a pained look on her face. "Yes."

"And you told me there's no such thing as magic?!"

"She threatened us!" Maple said. "For some reason she especially didn't want you to know. That's why she keeps you in the smokestack by yourself!"

"She told us she'd push you out your bedroom window." Thorn said. He looked guiltily at Flora.

She shook her head at him in disbelief. She couldn't believe he'd said nothing, after all they'd talked about.

"It looks like you've been keeping plenty from us, too, Flora," Ermine said tersely.

All of Flora's anger drained from her. She *had* been keeping her magic a secret. "Oh...yeah. That."

They were at a standstill.

"Yes!" Maple jumped up and grabbed Flora's hair, inspecting the ends. "What *was* that light?" Then she let out a great big yawn.

"It's late," Ermine said, "and Madame Cribellum will probably check on us after inspecting the web. We'll have to get Flora to explain what on earth that was tomorrow."

Flora gave them a sheepish grin. "Fine, I'll tell you tomorrow. But only if you tell me everything you know about Madame Cribellum."

Ermine nodded. "Deal."

Flora tried to get up but fell back down in the path. She was too weak to walk after using so much energy for her light. The others helped to lift her back up. As they made their way into the hall, Thorn said to the others, "I'll take her up to her room. I'll be able to get back without being seen."

He put his arm around her to keep her upright, and she put her arm around his shoulders. He felt so warm, she wished her staircase was never-ending. But they did eventually get to the top of her smokestack tower and he released her.

Flora looked nervously at Thorn. He was staring at her with a strange look on his face. Was it dismay? Bewilderment? She couldn't place it. "What?" she said.

"I knew there was something special about you." He smirked and nudged her with his elbow, then practically flew down the steps in silence.

Flora should have been terrified of what had happened on the roof. She should have had nightmares of sticky webs and frozen limbs. Madame Cribellum was practically a spider! But she couldn't help smiling. Thorn thought she was *special*. It was the best kind of magic she'd encountered yet.

15

SECRETS

*F*lora stood in the center of the conservatory in almost complete darkness the next night. The other children stood behind her like a small audience, silently waiting. She put a cupped hand out, palm up. The others shuffled closer, squinting, trying to see what was in it.

Flora looked up at the conservatory's glass. Soft glimmers limned the panes where light from the mill reflected. The crystals Ermine had strung sparkled in the shadows as they spun slowly on their threads. Flora could now almost shift her eyesight to just seeing the world in light and dark. She absorbed glints and shimmers, and they seemed to speak a language she felt only she could understand. Once she felt that the lights had given her all they wanted to say, she blew lightly into her hand. A light pooled there. It wasn't flame, and it wasn't liquid. It was just…light. It was dull, not too bright. And it had the faintest blue tint, like the center of a candle flame.

Flora slowly turned around so the others could see.

"What the…" Thorn stood back.

Flora laughed.

"What is it?" Maple asked, getting closer.

"Light," Flora said.

"How do you do it?" Ermine asked. "Is it magic?" She furrowed her brow. "Is it dangerous?"

"It's…I don't know. My Gran told me it's available to anyone who spends time in nature. She used to use a *little* magic…but not like this. I think hers was more of a spirit…more of a thought. Mine is like a reflection. It comes from things that give off light, like the stars or a candle flame. Anything that gives off light, really. I have to focus on it really hard, then I can whisper or blow out a little or, I guess it can leak out of me like last night. It isn't very much, and I can only do it about once, maybe twice a day. That's why using it to get off the web was so exhausting. But a little can go a long way… watch this!" She threw the pool of light into the air, and it splashed up into a thousand little pricks suspended in mid-air. The room looked like it was filled with blue fireflies. The children gasped and clapped with delight.

Maple tried to catch one, and it fell onto her nose. "Flora, *you're* like a prism! Only better…"

Flora's heart caught at the thought. She *was* like one of those crystals she'd always loved to make and hang in her window. She

imagined her insides faceted and sparkling, and smiled. Then she frowned. She wished her light could somehow help them.

"I think there's an even greater light I'm supposed to find, though," Flora said. "In my Gran's note she said I would find it if I found the Mother. I think now she meant Henry...Henry's story. He found the moth fairies. Maybe that's what she wanted me to find. Maybe if I could find their light, I could use it to escape."

They all huddled together on the floor and gazed up at the sparks all around them. Flora's magic was intoxicating for these friends. She had a sneaking suspicion they had more to do with the moths than they realized. She could keep them lured with a little light. She hoped she'd snared them enough to get them to spill their secrets.

"All right. Tell me what you know about Madame Cribellum," she said.

Ermine furrowed her brow and took a deep breath. "We know she has magic. I got caught in the web ages ago, but she made me swear that I wouldn't tell anyone or someone would get hurt. Ever since I found out, I've been so careful to make sure everyone stays on task. I've always known what she's capable of. It's been exhausting."

"And I saw the whole thing," Maple said. I was watching from a window. "I'm so bad at keeping secrets, Ermine has had me under her wing ever since to make sure I don't say anything stupid around Madame Cribellum or to any of the other kids."

"She's let it slip to most of us already," Thorn quipped.

"But is that it? Just a web? Do you know anything else? What other magic does she have? Besides making you all forget your pasts and making everyone do anything she wants them to. Because that's obvious."

Ermine shook her head. "I think she must be the...what is it called? The moth with black wings with purple and silver chevrons? They look just like her silver hair and violet eyes."

"OH!" Maple squeaked.

"Me too! And think about it" Flora said. "The spider was jealous of the moths. She hated them. Especially how colorful they were. Who else do we know that hates moths and color?"

"Madame Cribellum!" Maple said.

"Yes. But I don't know for sure," Ermine said.

Maple shivered.

"Tell me again about the moth creature things..." Thorn said.

"It's an old fairy tale about why moths are always searching for light." Flora said, "There was a race of fairies with moth wings in Silkwood called the Giltiri. They weaved beautiful silk and shared their magic with the people who lived near the forest. But then a spider came and was jealous of their magic. When they wouldn't give it to her, she took the dust from their wings. Then she spun herself a cocoon out of spider silk and sprinkled the dust on herself so she could become a moth. Then she turned all the Giltiri into moths. And now that I know Madame Cribellum has a giant WEB... it all makes sense! She must be the spider."

"The one Henry was holding in the picture with his mother!" Thorn said. "And what did she say last night? That she wanted to help him destroy them?"

"She was in Henry's windowsill when he opened the cocoon, and the moths got mad," Maple said.

"She really is a spider," Ermine said. "The Witch Moth!"

"She must be," Flora said solemnly. "She's the Sorcier Noir. The Mariposa De La Muerta. The Butterfly of Death!"

"Mariposa is even her first name," Thorn snorted. "She really wasn't hiding anything, was she?"

"And did you hear her?" Flora asked, "She said she'd stolen their children. The Giltiri children! Do you realize what this means?"

"Don't say it…" Ermine said, "It can't be true!"

"You must be moth fairies!" Flora exclaimed.

"Moth fairies?" Maple asked in awe.

"I guess we have to be," Thorn said. "Unless she's got some other kids hidden away somewhere."

"I guess that could be true," Flora said. "I mean…you don't have any wings. Or magic."

The children sat in silence, absorbing everything.

After a long while, Maple's quiet voice spoke from the dark. "Ok, I have to tell you all something."

The others propped themselves up on their elbows to give her their attention. "I think I might have magic, too," she said. "Nothing like what Flora has, but I've noticed it more and more since Flora came. Actually, ever since she gave me the pink rose. She makes me want to be more brave…It's more like how Flora described her Gran's magic. Like a thought."

"I think I know what you're talking about," Flora said. "When you made Madame Cribellum look all confused when she grabbed me. There was more to it than the look on your face, wasn't there?"

"Yes! I don't know how…but the rose you gave me… somehow it helped me to feel…I don't know, to feel outside of myself. When I blush it's like the pink comes out of me and goes inside another person."

"I used magic to make the rose!" Flora gasped. "I used pink magic from the sunset!"

"I think that's what it is, then. It feels like a sunset inside of me! And it can make other people feel the same way. I've always

172

sort of felt like I could do it in tiny ways, like giving someone a hug to feel better or getting Ermine to help me with a pout, but the rose made it much stronger. "

Ermine shot up into a sitting position. "Maple, if you've been manipulating my emotions, I am going to…"

"Only a little!" Maple hid her face under her arms.

"MAPLE!" Ermine poked her.

Thorn laughed, "What do you mean, she can control thoughts?"

"No…just feelings. I sort of reach out with feelers…to the other person's feelers…"

"Like antenna," Flora said, with a knowing grin. "Maple, you *are* like a Rosy Maple moth!"

Ermine was fuming. "I knew it, you little…"

"Like you can't control silk?" Maple shot back, "I know you can! You say you just take apart knots like it's nothing, but I *know* you have some kind of power over the string, so weaving is faster for you! I've seen you thread yarn through the shuttle without your fingers. Explain that!"

Ermine gave them a sheepish grin.

Flora looked up at the ribbons weaving impossibly in and out of the tall trees, then pointed at Ermine. "You DO have some kind of magic!"

"Ok, I admit it. I didn't start out with it, though. I really do weave the fastest! But one day as I was working, I didn't have to grab the silk…it sort of just lifted up into my hands."

Flora's mouth was agape. "How?"

"At first, I thought it was static. It was right after I'd gotten a static shock from the fabric you were embroidering. Remember the stars?"

Flora thought back to when Ermine had touched the magic she'd been blowing onto her embroidery. It made sense. "Yes. I

173

was using magic on those too! Light from the sparkles of frost in the windows."

Ermine grinned. "I thought I must just be extra electric that day…but it kept happening. And it was only the strands I wanted. Eventually, well….look." She pulled out a tiny ball of iridescent white silk. She held it out for them to see, then let her hands fall away from it. The ball stayed in midair. Ermine moved her hands in an arcing, poetic motion and the ball began to unravel. Then she fluttered her fingers, and the string started looping into itself, over and under, in intricate knots. Soon it

moved so fast, it was difficult to see its movements at all. In a manner of moments, there was no longer a ball of yarn, but a fully formed ribbon floating as if it were underwater. Ermine grabbed it and said, "I've been practicing."

The others stared at her wide-eyed. Then Flora let out a knowing "Mmm hm. *Of course*. You're just like an Ermine moth, able to weave silk over trees."

Ermine gave her a look that said she didn't believe in that sort of nonsense.

"You were keeping *that* kind of magic a secret, and you were upset with *me*?" Maple asked.

"At least I wasn't in your head!" Ermine bit back.

"How else am I supposed to untie knots?"

"I'd do it for you even if you didn't whine so much!"

"Woah! Girls. Stop!" Thorn touched their shoulders. "Just forget about how upset you are for a second and think about what this means! You all have magic!"

Maple glared at him with pink cheeks, and Thorn frowned. He turned to Ermine and said, "Well, maybe you shouldn't have kept it a secret for quite so long."

"Maple, no fair!" Flora laughed, "stop using your blush on Thorn."

They all looked at Flora. Maple said, "My blush?"

"We should call it something, right? Feelers...or blush? Whenever you use your feelers, you turn pink! Let's call it your blush. Nobody will suspect that word."

"What should we call mine?" Ermine swirled the ribbon in the air.

"Stringy fingers?" Maple asked.

Thorn laughed. "String puller?"

They both giggled.

"Very funny," Ermine crossed her arms over her chest.

"A silk spinner?" The others stopped laughing.

"It'd be better shorter…just spinner so nobody knows what we're talking about," Thorn said.

"Good idea. I like that!" Ermine said. "Nobody will suspect it in a mill especially."

So the other girls had magic. Flora wasn't alone in her secrets after all. She was happy for her friends, but felt a little pang of jealousy too. She looked over at Thorn. Would he still think she was special?

He looked back at her. For some reason, he looked a little bit guilty. Was he hiding something too?

The children laid down together among the cushions under the glass dome. Flora's lights flickered all around and above them like a giant snow globe. Flora's head rested close to Thorn's. She could smell his forest floor scent, and it reminded her of home. They would get up and return to their rooms before it became too late. They would just wait until the last light flickered out. But slowly, surely, they each fell asleep.

16

A RAINBOW OF DYE

adame Cribellum's voice screeched from somewhere in the mill, "FLORA!"

Flora jolted up. The children were all still sleeping in the conservatory. She frantically shook the others awake. "She knows I'm not in my room! Quick!"

Thorn and Ermine leapt to the door, dragging a half-asleep Maple.

But it was too late. Madame Cribellum flung the door open, and the children cowered back. Maple retreated into the greenery near her.

"It's my fault, Madame Cribellum." Ermine croaked. I let Flora out early so we could work on…" She stopped short, as if no ideas would come to her.

"A bunch of dusty, wilted plants?" Madame Cribellum rolled her eyes. Then she opened them wide and surveyed what the conservatory now looked like. She took in the pillows, the ribbons strung with crystals, and the teacups stacked. Anger pulsed in the veins at her neck. She took a deep breath, trying to calm herself. "Well, I see you four have too much time on your hands. How about you get down to the basement for a double shift."

"Oh, come on!" Thorn said.

Madame Cribellum glared at him, and he quickly shut his mouth.

Flora shuddered at the thought of the dark underbelly of the mill. She had never had to work there, but she had heard frightening tales.

"We're soooo tired! Please don't make us!" Maple whined. Flora could see the blush in her cheeks forming, but then it receded as Madame Cribellum seethed.

"Enough!" She snapped. She twisted her face into a menacing smile and turned to Flora. "You and your little friends can dye the entire order for the Parisians tomorrow…it should only take you all night."

Flora sucked in a breath. *The entire order?*

"And I don't want to hear a peep from you until the work is done! I'll let the groundskeeper know he has some work to do in here. We'll get rid of your disgusting tattered pillows and ribbons and…" She touched one of the hanging crystal prisms, sending jangly rainbows over her face. She winced and made what sounded like the guttural sound of a frightened animal.

Why does Madame Cribellum have such a hard time with the light from the crystals? Flora thought.

Madame Cribellum yanked the crystal off the ribbon and threw it into the bushes. She tried to compose herself and walked to the door with her head held high, but Flora could see she was hiding a grimace. "We'll have to board this door up from now on. Now OUT, all of you!" With that, she whirled off down the stairs, covering her face.

Maple began to cry.

"Don't worry, Mape," Thorn said, "We'll be able to remove a few boards."

"But what about all our treasures?" Maple asked. "Maybe we could find a place to put it all before she comes back…"

"No, we'd better get down to the basement before she notices us dilly-dallying," Ermine said, like a wilted flower. "Come on, Maple."

"You girls go get ready for the shift. I'll try to salvage what I can in here." Thorn said.

"I can help…" Flora said.

"No, go on up with them. I'm just going to…sort of hide it all." Thorn said. "It won't take long."

The girls relented, then put their arms around each other and walked forlornly out the door. They would go to their rooms to change, then meet at the basement steps. Thorn disappeared into the foliage.

Flora trudged a few steps down the passageway, then changed her mind. She didn't care if she was wearing her nightgown under her sweater for her shift. She went back through the conservatory door to get one last look at her beautiful garden bubble in case they were barred from it forever. It was nothing compared to the forest, but it was all she had of the green world she loved so much. She felt like the glass of the conservatory was being shattered. "Ragwort!" She screamed. She could feel a heat within her like a sparkler. As she fumed, she gathered all the dye specimens she'd gathered over time and smuggled them into her sweater pockets. She had an idea for a way to get back at Madame Cribellum. When she finished, she made her way back to the center of the conservatory, where the table was. But it was gone. All of their treasures were gone.

"What happened to everything!?" she sputtered. "Thorn couldn't have hidden it all so quickly!"

"I've had some practice at hiding," came a voice from in front of her. Flora looked into the red and brown bark of one of the largest trees in the conservatory. She could just barely make out a shape there. Then the leaves and twigs seemed to move.

Did that tree just talk to me? She thought. The tree was changing color, or at least the shape was. Suddenly, she realized it was the shape of a boy! Thorn's messy auburn hair was mixed with leaves, and his face was mottled like bark as he stepped away from the tree toward her. Even his clothes looked like the foliage surrounding him.

"Ummm…" Flora looked at him in shock. "Did you just change color?"

"Maybe."

So Thorn *did* have magic. Some kind of camouflage! He was like the Purple Thorn Moth, disguised like a leaf. "Why didn't you tell us?!"

"I was trying to find some fun way to surprise you with it."

She punched him in the shoulder. "I can't believe it. I mean… you always seem to be coming out of nowhere, but…Thorn!"

"Don't tell the others. They're due for a good trick."

Flora giggled. "Ok!" Then she looked around. "Wait… Where did you put everything?"

"It's all still here." He waved around the room. "I can make things blend in with their surroundings. It doesn't last forever, but it should last long enough for the groundskeeper to come in and see that there's nothing to do besides trim a few things. Our things have a sort of magical shield…even if he bumps into them, he won't notice. Only someone who knows what to look for would. The way you saw my shape on the tree but couldn't see me. Talking to you ruined the illusion."

Flora shook her head at him and smiled. Then she sighed, "Come on, we'd better get to the basement. I have a surprise of my own."

Flora, Thorn, Ermine, and Maple lumbered down the spiral basement stairs past thick stone walls. It looked like something had bored a hole right down to the center of the earth. The smell of wet dirt and rotting fruit rose from beneath them. Flora's nose tickled. The children in the mill talked about the basement as if it were the mill's own underworld. Madame Cribellum would choose the children who displeased her most to work down there. It was where the dye room was, so it had to be done. And unfortunately for Flora, she was now one of the chosen.

Maple whined as they took the rickety steps down into darkness. "My fingernails were black from dye for a whole week last time! I hate the basement! I swear there are rats the size of dogs down there!"

Thorn slid past them on the banister, pulling one of Maple's ringlets as he went.

"Ow!" Maple yelped.

"It could have been a lot worse." Ermine shrugged. "She could have left us in our rooms for a few days. I'd rather get some work done."

"Speak for yourself," Maple trudged more slowly. "We could have gotten some sleep!"

"Touché," Ermine yawned.

They came to the last step, and a long, low-ceilinged corridor stretched before them. There was a lantern with a candle and matches on a shelf by the stairwell. Ermine lit the lantern, and a soft yellow glow arced around them. They heard a scurry at the far end of the hall.

"Oh, Goodness. I'm going to faint!" Maple leaned into Flora.

"Careful, I might, too." Flora winced.

"They say the basement connects to underground caverns," Maple whispered. "Do you think anything could be living down there?"

"There's nothing down there but the end of the hall." Ermine said. "I've been to get things from storage."

"Caverns?" Flora squinted her eyes and searched the darkness. "I wonder if they're anything like the caves Gran used to search for minerals to make dye. If they are, then there might be something living in them. She would never let me come with her when she'd go. She said it was too dangerous, but I never knew why." *If there are caverns under the mill,* Flora thought, *maybe we have a way out!*

"Relax, you guys. It's just right here." Ermine led them into the first door, and before them was a stone room filled with big vats of steaming liquid, reams of cloth, and ten or so skeins of yarn. Hundreds of candles lined the walls in small alcoves. Their wax had dripped down the walls for what looked like centuries. Thorn went to light a few near the door.

"Come on, let's get to work." Ermine said as she opened a large armoire filled with glass bottles of all shapes and sizes. Most of them were empty, but you could still see the faintest bit of dried-out color in their bottoms. She brushed her fingers over a few bottles and pulled one out with daisy etchings and a crystal stopper. It had a murky brown liquid inside. She dropped its contents into one of the vats. Swirls of brown color streamed through the water. "Maple, grab that pile of cloth," Ermine instructed.

"Oh!" Maple whined, "Can't Thorn do it? They always have spiders under them."

Thorn bowed dramatically and said, "M'lady," then slowly lifted the cloth and looked under it to see if there were any spiders.

"BOO!" He jolted toward Maple, and she screamed.

"Thorn!" She swatted at him and he jumped out of the way.

Thorn laughed and dumped the cloth into the vat.

"These vats are also connected to the hot spring. That's how the water is always hot," Ermine said as she went to put more drops of dye into another vat.

Flora stopped her. "Wait! Ermine, I know you're going to hate this idea, but what if we dye the fabric with something else?"

Ermine furrowed her brow. "What are you up to, Flora? The fabrics are supposed to be brown, grey, and black."

"I know…but that's so boring! What if we gave the Parisians something spectacular? Something colorful!"

Ermine shook her head. "Are you crazy? Madame Cribellum would kill you!"

"But not *really*," Flora said, "I mean, what's the worst she could do to me that she hasn't already done?"

Ermine scoffed. "Did you forget about the big burning web you were in just the other night?"

Flora bristled. "I don't care. She's already taken everything from me. From all of us!" Flora put her arm around Maple. "I've been meaning to get her back for being so cruel to Maple when she cut her rose."

Ermine looked over Flora sadly. "Well, even if I did let you, where would you even find colorful dye? We only have about a hundred shades of brown and gray anyway."

Flora gave her a big grin. "Look what I grabbed from the conservatory!" She dumped out her pockets and displayed the treasures she'd gathered before they left. "We have everything we need to make as many colors as we want!"

Ermine looked over the leaves, berries, and flowers, deep in thought.

Flora held her breath, then let out a small, "Please? For all we know, we'll be working here for an eternity. Why not have a little fun?"

"Madame Cribellum will be furious," Ermine said.

"I hope so," Thorn said. "Flora's right. We can't just let her treat us the way she does. She deserves to know that we won't put up with all of it so easily anymore."

Ermine stood with crossed arms, pondering.

"What do you think, Maple?" Flora asked, "We won't do it if it scares you too much."

Maple winced. "I don't know… I don't want to get in trouble, but…" She stomped her foot. "Let's do it!"

Ermine threw her hands up. "Fine. But we'd better dig some graves while we're down here, because that's where we're going to end up."

"Oh, thank you, Ermine!" Flora immediately got to work, smashing berries and cutting up leaves. She found all the necessary tools in the storage down the hall under some old, dusty cloths. The others helped her test the colors and cut up specimens. They delighted with her over the colors that blended into the vats as they worked.

"Look at this purple! It's like the violets in the forest!" Flora cried.

"This yellow is so sunshiny!" Maple gleamed.

"I can't believe this pink came from that bark," Thorn mused.

And despite her caution, Ermine took a particular liking to the light blue color they got from dried cornflowers. "It reminds me of the sky," she said. "I wish we could have just one moment outside to really appreciate it. But this is the next best thing."

It angered Flora to her innards that Madame Cribellum had kept beauty and color from them. Things that used to give her pleasure, like the sound of a loom and the touch of silk, had turned into monotonous tasks. Maple wasn't allowed pink when it was her favorite color, and Ermine's creative gifts had turned to schedules and work bells and keeping quiet. Their spark of joy had turned to ash. She wanted to free them all from Madame Cribellum's exploitation—her sucking the life from them like a greedy, hungry spider. She looked down at the swirling color in the vats. Madame Cribellum was about to get Flora's perfect revenge. The dye was beginning to set, and there was no turning back.

17

THE MOTH

he children worked late into the early morning, drying, pressing, and packaging their fabric. Ermine even swirled some embroidery into some of the reams, and Flora used her light to make it shiny. Stars, trees, vines, and even a few little creatures sprawled over their canvas of silken cloth.

Maple would walk between the drying folds of fabric and touch them with her fingers... to her delight, the color would brighten just like her blush as she passed.

Thorn whispered to Flora, "I bet I could make some of these cloaks of invisibility, but that might be a little too much."

Flora gaped. Then she smirked. "We'll have to save that for another time!" She whispered.

Flora's nerves tickled as she put the fabric into boxes and tied them with velvet ribbon. She hoped Madame Cribellum wouldn't peek inside.

When Flora finally climbed back up out of the basement and fell into the curve of her round bedroom window, she heaved a great sigh. She was exhausted from all their hard work. "If I have to tie one more ribbon on a box, I'm going to rip Madame Cribellum's bun right off her..." Her words trailed off as she slipped into slumber.

Flora had restless dreams of Madame Cribellum's anger wrapping her friends and her in sticky webs. And then, in her sleep, Flora heard a rustle. She opened her heavy eyelids and looked up to see where the sound was coming from. A bundle of gossamer glistened in the setting moonlight. Flora focused her eyes and saw…

The cocoon was moving!

A large white silk moth slowly bit its way out of the cocoon. It had a luminous furred, body and feathery antennae. Flora sat up sleepily and patiently let it crawl onto her finger. She held it up to the starlight so she could watch it slowly grow in strength. Its soft wings shuddered as it pumped the blood that would enlarge them. When the moth lifted its wings, it revealed two

large pink rings circling black spots on its underwings, like the eyes of an owl.

Flora smiled. It reminded her of her grandmother, with her round glasses and wispy hair. And its plump, fluffy body was like Gran's hunchback. It even had speckles like Gran's freckles!

"You glitter the way Gran once did," Flora whispered. She gently touched its soft head. "Are you looking for light little one?"

The moth looked up at her and said, "No. I've found it!"

Flora was shocked. *Did this moth really just speak?!*

But before Flora could respond, she heard Madame Cribellum's loud shriek. "Flora!"

"Quackgrass!" Flora realized she'd slept in. "You'd better hide!" Flora whispered to the moth, "Madame Cribellum *hates* moths."

The moth fluttered up into the air in a tizzy, a shadow against the moon. Flora meant to warn it not to get caught in Madame Cribellum's web when she was startled…

"FLORA! The Parisians will be here very soon!" shrieked Madame Cribellum. She was coming up the stairs. "I want everyone up and ready for them when they arrive!"

Flora held her breath as the moth flew beyond where the invisible strands of the web waited. She let out a sigh of relief. It was small enough to fit through the gaps! Its wings caught the starlight as it sailed out over the forest and glimmered through the dark branches as Flora heard it plead, "Flora, you must use the Giltiri light! It is the only way for you to escape. I will be waiting for you when you succeed!"

Her voice was so familiar.

"Wait!" Flora cried, "What do you mean?!" She had so many questions. How did the moth know so much? Had it really been listening and watching as a caterpillar? Flora watched it fly toward a pink smudge in the distance. Spring had come to the forest, and her cherry tree was blooming! Flora's heart ached to fly towards it with the moth.

"You must shine!" The moth called from far away, barely a glint of moonlight in the night sky.

Madame Cribellum threw the door open. "WHAT are you *doing*?"

Flora was leaning out of her round window, clinging to the stones. She wished she could see the first flowers in her meadow. She imagined her star flowers clustered along the creek. She would give anything to have wings!

"I'm sorry, I'm coming," Flora said, distracted. "I just didn't get any sleep last night."

"And whose fault is that?"

Yours, she thought, but said, "Sorry, Madame." She rolled her eyes inwardly but curtsied outwardly.

"Do try to look your best, Flora." Madame Cribellum looked at her with faux pity, and said, "I know that's hard for you."

Flora cowered. "I have a dress I made that would probably work well." She pulled out the dress she'd worn on market day, all gray and brown fluff, and held it up proudly. Madame Cribellum looked horrified. "That's hideous!" She laughed. "Wear something simple if that's all you have."

Flora looked at her dress and frowned.

Madame Cribellum whirled, and Flora listened as her heels tapped down the hallway.

"What does Madame Cribellum know about fashion?" She took a second look at her dress. "Well, maybe it is a little silly." Flora tried to push back her embarrassment, but she couldn't help but let a few tears out.

But then the moth's words echoed back to her in her mind: "You must shine!"

Her mind raced…

Had the moth really spoken to her? She was so tired. She thought she must have dreamed it all. But the cocoon was empty. Had she been sleepwalking? Sleep talking?

She thought about what Gran had said to her about Geodes. How Flora sparkled like them. She certainly felt like the *outside* of a geode, hunched and weak. She felt her back. The lump had grown bigger. She winced.

"But geodes have hidden beauty within." Flora put her gray dress on with her blue petticoat underneath. Then she put her sweater on over it. She fluffed her tangled hair down her back and set her jaw.

She was determined to shine.

18

THE PARISIANS

arisians had come to Nuthatch Estate, and everyone was in a tizzy. Madame Cribellum was screeching at the children to be on their very finest behavior. She told them to wear their nicest clothing and gave them the morning off in order to get ready and look presentable. The girls were getting ready in Maple and Ermine's room in the dormitory. They crowded around a tiny silver mirror on a bare desk. The girls had very few belongings but made do with what they found in the mill's closets.

"It's all just a show for the Parisians," Ermine said while smoothing Maple's yellow ringlets into smooth curls. Maple wore a cotton candy pink dress and a pair of marigold tights. She pinched her cheeks to make them more rosy.

"Madame Cribellum never lets us wear our prettier, more colorful things unless there's someone to impress," Maple said. "We all still have a few things our parents must have left for us. But nobody really knows where we got them. I wish we could remember."

Ermine wore a white dress and white tights with black spots. She wore a small stole of white fur around her neck and shoulders. She touched the soft fur. "I think this was my mother's, but I have no idea."

"Hmmm," Flora said. "You must have brought them from your home in the forest… Maybe she let you pack, and you don't remember. That stole looks just like an Ermine moth's fuzzy white body." She giggled. "I wonder why I still remember everything from my past… maybe because I'm human."

Ermine untied her usual two braids. She waved her hands and unfurled her fingers in delicate patterns. Her black coils unspooled and then wove themselves into an intricately braided crown around her head.

"I didn't know you could use your magic on your hair!" Maple gasped.

"It's pretty much like string, isn't it?" Ermine shrugged and winked at her. Then she took some charcoal she'd gotten from the fire, mixed it with some water and, delicately lined her eyes like a cat with the end of a knitting needle. She was already a beautiful girl, but this made her look striking.

Flora looked on in jealousy. She tried to smooth her matted hair, but it was untamable. "Ugh! It's like it's straight and curly at the same time," she huffed. She finally decided upon letting her mass of wavy hair fall down all around her and sighed. She realized that with her hunch back getting bigger and her hair in her face, there wasn't much that could make her look better. She slumped onto Ermine's bed.

"I can understand your frustration," Ermine said. "Before I realized I could use my magic on my hair, it would take me forever to braid it. Here. Let me help." She stood behind Flora, and Flora could feel the magic resonate and tingle over her scalp. The hair falling down into Flora's face was pulled up into a side-swept French braid, and the hair that fell around her shoulders smoothed out into soft waves that curled at the ends.

Ermine took a blue ribbon from her belongings and used her magic to swirl the ribbon into a bow to hold the braid up on the side of her head. "There."

"That's pretty!" Maple exclaimed. "It matches your eyes!" She put a hand in Flora's and blushed almost imperceptibly.

195

Flora knew what she was doing, but it still made her feel warm inside. Her cheeks turned a faint pink too. She managed a smile. "Thank you, girls."

The front entrance of the mill was dusted and gleaming thanks to all the children's hard work. Flora didn't realize the chandeliers could sparkle so brightly. The parlor was set up with a few new white furniture pieces and spiffed to perfection. With its light blue walls and golden millwork, it looked as lovely as a music box. Madame Cribellum wanted to give the impression that the place had some refinery and repute.

Flora was to be one of the children who would present the fabric to the buyers. She helped pile boxes and boxes of the fabric they'd dyed the night before. Inside lay the most beautiful array of colors. Sultry purple, emerald green, bright yellowy orange, crimson red, and pale blue. And of course, a blush pink. They had somehow gotten away with it so far. Madame Cribellum hadn't seen or heard about the fabric yet. Everyone assumed Ermine would know exactly how the fabric was meant to be, and Madame Cribellum had been too busy entertaining her guests.

She had ordered many little delicacies for the Parisians. A large decorated cake, petit fours, cream puffs, macarons, and tiny sandwiches were brought into the parlor on silver plates. Flora waited outside the door with the others as Madame Cribellum tried to croon her way into the good graces of the ladies, then her heart lurched when she heard herself called in.

Madame Cribellum's super sweet sing song voice called out, "And now may I present to you the fabric we have painstakingly worked on since your gracious order... Flora!"

Flora brought in three boxes that engulfed her tiny frame and set them down on the ground before the ladies. Maple and Atlas came in after her. Atlas was so tall he was able to carry six boxes between his broad shoulders. Maple had two.

"You may go now, children." Madame Cribellum nodded.

Maple and Atlas shuffled out the door, and Flora had every intention of getting out of there as quickly as possible, but as she looked up, she saw before her the Parisienne ladies and froze.

Flora had never seen such delicate, detailed, lovely dresses in all her life. And their jewels! They were dripping with sparkly bright colors. Pearls, rubies, diamonds! They looked like flowers covered in dew drops. One of the ladies had on a pair of satin slippers drizzled in swirls of golden string and accented with big fabric pom-poms. The other had a hat with enormous plumes of silk flowers. They were like the rose Flora had made! She was in awe of their intricate folds and shiny petals and leaves. The ladies tilted bored heads toward Flora.

Flora curtsied and stared.

"That will be *all*," Madame Cribellum said.

"Your dresses!" Flora squealed. "Your shoes! Your hat! Oh I could look at you for forever and never need to see the stars or flowers again!"

The ladies, who had been languishing in Madame Cribellum's presence, laughed. "Merci beau coup!" one said. They stared at Flora with wide, adoring eyes, as if this little girl was the most fascinating treat presented to them so far.

"I'm sorry. Please ignore Flora. She is leaving now."

"No, no! Please, let her present the fabric to us," the lady with the flower hat said.

"Fleurs!" the pom-pom shoed one said. "I have never been compared to a flower!"

"As you wish," Madame Cribellum said. "Flora? Present these fine ladies with their fabric." She spoke with a smile through gritted teeth.

Flora curtsied again. She could not remember which box had which color. She grabbed the one on top of her stack. She untied the ribbon and closed her eyes as she pulled the lid off.

She heard the gasps before she opened her eyes.

"Rouge!" the ladies said together. "We did not order pink!"

Inside was the most vivid pink Maple could produce. Ermine had embroidered it with little golden moths flying through leaves. It practically flung itself out of the box. Madame Cribellum flinched back like a spider terrified of bright moth wings.

"Ce'st parfait!" the pom-pom shoed lady said.

Madame Cribellum's face looked like it might burst. The veins in her forehead bulged, and her eyes were so wide, Flora thought she looked like a big fat spider.

Flora beamed. Her revenge had worked!

Madame Cribellum clutched at the fabric box, her skin turning a rich shade of purple. She began to gurgle and then erupted with a loud growl. "PINK!" she screamed. "This wicked girl has been dying things pink and embroidering marks on my good fabric, and now she has *ruined* your order!" She got up and reached for Flora.

Flora took a step back.

"No! Margeaux says it is *perfect,*" the plumed one said.

Madame Cribellum stopped dead in her tracks and looked at them in shock.

"There's more!" Flora untied the ribbons on the next boxes and grandly opened their lids. "Marigold! Cornflower! Violet! Emerald... I made the dye with plants from the conservatory!""

Madame Cribellum screamed. "Oh, I'm so sorry, Madames! I know this is not what you wanted. This girl had been nothing but a nuisance since coming to the mill." But the ladies clutched at the colors as if a rainbow had erupted into their very hands. The pom-pom shoed lady began weeping for joy.

"And you embroider!" the flower-hat one said to Flora, "I have been looking for a good embroiderer for ages! My dear girl, perhaps you could come and help make us couture dresses! What do you think, Pippa?"

"Oui oui! Oh, look at her. Did you make your sweater?" Pippa grabbed Flora's hand and patted it.

"I did!" Flora yelped. Then she took it off in a swoop and brandished her dress underneath. "And I made this too!"

Feather-hat touched the bunny fur collar and let out a squeak of pure delight. "Tres chic!" She marveled.

"Couture!" said pom-pom Pippa, "Little darling, you could come live with us and embroider all you want!"

Flora beamed.

The ladies clasped Flora and each other and began scheming. "We would love a little poppet to dote on! We would make you dresses as silvery and lovely as the moon, my dear!

Flora gasped. "Would you?!" Her heart nearly exploded. This was it! She was going to get out! She'd find Gran. And even if she couldn't, anything would be better than staying in the mill with Madame Cribellum!

But Madame Cribellum seethed, "How *dare* you! You can't take Flora. She belongs to me!" She grabbed Flora by the arm and shoved her toward the door.

"Oh, but we thought they were all orphans… Does she not need a home? And she seems to disappoint you, so…"

Flora suddenly felt a pang of guilt. They were *all* orphans. She couldn't leave Maple, Ermine, and Thorn, could she? She pictured her friends slowly withering away in the mill, forgetting everything. She pictured little Maple's fingers raw to the bone, spinning for an eternity. She pictured Ermine closing up inside herself like a bud who didn't know how to blossom. She pictured Thorn forgetting who she was…and that broke her heart to imagine. She could not leave them.

When Madame Cribellum grabbed her and shoved her toward the door, she didn't fight or speak. She shuffled willingly toward her friends.

Madame Cribellum yanked the blue ribbon out of Flora's hair and whispered in her ear, "I'll deal with you and your little friends later." Flora could feel a darkness emanating from her. It was nothing like the anger she'd sensed from her before. Madame Cribellum's words seethed with hatred. Whatever she had planned for Flora was going to be very unpleasant.

She threw Flora's sweater at her and slammed the door in her face.

"We need to hide!" Flora whispered loudly to the others as she ran down the hall, pulling her sweater back on. "Hurry! To the basement!" The children scrambled down the steps, and they all talked over each other.

"I knew it was a bad idea!" Ermine said.

"What did the Parisians think of our fabric?" Maple asked.

"What did *Cribellum* think?" Thorn snickered. He took two steps at a time down the basement stairs.

Flora told them what had happened as she gasped for breath at the bottom of the stairs.

"It was so hilarious. I wish you all could have seen her too. She was livid! But the Parisienne ladies LOVED it! They loved it so much they wanted to take me with them!"

Maple swooned. "Oh, how lovely!"

"No… it's bad. Much worse than usual." Flora shook her head with desperation in her eyes. "Madame Cribellum wasn't just angry… It was almost as if she was frightened. And I could feel her magic coming off of her. She seemed desperate…"

They all began talking at once.

"Everyone be quiet! What are we going to do?!" Ermine bit her lip. "Maybe Maple could use her blush on her…"

"I think she'll plough right through Maple's feelers and cut our dresses up or starve us for a week," Flora said.

"Let's get some of those geodes from Floras spring and start a war!" Thorn joked. He motioned throwing a rock.

"No." Ermine said. She was nervously playing with her hair, unraveling it with her magic. Finally, she bunched it into two cute puffs and set her jaw. "We're stuck in the mill with no way out. We have to think of a way to get out of this sensibly. Maybe we could say the dye bottles got mixed up, or that we got the wrong order."

"That's dumb; Madame Cribellum is the only one who gives us orders." Thorn said.

"Yes, but maybe if we could find some old order, or, I don't know..." Ermine started rummaging around by the dye armoire, pushing it away from the wall. "We could say the dye got mixed up..."

"No... It was pretty clear that Flora was proud of the work she'd done. And Madame Cribellum isn't that stupid." Thorn said.

"You guys... shhhh. Look." Flora pointed at the wall behind the armoire where it had been pushed away. There was a large gaping crack in the cement. From inside, layers of glittering purple crystals shone.

19

WINGS

t's a secret passage!" Flora stuck her head in through the crack. "Or a cave… I'm not sure which. Let's see where it leads!"

"Sheesh, this place is full of secret passageways," Thorn said.

"How long has that been there, right under our noses?" Ermine said.

"It must be the entrance to the underground caverns!" Flora exclaimed. "This might be a way out!"

"I don't want to go in there!" Maple said. She hid behind Ermine's dress.

"Would you rather face Cribellum's anger?" Thorn motioned toward upstairs.

"It looks dark!" Maple whined.

Flora rubbed her hands together, and little sparks flew into the air. She carefully molded a ball of light in her hands and held it up. The light reflected like embers in her eyes.

"Is it hot?" Maple reached out to touch it with a grimace on her face. But the little orb was cool. She gave Flora a big smile.

"Can you make one for everyone?" Thorn asked.

Flora blew into her other hand. "No. That's all I've got. I used up most of my light when we dyed the cloth."

Thorn looked into the tunnel and gave her a squeamish look.

"Let's just see where it leads," Flora urged, looking to Ermine for approval.

Ermine took her ball of silk out of her pocket. She tied one end of the string to a nail on the back of the armoire with a wave of her hand, and unraveled the ball as she moved down the passageway. "This will help us find our way back. If it doesn't lead out of the mill, at least we'll be able to hide for a while until Madame Cribellum's anger wears off."

Flora stepped onto the polished floor of the tunnel. It seemed to go on and on, with no end in sight. All the children could see was whatever Flora's light touched, and the crystals burst dangling points of reflected light in return.

"It's like walking into a geode!" Flora marveled.

A thin mist crept at their feet. They clutched each other, full of nerves. Very carefully, they edged down the tunnel. When they reached the first curve, Flora looked back. The strand of Ermine's silk glowed in the light, leading back to the dye room.

"I hope we find our way back," Maple whimpered.

"Of course we will," Ermine reassured her, but then she looked at Flora nervously and shrugged.

After several minutes of frightened steps, Maple whispered, "Where's Thorn?"

"What do you mean, he's right…" Ermine stopped. "Wasn't he next to you?"

Flora shook her head. "I thought he was on your side."

The girls looked back. There was nothing but darkness and deep amethyst pricks of light.

"Ragwort!" Flora swore.

"Maybe he went back to grab something." Maple shivered.

"Why wouldn't he tell us?" Ermine asked.

"Because it's Thorn," Flora said. They all giggled. "Seriously though…"

"Come on, Thorn, it's not funny. Where are you?" Ermine huffed.

The girls screamed as something broke off from the crystal ceiling and dropped down right in front of them. It had a human

shape and was covered in a layer of dark crystalline crust. It moved swiftly toward them, growling. The girls jumped back. The creature shook out his head of purple crystal hair. Before their eyes, it morphed into…

"Thorn!" Ermine gasped.

"You piece of gum!" Maple stomped her foot.

Flora laughed, "I nearly forgot about your camouflage!"

Thorn raised his eyebrows and sauntered up to them. He looked like someone had gotten him wet and dipped him in purple sugar. He sparkled all over, just like the cavern walls.

Ermine shoved him. "Ok, so you're special too. Can we move on?"

The others sputtered laughter, then linked arms.

"How long have you been able to do it?" Maple asked Thorn.

They spoke quietly as they moved slowly down the tunnel past long stalactites dripping water into dark pools.

"It started around the same time Flora came," he said. "I uh…was sort of spying on her."

"What?" Flora said, taken aback. Maple nudged Flora with wide eyes.

"I mean… You were new, so I was curious! One day I was waiting for you outside your room, and you opened the door… I was so embarrassed you'd notice me lurking, but you didn't seem to see me. You just walked right past. I looked down to see if I was invisible, just as a joke…but I WAS! Well, not really. I was the color of stone. My body had mimicked the wall. After that, it was just a matter of experimenting. My clothes had changed, too, so I tried to see if I could make it happen by just touching something. See…." He touched Flora's hand, and it suddenly turned purple. She yelped and pulled it away from him, then held it up in front of her face. Before her very eyes, her fingertips and nails grew glimmering crystals.

"You mimic things," Flora said. "Like a moth. Remember the moths that looked like bark? We should call you a mimic."

"That's perfect!" Maple said, "A mimic, a blusher, a spinner…and what's Flora?"

"Something to do with light…" Ermine said.

"Maybe she just *is* a light," Thorn said.

"No, it's more of a reflection. A reflector?"

"That doesn't sound nearly as amazing, though," Thorn said.

"A blusher, a mimic, a spinner, and a light." Maple nodded her head triumphantly.

"Moth Magic." Flora said.

"Oh, come on... It can't be!" Ermine scoffed, "I don't know what it is, but it definitely has something to do with you, Flora. All our magic started with you."

Flora let out a clipped "hmmm." She had to admit that was true. "But I think your magic is much stronger than mine. I'm pretty much certain *you* are all moth fairies. I just sort of helped you along with it using borrowed magic from nature." She stepped gingerly around the edge of a pool that seemed to have a fathomless depth. What she didn't say was that she had a sneaking suspicion her grandmother was right. If she showed others her light, it could be stolen. She chewed on the thought. Could it be that her light would be stronger if the others didn't get their powers from her? Were they draining her? How deep did the pool of *her* magic go? She always had a little bit of light inside of her. She could feel it flickering at all times. But if it went out...would it be gone? She put the thought out of her mind and squinted into the darkness.

"Maybe we should go back," Ermine said.

"To Madame Cribellum? And then what?" Thorn asked.

"I think I'd rather be confined to my room than get lost in some cave!" Ermine snapped.

Flora held up her light to see what was beyond the pool. There was another cavern beyond. She threw the orb into it and the cavern they were in was plunged into darkness.

"Flora!" Maple squealed.

"I think I see something!" Flora ran forward. Something colorful in the next cavern had caught the orb's light. She wanted to know what it was.

The children followed her into the cave. Black rock walls stretched high above them. Strung from dangling stalactites was a giant, looming web. Its strands were the thickness of their

fingers, and it glistened iridescent hues. In the web countless large wings were stuck.

"They're giant moth wings!" Flora cried. She ran up to the web and touched a large, shimmery one. It was almost as big as she was, and had brilliant silvery dust and fur on its edges, the size of down feathers. "Look how big their dust crystals are!"

Flora touched the wing, and a handful of small crystals came off and into her hand.

"Careful!" Ermine said. "Won't Madame Cribellum feel you tug on the web?"

"This one isn't attached to anything but the walls," Thorn said. "I think it's safe."

"They're large enough we could wear them!" Maple said.

"Maybe they are for people… Maybe they're costume wings. Did the mill ever make costumes?" Thorn asked.

"They're way too realistic to be costumes," Ermine said.

Something clicked inside Flora's brain. "These must have been the moth fairies' wings!"

Maple gasped.

Ermine was shaking her head, eyes wide.

"This must be where Madame Cribellum kept all the wings when she was a spider!" Flora said. "And used their dust to make herself a cocoon!"

"And then she became the Witch Moth," Maple shuddered.

"She still uses moth dust… She has it in a jar on her vanity! I don't know why these wings are so big. They must have fought her in human size… or she made some wings bigger with magic or something?"

"Like trophies," Thorn said with a grimace.

Flora tugged at a large, sunset-colored wing, and the entire web jangled. The wings glittered as they shook, like a swarm of moths flying in the golden shafts of light in the forest. Flora felt like her heart was flying with them.

Ermine was shaking from nerves, but her jaw was set. "Ok. So what if it's all true? We're really moth fairies; Madame Cribellum is a spider. What do we do about it?"

"Do you really still doubt it?" Flora asked.

Ermine sighed. "No… it's just… I mean, it *is* pretty unbelievable!"

"We have to fight her," Thorn said.

"Or escape somehow," Flora said.

"How would we get past the web outside the mill, though?" Maple asked.

Flora thought hard. Her light had helped her unstick. But she didn't have enough to make it break apart. But if there was some way to magnify her light, or use some other kind of magic…

There was a long, nervous silence, then…

"Crystals!" Flora shouted. Her voice echoed against the cavern walls.

"What?!" The others were startled.

"These scales on the wings…they're crystals." Flora began pacing, thinking aloud. "My geode came from the spring, and the spring comes from the cherry tree. There's always so many cocoons and caterpillars and moths in it. They fly in and out of holes in the tree. And this morning, when I woke up, an Emperor Moth crawled out of a cocoon in my window. It…" Flora thought better of telling them that it had spoken to her. She still wasn't sure if it was real. She had worked all night, and then she had just awoken. It might have been a dream. She continued, "It flew toward the same tree. I think that it must be where the moth fairies once lived. The geodes must have come from the moth dust and magic that came from the tree!"

"Maybe that's where that light came from inside your geode!" Thorn exclaimed.

"Yes!"

"Flora, we should get back. We're never going to find a way out of here. Madame Cribellum is sure to figure out where we've gone, and if what you're saying is true, we could be in even bigger trouble than we think." Ermine edged toward the way they'd come.

"Wait," Flora said, pulling a wing off the web. "I have an idea! Grab these wings with me. I think we could make a big crystal with them!"

"How are we going to do that?" Maple scrunched her face up.

"I used to make crystals out of sugar all the time. I even wondered if I could do it with moth crystals once. But I never would have been able to get enough dust!"

"Well, now you certainly can!" Thorn jumped up onto the web, pulled a large gold and brown striped wing off, and handed it down to Flora. They were so delicate, they dropped little shining crystals as she stacked them in her arms.

"Why are we doing this?" Ermine said with a huff as she and Maple stacked a few wings in their arms too.

"Madame Cribellum always seems freaked out by the light coming from crystals," Flora said. "Remember how bothered she was by the prisms in the conservatory?"

"And she nearly lost it when Flora threw that geode at her!" Thorn said.

"If we can make a crystal from these, it might be big enough to scare her off for good." Flora hoped she wasn't out of her mind.

Between the four of them, they managed to dismantle and carry all the wings. Thorn's feet and hands kept getting stuck to the web, and the girls would have to pull him off, but it wasn't the stinging, freezing kind that Madame Cribellum had put around the mill, so it wasn't too difficult to free him.

They quickly made their way back through the cave tunnel by following Ermine's silk. Maple kept stumbling, but the others

would catch her. Sparkling powder and chunks of crystal dropped in their wake.

They squirmed their way back into the dying room, shuffling over piles of fabric to the vats of hot water.

"Quick" Flora rushed to one of the vats and shook a wing over it. Glittering scales dropped into the bubbling water. "Scrape the dust off into here!"

The children looked at each other and shrugged, then did as Flora asked. Different sparkling colors dropped into the water, swirling together.

"Woah!" Thorn exclaimed.

The children were surprised as the dust dissolved almost immediately.

"I need some string!" Flora searched the room.

Ermine gave Flora a pointed look. "Obviously I can help with that!"

Flora instructed her to tie one end of her string to a rafter in the ceiling and hang the other end down into the vat.

"Now turn off the heat!" Flora said. "Now we have to wait for the water to evaporate."

"Oh! It's just like how you make crystals with sugar!" Maple squeaked.

"How long will it take?" Thorn asked skeptically.

"A few days usually."

"Flora! We don't have days! We don't even have hours!" Ermine yelled.

Maple began hyperventilating.

Flora scrunched her face up apologetically.

"Look!" Thorn pointed to the vat.

The children watched as the wing crystals began clumping together onto the string. They slowly started to morph together and grow. Rainbowy whorls formed and hardened as the crystal got larger and larger. Then the water began to evaporate.

"It's happening so quickly!" Maple said.

"The dust must have had magic!" Flora said.

When the water was completely gone, the inside of the vat was lined with a thin crust of crystals, and on the string, a large chunk of crystal had formed, about the same size as Maple. Thorn and Flora held it in their arms as Ermine untied the string with her magic.

"What do we do with it?" Ermine asked.

"Let's throw it at Madame Cribellum!" Maple piped.

"I have an idea," Flora said. "But we have to get it to my room."

"Here, let's cover it with this." Thorn grabbed some dark fabric from the discard pile in the corner of the room.

"Hey, it's the fabric Flora got in trouble for embroidering!" Maple touched the iridescent silk stars on it. "It really is so pretty. Madame Cribellum must have thrown it down here that day."

They covered the crystal with the starry fabric. Flora could have sworn she saw sparks come out of the fabric as they secured it, but there was no time to ponder why.

"Ok. Let's take the crystal up to my room. I have the perfect spot to put it," Flora said.

Ermine crept upstairs to see if the coast was clear.

She came back down and sighed. "Madame Cribellum is *still* chatting with the Parisians."

"Probably trying to get them to make another order." Thorn said. "Come on, let's get this upstairs before she's done." The children quietly snuck the crystal all the way up to Flora's room. The sun was low in the sky. Citrine light lit their faces as they set the fabric-wrapped crystal in her round window.

Then they waited.

Maple got bored and took off her tights and shoes. Ermine shook her head and bit her lip. "If the sun sets before she gets here, this will have been a whole lot of work for nothing."

They heard voices out the window. Au revoirs and goodbyes. Then the wheels of a carriage creaked, and horses clopped down the drive. The Parisians had left.

The front door slammed.

They waited more.

Chill air crept into the room as the sun began to set. Flora put her golden sweater back on. Its warmth made her feel a little safer…her soft hug from Gran.

"What's taking her so long?" Thorn asked with a huff.

"Ssshhh. She's looking for us." Ermine said.

"If they loved the fabric so much, maybe she won't be angry anymore," Maple whispered, her brow furrowed.

A scream echoed from deep in the mill.

"She is." Thorn gulped.

"Oh no… I think she's in the basement!" Ermine's eyes were wide.

"FLORA!" Madame Cribellum's voice shrieked.

"She's seen all the discarded wings…" Flora took a deep breath.

They all braced themselves. Maple grabbed Flora and Ermine's hands. Thorn grabbed Flora's. They didn't even hear footsteps. They could only feel a dark power rising from the stairs below them, like a buzzing electricity.

20

THE CRYSTAL

 chill swept over the room. The children held their breath as the door creaked open. Then a black and purple moth flashed into the room, startling them. Its wingspan was as wide as a bat's.

"Ragwort!" Flora swore.

"What is it?" Ermine flinched.

"The Witch Moth!" Flora grabbed Maple and shoved her behind her.

The moth made a long, large circle around them, then fluttered in place near the other end of the room, near the door. There was no escape.

Then, as the children watched in horror, it began to grow. It pulsated and morphed into a black dress and tall, lanky limbs. Amethyst sparks spiraled and ricocheted across the room. Soon, Madame Cribellum was standing before them.

"I KNEW it!" Flora said, triumphantly, forgetting her fear for a second.

Madame Cribellum threw back her cloak, and giant Witch Moth wings fluttered up and out. The silvery lines matched her hair, and the purple chevrons matched her eyes.

Madame Cribellum pointed with her long finger. "Yes, Flora. I am the Sorcier Noir. It was I who flew in through your window the night your grandmother disappeared!"

"Mariposa de la Muerta," Flora whispered.

Mariposa Cribellum leaned against the door frame in a lackadaisical manner. A spider, who knew her prey was already caught. "When that woman at the market place told me there was a little girl with a weaver grandmother too old to care for her, I couldn't believe my luck. Could it be true? After all these years? I thought she had died, the great fallen emperor… It was just too easy for me to spot you and follow you as the Witch Moth. And then there she was… hiding her wings in a hunchback, ha!"

Flora was startled. *Wings? Emperor?*

"I knew you were in that carpet. I'm not stupid! But there were powerful talismans in the patterns. I couldn't touch you then. So I followed you to your cottage. It had been hidden from

me by your grandmother's camouflage spells. But once I knew where to look…"

"What did you do to Gran!?" Flora screamed.

"I obliterated her!" Madame Cribellum cackled.

Flora's heart shattered. It couldn't be true. Not Gran—not her fluffy, twinkling Gran. Flora felt like she would know if she was truly gone. She would feel it. She wracked her brain… The speckled Emperor Moth in Henry's journal had pink eye circles. And Gran had acted like she'd been there when the moths attacked. As if she knew more about the story of the Giltiri than she was letting on. Gran had speckled arms and pink glasses…

"After seeing me, Maja should have taken you far, far away from here, my dear!" Madame Cribellum giggled. "Then I wouldn't have been able to catch you. Her simple magic, born from nature, was nothing against mine! I'd stolen the Giltiri light years ago!"

Flora was lost in her swirling, foggy thoughts. She was so confused. She'd always thought it was strange that there was a caterpillar in Gran's bed with a note. And the moth that came from its cocoon was an Emperor Moth… It was white, but so was Gran's hair now that she was old. It had reminded her so much of Gran…

The note! Her Gran wanted her to find the mother. But Henry had gone to Luna in the forest. That was the end of his journal. But if he really had gone to Luna, why would her Gran tell her to find him?

Flora bit her lip and asked nervously, "Madame Cribellum, do you know what happened to Henry Nuthatch?"

"Oh, my dear girl," Madame Cribellum said, looking at Flora with wretched pity. "Henry Nuthatch has been close to my heart for such a long time. I was his first love, you know. I was the first creature he brought home from the forest." She looked off into the distance, remembering. "His own little pet spider. I thought that he would be so happy when I destroyed the moths for him. They ruined his family, his home. I only did what he asked of me. I always wanted to share in their power, but they would never let me, throwing me into puddles, destroying my webs! I was just a child when your grandmother nearly killed me! All I'd done was ask for some of their magic…" the vein in her forehead looked like it might pop. She looked as maniacal as she'd been on her web, spewing about Henry.

"The day the moths attacked, I caught some of the Giltiri. It was only natural, with the swarm writhing near my web. I took some of the dust from their wings so I could use its power of metamorphosis for myself. Then I spun myself a cocoon and waited for my revenge."

She went on, a glazed look in her eyes, almost speaking to herself. "After all our time together… all those years. I thought when I came to Henry as a woman, he would take me in his arms and love me all the more. I was so helpful to him. I got him everything he needed for the mill; I soothed his aching heart after his mother's death. But he left me before we could even get started spinning." Her eyes welled with tears.

"One evening, he asked to meet me in his estate to discuss plans for reopening the mill. I was so thrilled. Blinded by love, I had the stupidity to think it was a ruse. That he was really going to ask me to be his that day." She choked. "But he did not show up. Instead, I found a letter taped to the door. He said he was leaving forever and wanted me to take care of the mill for him. I knew where he was going. He was going to let them change him. I'd watched in horror as he chose a life with them. He'd had a… baby…with one of them!"

Madame Cribellum looked at Flora, eyes narrow.

Understanding unraveled in Flora's mind. If her grandmother was truly the Emperor of the moth fairies, that meant...

"Me?" Flora whispered.

The children gasped.

"That's why I've kept you here. Mercifully keeping you alive, spinning my webs with the others. I'm not a monster...You were his, too, after all. I owed him that much." She cradled the amber pendant around her neck and sighed wistfully.

"Henry and Luna are my parents!" Flora's mouth was agape.

Madame Cribellum sneered. "He'd fallen in love with a *moth!* Those disgusting, dusty things! They had destroyed his whole life! I couldn't let him do it. Henry was fairywinked, and all the townspeople could tell." Madame Cribellum began to shake, and the children took a step back.

"The Giltiri deserved to die for putting him under their spell! They'd killed his mother with grief. They'd destroyed his father's mill! How could they take him after all of that? I spun webs to unleash my anger. I filled every corner and cranny of Nuthatch Estate and then crept into Silkwood. I would make them pay for what they did to my boy. I loved him. I loved him so much, I would rather wrap him up inside my webs forever and ever than see his heart stolen by one of their kind.

"But I thought you cared for Henry!" Flora said, desperation clawing at her. "How could you harm him? I thought you said he was close to your heart!"

"He is!" Madame Cribellum held up her amber necklace so Flora could see it clearly. "He'll stay right by my heart forever!" Inside the amber, trapped in its frozen golden liquid, were two figures shrunk down to the size of mosquitoes. A man with dark hair and glasses locked in an embrace with a woman with long pink hair and tattered green wings. Luna.

The children shuddered. They had always been so terrified of Madame Cribellum, they'd never bothered to look closely at the jewel around her neck. It was a prison. Or was it a grave? Maple covered her eyes.

Flora cowered. "Are...are they dead?" Somewhere deep inside she still hoped they might be alive, just waiting for her. But they weren't. They were trapped in amber. How could she defeat Madame Cribellum if her own parents couldn't? Her mother even had Giltiri magic! Flora felt like her whole world was slipping away.

"Do you think me so cruel?" Madame Cribellum asked, "They're in a deep sleep."

"But why?!" Flora yelled.

"I didn't want to do it! I gave Henry a choice! But he was so enamored, so determined, to stay with the mother of his child! You see, Flora? You are the reason for all of this! You were the baby Henry left me for! If you didn't exist, everything would be just fine!"

Flora looked at her friends in shock. They looked at her with the same faces that said *Madame Cribellum had lost her mind.*

Madame Cribellum spoke in a strange awe, "And you, Flora, have proven to be nothing but trouble. I don't understand it. I can feel my power draining. I can see the other children gaining their strength. That cursed forest has come back to life. And it all began when I brought *you* here."

Flora blinked. What did *she* have to do with it?

"I think I'll make myself another pendant," Madame Cribellum said sweetly. "There's plenty of sap where this came from. You'll make a perfect bauble for my collection!" She stuck out her pointed finger and lunged at Flora.

"NOW!" Thorn yelled.

The children let the fabric on the crystal fall to the windowsill, and the orange sun bathed the crystal with light. It refracted it like a prism, and hundreds of rainbows filled the room. A searing beam of light shot out from the crystal, hitting Madame Cribellum. She flung back against the wall and screamed.

The light pulsated and the smell of singed hair filled the room as steam curled off Madame Cribellum's throbbing body. Hairy black legs began to grow out of her waist, and her eyes multiplied. Her wings withered.

"It's working!" shouted Thorn.

"You wretched brats! I'll squash all of you!" Madame Cribellum screamed. "I let you live… How could you?!" Her mangled body crumpled.

But the light began to dim. "Oh no!" Ermine cried, "The sun is setting!"

Madame Cribellum held up a withered hand toward the beam of light, darkness emanating from her curled fingertips.

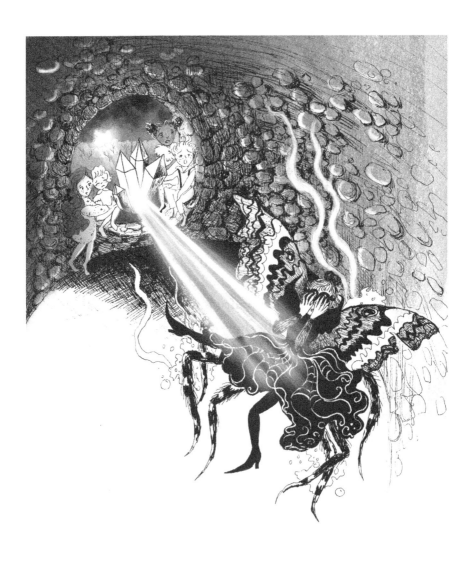

"Just a little longer… don't stop now!" Ermine urged the light to keep working.

Madame Cribellum was shrinking down to spider size. But the bright orange glow on the horizon grew smaller and smaller.

"No!" Maple squealed.

Suddenly, the light went out. The sun had gone behind the tree line. Madame Cribellum slithered up out of the corner and gathered herself. She held up her finger again and pointed at Flora. "You wretched girl!" Her magic hit Flora like an invisible wave of inky water.

"Flora! Your light! Try using your light!" Thorn yelled.

Flora jumped up onto the windowsill and held her hand against the crystal. She took a deep breath and closed her eyes. She thought of the setting sun and its orange light pouring into the room. She thought of it warming her in the forest, the way it would light up her eyelashes. As she absorbed its beauty, a faint stream of light poured from her hand, and the crystal began to glow.

"You have light?!" Madame Cribellum laughed maniacally as she gained her footing. She stumbled toward Flora, still shrinking but getting closer.

Flora broke her concentration and looked up at Madame Cribellum in terror. She faltered, and the light shining from the crystal dimmed. *Never let anyone take your light*, she remembered her grandmother saying. Would Madame Cribellum be able to steal her light?

As she stretched toward Flora, Madame Cribellum was able to reach out with her spindly fingers and breathe a curse at the children.

The crystal seemed to suddenly get larger. The window was twice its size and growing still!

"She's shrinking us!" Flora cried. The children shrank down, down, down to around three inches tall. They still stood clutching the starry fabric on the windowsill, but the room had grown to an enormous size. The starry fabric was now like a large carpet.

But their size was not the only thing that had changed. Flora was astonished to find that the other three now had *wings*! With Madame Cribellum's weak magic, they had taken on their true Giltiri form. Maple and Ermine pointed at each other and brightened.

Both girls exclaimed, "We're fairies!"

"Your wings are beautiful!" Maple said.

"And yours are adorable!" Ermine rushed to her and touched them.

Maple's wings were pink and yellow, and fuzzy as a bumblebee. Two fat yellow antennae sprouted from her curls. Just as Flora predicted, she was a Rosy Maple Moth. She squealed with glee at the sight of herself.

Ermine's wings were white with black spots, just like an Ermine moth. At their base and between her shoulders, a thick layer of fluffy white fur grew. With her ermine collar and her fuzzy white wings, she looked like she was wearing a fashionable fur coat. She spun elegantly, touching her svelte black antennae.

Thorn's wings were like two crumpled leaves, the fiery, earthen colors of autumn, with tiny white crescent moons tucked into their deep auburn pattern. The wings of a Purple Thorn moth. His swirly brown antennae blended perfectly with his ruffled auburn hair.

But there was no time to truly process what had happened to them. Madame Cribellum huffed and crawled toward them slowly, squinting against the light of the crystal.

Ermine saw that Flora had a spool of thread on her windowsill. Using her magic, she lifted the string, as large as rope, and tied it to a jagged piece of stone. "Hurry!" she said. "We can climb down this! Maple and Thorn shimmied down the silk as fast as they could behind her.

"It's not long enough, though!" Flora said, "Maybe you can fly!"

The children looked at each other worriedly.

"We don't know how!" Ermine said.

"Besides, we can't leave without you!" Thorn yelled.

Flora was still holding onto the very bottom of the crystal, still trying to shine. But her light was going out. The crystal had taken most of her power.

Madame Cribellum looked up at Flora and grinned a luminescently wicked smile, her jagged teeth lit up in the crystal's light.

Flora felt herself drained with a terrible thirst. It was as if she hadn't had a sip of water in days, but she didn't feel it in her mouth… she felt it in her heart.

"Flora! Hurry! Come this way!" Thorn yelled to her from the silk rope. Madame Cribellum tried to snatch her, but Flora stumbled back and grabbed hold of the rope to slide down. Thorn caught her in his arms as she slid. "Are you okay?"

"I think so…" she said, dizzily looking down at the ground below. She willed herself to focus and held onto the rope tighter. "I'm okay. I just used more light than I usually do, that's all."

"Get them!" They heard Madame Cribellum command. From above, a hissing sound came from the window. The children looked up to see several spiders pouring out, crawling along the smokestack stones. They were a jangled mess of furry legs and fangs.

Maple screamed.

They kept shimmying down the rope until they reached its end.

"We have to jump!" Thorn yelled.

"It's too far!" Ermine yelled back.

The spiders were getting closer.

Flora was so scared, she closed her eyes and yelled, "Help!"

A flash of iridescent light burst toward them from above. Silver and gold stars on a current of dark gray flooded their vision. Flora's fabric, the children used to cover the crystal, came bursting out of the window in a flurry of sparks and jerked to a stop in midair under the children.

"What the..?" Thorn exclaimed.

"My star fabric!" Flora was shocked. "It's flying!"

"How?" Maple asked.

"There's no time to worry about that now!" Ermine said. "Get on!" Ermine jumped onto the shimmering thing. Flora and Thorn jumped on, too, as some spiders lunged at them and missed, falling to the ground below.

"Come on, Maple!" Ermine screeched. "Jump!"

Maple looked down at the ground below and winced. "I can't!"

"You have to! Watch out!"

Maple looked up to see a spider edging toward her, its fangs rearing. She screamed and leapt onto the carpet just as the spider lunged. She crumpled into the carpet and let out a moan. Flora put her arms around her.

"How do we fly this thing?" Thorn shouted.

Ermine stood up and swished her arms. They jolted forward. "I can control the threads inside!"

They were suddenly flying at an alarmingly fast pace.

"Wait! The web! We'll be stuck!" Maple screamed.

But the magic carpet shot right through the invisible strands, shining like a golden leaf blown in the wind. Sunset colors erupted all around them in a vast, unending expanse. They were free!

"Magic silk!" Flora exclaimed. "My Gran told me that the moth fairies could make magic fabric! It didn't seem like much when I blew a little bit of light into the stars to make them shine. But maybe that, combined with the rainbows from the moth-wing crystal, turned it into a magic carpet!"

"Do you think you have any *healing* magic?" Maple asked.

They all turned to her. "Why?"

Maple lifted one of her new wings up to show two fang marks in its fuzzy yellow membrane. "That spider got his mark."

"Oh no!" Ermine said, trying to keep her eyes ahead as she steered.

"It's not so bad," Maple said. "I mean… I can barely feel it anymore."

"Probably because it's going to paralyze her," Thorn said darkly.

Maple's eyes looked like they'd pop out of her face. "What?!"

"Don't worry, I'm sure it won't." Flora shot Thorn a warning glance. "Everything will be fine. Here, maybe I can do something."

Flora put her hand on Maple's wounded wing and took a deep breath. She closed her eyes. It was worth a try. If her light could make the carpet fly, maybe she could heal Maple's wound.

Humming one of her Gran's magic incantations and looking up at the first star winking down from the heavens, she willed all her light into the bite mark. And…

Nothing came. Where once there was a spark, nothing but darkness remained. Flora searched inside herself for the flame… but there was nothing.

"I don't have my light anymore!" She gasped.

"Oh no!" Maple cried.

"Did you spend it all on the crystal?" Thorn asked.

"It might come back," Ermine said softy. "You had to use a lot to help us. Just give it time."

"I usually have something…even just a spark." Tears welled in Flora's eyes. She had let the one thing her Gran had warned her not to let happen come true. She had worried so much that it would run out, and it finally did. Her heart ached at the thought of it. What had she done?

The children all jumped as they heard the crystal crash to the ground behind them with the wretched screams of Madame Cribellum. They turned to look as she crawled out of the smokestack window with the last of the spiders. She was coming for them. And Flora's light was gone.

21

THE MEADOW

The magic carpet whizzed into the dark forest until frothy branches shielded them from view, then it lazily caught a warm current of air and wove between branches under a sky full of rosy clouds and a cinnamon scatter of twinkling stars. Flora stared, exhausted, at the dim expanse of forest all around her. She wanted to run her fingers along each leaf to smother her face in moss. She had looked out at her forest for so long from her window, longing to touch it… and she was finally there inside her emerald world. The children held each other close in the center of the carpet, in disbelief that they had escaped.

"So your parents are Henry and Luna." Thorn said, "I did not see that coming."

"Me neither," Flora said. "To think that I had found my own parent's initials carved in the cherry tree that day." She shook her head in disbelief. She pondered the truth of everything she had just learned. Her Gran, the children in the mill truly being moth fairies, her parents trapped forever in amber… She found herself holding her breath with the strain of it all.

"So that means *you're* half Moth Fairy!" Maple said.

Flora smiled slightly. "I guess that's true!" She hadn't grown wings with the others, so she figured it must not be very dominant, but it did make her happy to know she was one of them.

"Too bad you didn't get your mom's pink hair!" Maple squeaked. "Can you *imagine?*"

"And I think technically that means that Nuthatch Estate belongs to you," Ermine said over her shoulder. "If we ever find a way to prove it and figure out how to be our normal size again, I call dibs on being in charge of the mill."

They all laughed.

"Ermine, if Flora owns the mill, we won't have to work at all! We're just kids!" Thorn said.

"Oh right!" Ermine laughed.

Despite the weight of what they still faced, Flora felt like their current circumstances were too good to be true. Being back in the open air, and the hope of actually being rid of the mill and never having to work tirelessly for Madame Cribellum again was like a drink of warm honey.

"Smell that?" Flora asked. She breathed in deeply. The smell of green and new forest flowers filled her lungs. The smell of the woods after the rain. "That's the smell of spring!"

Thorn and Ermine breathed in, and Maple giggled.

Everything in the forest seemed to be coming alive. Fronds unfurled, leaf buds in brilliant hues dotted the branches, and crocuses opened in soft wonder to the cool air.

"I think our magic carpet is losing its power," Ermine grunted. She tried to gain more lift with her hands, but found it impossible. "I'm going to have to land us." She eased the carpet down gently through the trees to the forest floor. The ground where they landed was covered with clovers so fresh and green they were still bright in the dim canopy light. As they landed, the carpet let out a spray of golden sparks, and the children tumbled off. Flora carefully folded the fabric, now light and airy. She couldn't believe they were able to ride on something so flimsy. She tucked it into one of the deep pockets of her dress.

Since the children had shrunk, the clovers were like a blanket
of knee-deep snow to them. They collapsed in relief, alighting on
the leaves like a feather bed.

Ermine was finally able to focus on her new wings. She
gently touched the white fur along her shoulders and smiled at
the dotted pattern that matched all her clothes. She touched one
of the spots and lifted a finger to find black matte crystals there.
Dust.

"I knew you were Giltiri! And look at you all. Your wings are
the exact ones I predicted!" Flora felt proud and delighted. She

made them each spin around so she could inspect them. "Can you open your wings?"

In response, Maple fluttered her pink and yellow wings and lifted off the ground a foot or two. Flora grabbed her hands and brought her back down.

Thorn sauntered over to the crackled bark of a fir tree as large as a castle. He unfurled his auburn wings and covered himself with them. He matched perfectly. It was hard to tell where his wings started and the bark ended. "This will come in handy." He smiled with an eyebrow raised.

"Look how high up the branches are!" Ermine held her own face in her hands, looking filled to the brim with happiness at the sight of the forest. Then her responsible self kicked in. "We'd better not try to fly any time soon. Madame Cribellum's webs could be anywhere. Flora, do you know where we are? Are we close to your cottage?"

"I don't know if we should go to my cottage. Madame Cribellum will know to look there, but…" She looked all around her, puzzled. "Everything is so different when you're tiny!" She saw a gnarled, heart-shaped hole in one tree. "Oh! That's the barn owl's home! I know where we are. We aren't far from the meadow at the center of the forest. That's where the giant cherry tree is. Maybe if we go there, we can get some answers… and maybe even find a way to help the other children in the mill." Flora hated to admit it, but she didn't know what they would find, if anything. They were lucky enough to get out of the mill themselves. She didn't know how they could ever get the other children out.

"We'd better get there quick." Ermine glanced at Maple. "That spider bite might be poisonous."

"I do feel a little weak," Maple said. She examined the bite mark. "EEEW, gross!" The wound was green, and the wing around it had turned a purply bruised black color. She made a face. But then she shrugged and took a few steps. "But I can walk just fine."

Flora folded the starry fabric up and hugged it. They were lucky its magic had lasted for the few moments it took to escape. "Thank you for saving us," she whispered to it. She stuffed it into one of her big dress pockets with the hope that she might be able to use it again. Maybe her light would come back. There was no way to tell.

The children made their way over enormous roots and rocks. They waded through spongy masses of moss and under tall gilled mushrooms and frilled ferns, sometimes with great difficulty because of their small size and Maple's weakness. Thorn, Ermine, and Maple had to get used to the weight of their new wings, though they were so light, it didn't take long. They worked together, sometimes taking turns carrying Maple on their backs when her feet grew too tired.

It was a moonless night. As the sky grew midnight black, the stars overhead somehow seemed bigger and brighter than they had ever been to Flora. Their steady, cold glow cast long shadows. Every once in a while, she would try to absorb them to create a little light in her fingers, but nothing ever came. *It really must be gone*, she thought. She wished she'd paid attention to it the last time she'd used it. She would have savored it somehow. But it was too late for that. And she knew there were more important things to think about. She needed to find the light the Emperor Moth had told her about. Clearly, the moth dust crystal wasn't bright enough, and her own light had been snuffed out, so *she* couldn't be the light. She had to find the magic that disappeared so long ago.

Nature magic.

Eventually they rounded a corner of large roots and crested a bramble-covered hill just above the meadow. They looked out over it in astonishment.

"This is a meadow?!" Thorn asked. It was enormous. The weeping cherry tree stood at the other end like a lady with long, flowing hair. But now it was miles and miles away because of their small size. The spring that flowed out of the tree and glittered through the meadow was no longer a creek; it was a raging torrent rushing and splashing over rocks as big as boulders. Every flower looked like some giant confection or decoration of crepe.

"It's like a whole forest inside the forest!" Flora cried.

"Well, we'd better get going if we want to get to that tree." Ermine set off down the slope.

They journeyed under dewy flowers, all glittery in the starlight. Candelabra primroses plumed high above them, violas unfurled beside their long quill-like leaves, and bluebells rang their silent song in the light breeze. Every once in a while, one of Flora's favorite star flowers shone like a shooting star in the murky depths. Flora had spent so many afternoons in this very meadow, examining flowers and moths. It was so strange to see it from such a tiny perspective! It used to take a few bounds, and she'd be across it. But now it would take hours and hours to get across. Maybe even days.

"Your face looks so ashen, Maple." Ermine had been keeping an eye on her.

Flora was worried too. Where was her usual rosy hue?

"Yeah, Maple. You're usually either whining about something or overly delighted by something that's ridiculously cute. But we haven't heard a peep out of you for hours." Thorn laughed uncertainly.

He was right. Maple would have lost her mind with joy over the giant flowers if she were feeling well. But she was silent. She dragged her feet over the moss. Finally, she lost her strength completely and slumped to the ground.

"Here, lie down. You can't walk anymore." Ermine had
Maple put her head in her lap. Her face was covered in beads of
sweat.

Flora looked around. Gran would know what to do. She was
always making tinctures and potions from things in the forest.
She tried to think about what Gran would have gathered. She
would make sure Flora was hydrated. She was always having
her drink more water... Then something occurred to her.

"I know! Maple, I bet you'll feel better if you drink nectar
from one of the star flowers... Here!" She grabbed a leaf and

cupped it in her hands. "Thorn, can you help me? Pull on the stem." Thorn climbed up one of the giant stems and pulled down a flower as big as herself. Pollen sprinkled onto her hair and stamens brushed her cheek. She grasped the tail of the flower and ripped a small hole off the end. Globs of sugary syrup poured out into the leaf she held.

Maple tried to drink, though her mouth was dry and her strength was so low she could barely lift her head. She sputtered, and it seemed like more of the liquid was ending up on her dress than in her mouth, but soon a little color returned to her face. "It tastes like liquid light!"

"Exactly!" Flora jumped up and down. "It must be because these flowers are fed by the stream that comes from the tree!"

Maple's cheeks grew pinker and pinker until she was the same old rosy Maple she normally was. She pulled her wing in front of her to inspect it. The purple-infected membrane had already lightened. The fang holes began to close up.

"Wow. That was quick," Thorn said.

The children took turns drinking from the star flower. As they did, they felt renewed strength and vigor. It was a soothing balm after they'd been walking for so long.

Thorn was suddenly determined. "Let's keep going! I bet we could get to the tree by tomorrow!"

"I know we could keep going," Ermine said, "but I think we should find a place to rest and get some sleep. The morning must be coming soon, and Madame Cribellum will be able to find us more easily in the daylight."

"That's a smart idea," Flora said. "Maybe we could find an old animal hole or something."

"Hopefully *without* an animal in it." Ermine shuddered.

"And something to eat?" Thorn asked.

The children continued their trek through the meadow, searching for a place that might be good for shelter. Soon they came to a puddle surrounded by tall blue forget-me-nots standing out like sapphires in the mist, hovering over the water. The puddle, really a pond for their size, was like a pool of mercury. It was so still it reflected the silver world above it. The children took gulps of water and washed their faces.

"It's so pretty," Flora said, staring at the circles of ripples fanning out slowly toward the other end of the puddle.

Then, out of the middle of the puddle, two bulbous green boulders rose to the surface.

"What are those?" Maple asked. "Rocks?"

"It looks like they're covered with slime," Ermine said, disgusted.

"I don't think those are rocks," Thorn said. "I think they're skin."

Sure enough, black slits opened in the boulders, and the children discovered...

They were eyes.

"It's a bullfrog!" Flora yelped, taking a few steps back.

The bullfrog slowly lifted his head above the water and stared the children down.

"Don't move!" Ermine said. "Maybe he won't see us."

"He's looking right at us!" Maple said. "Do you think he thinks we're tasty bugs?"

"We kind of *are* tasty bugs." Thorn grimaced.

"Can you camouflage us?" Flora asked Thorn.

"I think it's too late..." he said as the bullfrog opened his wide, wet mouth and his tongue came careening out. The children all leapt out of the way, but Ermine wasn't fast enough. The sticky tongue wrapped around her waist and began to snap back. She dug her heels into the ground and screamed.

The others grabbed her arms and pulled with all their might. But the frog was too strong. Flora's fingers were slipping, Maple fell to the ground, and Thorn lost his grip.

Ermine's eyes filled with tears. "Don't let go of me!" she said in a panic. "Don't let..."

Just then, a bunch of darts hit the bullfrog's tongue, and he loosened his grip. Ermine fell to the ground as she was released.

The bullfrog let out a loud "croaaaak!" And plopped off into the mist. The only sign of him was the rustling forget-me-nots in the distance.

"What was that?!" Flora said. "Ermine are you okay?"

"Those darts..." Ermine gasped for air. "They were like giant..."

"We finally found you!" An oddly gravelly voice spoke to them from above. The children looked up, startled.

22

CATERPILLARS

areening from a strand of silk, a large orange and black fuzzy caterpillar swung down to the children. Above him, three other caterpillars were clinging to a low vine of honeysuckle.

"We know of a hiding place nearby. Let us take you there," the orange and black caterpillar said.

"You're a Woolly Bear caterpillar, aren't you?" Flora was beside herself.

"Why yes, I am," he bowed. "Bear is my name. And this is Spindle." He motioned to a white caterpillar with black spots who also bowed. "He is a webworm." Spindle was much smaller than the others, but had the longest hairs.

"And I am Geo!" Squeaked a smooth green caterpillar. He inched a few paces down the vine and lifted his upper half importantly.

"You're an inch worm!" Flora curtsied. "I'm Flora, and this is Ermine, Maple, and Thorn." She looked up at another caterpillar with yellow and black stripes. "And what's your name?"

"Cinna," she said shyly. "I'll turn into a red Cinnabar moth."

Flora smiled brightly. "You'll be beautiful!"

Flora tried to step closer, but Ermine held her back. Her eyes narrowed. "How do we know they're not going to trick us?" she asked.

"Or eat us?" Maple gulped.

"They're caterpillars. They turn into moths, right?" Thorn said. "They probably want to keep away from spiders just as much as we do."

"We mean you no harm, little chenilles," Bear said. He lowered himself to the ground and dipped his head. "We only want to protect you."

"Chenille…" Flora cocked her head. "My Gran used to call me that."

"What does it mean?" Maple asked.

"It's a type of fabric with furry lines on it," Flora said. "I had a bed spread with chenille designs in bright colors. It kind of looks like frosting on a cake."

The caterpillars laughed. Geo said, "Chenille means *caterpillar*!"

Flora furrowed her brow. Then she began to realize… "Oh! The puffy lines on the fabric do look like fuzzy caterpillars!"

"Caterpillar is a strange thing to call your granddaughter, but I guess they are pretty cute." Thorn said. Flora felt herself blush.

"Because she doesn't have wings!" Maple said. "Her grandmother was calling her a caterpillar because she's a Giltiri!"

Flora laughed. Her Gran had been giving hints about her true identity all along.

"This is all beside the point," Ermine said, crossing her arms. "How can you protect *us*? You're just caterpillars!"

Bear reared up on his hind legs and stiffened. His body shuddered, and out of the orange fuzz on his back, about ten spikes shot out of his back like darts and embedded themselves in the hardy trunk of the honeysuckle plant.

"You were the one who saved me from the frog?" Ermine asked, wide-eyed.

"Don't be fooled by how cute we may seem, my dear. Caterpillars may be small, but there is more to us than meets the eye."

"Great things can come from tiny creatures!" Spindle squeaked. "Come, let me show you something my comrades and I have made for you!"

The caterpillars led them through a hole in the brush. It was dark and damp, and smelled like ripe blackberries and autumn bonfires. Flora thought perhaps it was the smell of stored goods from the autumn. Eventually, the twigs and vines that made up the walls of the hole turned to gossamer threads. Starlight lit the threads from behind, and it was as if the children were walking through a silvery cloud.

"It's like magical cotton!" Maple said.

"Is this…?" Ermine asked, touching the threads.

"Silk," Flora said with a small smile. She knew it immediately. It looked just like her Gran's golden threads. Like her sweater. It reminded her of home and it gave her a dull ache in her chest to think of it. "I used to collect silk for my grandmother to spin," she told the caterpillars. "This silk is more white than the golden cocoons I'd collect, but it's similar."

"This is one of the webworm tents." Bear said, "We have them all over the forest. Some are near the ground like this one; some are high up in the trees."

"We can weave one of these in minutes!" Spindle piped.

"I bet Ermine could too," Maple said. "She's the best spinner in the mill!"

Ermine tried to conceal a grin.

"Yes, we know!" Cinna said. "Ermine moths are what tent caterpillars turn into! I do believe you and Spindle are related!"

Ermine's face was covered in surprise. Her eyes darted to Spindle.

"There's no denying it!" Thorn said, "They both have spots!"

Ermine gave Spindle a nervous smile.

Flora held in the burst of laughter she felt. Not because she thought it was so awful to be related to a caterpillar, but because Ermine seemed to be having such a hard time with the idea of it.

But Spindle crawled over to Ermine and said, "It's okay! You can pet me if you like, and I can ride on your shoulder. That was what my ancestors did with the Giltiri of old. I think we could be great friends!"

Ermine put her arm out, and Spindle crawled up onto it. His body was as long as her forearm, and his white hairs were a good ten inches long. She pet his head carefully and, realizing it was silky soft, pet the rest of his body. She smiled. "I'd like to be friends with you, Spindle. Especially after seeing the amazing work you've done with your thread!"

"Here you are!" Cinna crawled over to some beds of moss covered with lamb's ear leaves at the end of the tent. "You can sleep on these and use these leaves as blankets!"

Maple ran over to one and bounced down onto it immediately. She laid out flat, and Cinna crawled up next to her. "You're sooo cute!" Maple squealed. Cinna bowed her head down shyly, then Maple grabbed her striped body and held her as if she were a puppy.

"Here are some pillows!" Bear rolled over four pincushion flowers. "And something for you to eat." He motioned to a giant blackberry on a leaf in the corner. Large, juicy seed pockets had been removed and set on a mint leaf. Thorn grabbed four and handed them to the others. Flora immediately sunk her teeth into the seed pocket, as big as a grapefruit. Purple liquid burst into her mouth. She hadn't even realized how hungry she was until she began eating. The blackberry filled her aching stomach.

"This is so exciting!" Geo said with a grin, "It's not every day that we get to attend to the Giltiri."

The children looked at each other's purple-stained faces. It was still sinking in that they were fairies.

"Am I really a Rosy Maple Moth fairy?" Maple asked. Her eyes glinted.

"Indeed!" Cinna squeaked.

Flora sat down on her bed and put her chin in her hands. She still hadn't felt her light return. Her magic must have truly waned. She couldn't help but sulk. "I'm not really a Giltiri, though," she mumbled. "Just half."

"Yes, we remember you, my dear," Bear said. He crawled up to her and rested several arms on her hand. "The little girl who loved our cocoons and saved us from the Barn Owl. We're honored to have you here too."

Flora brightened.

"We knew your father, too!" Geo squeaked. "Our kind watched him in the forest from the time he was a little boy, caring for creatures. He had the loveliest glow."

"He glowed like Flora?" Maple asked excitedly.

"Oh yes. Every human has a halo of nebulous light around them that animals can see," Geo said. "Some have more than others; some sadly have nothing at all. But Henry had a glow like a warm orange flame. Calming, pleasant, and caring. And all the creatures in Silkwood Forest could see. It was too bad that he took Luna's cocoon when she was little. Had he known she was inside, I'm sure he never would have. The moths never quite forgave him for that. Except, ironically, for Luna."

"Theirs was such a sweet romance," Cinna said dreamily.

"We helped keep watch as they danced under the silk lanterns, conjuring mushrooms in the night."

249

"Only her closest caterpillar friends knew," Geo said. "The Empress had forbidden Luna to see Henry. She even kept her pregnancy a secret, even from Henry, using magic to conceal her growing form until she had you."

"It didn't take long before he was perfumed with the scents of magic blossoms, and his perfectly parted hair started to grow long and curly, tucked behind his ears." Cinna said, "They had their secret places. Her magic could shrink him, disguise him, show the true glow of his heart."

"I remember her giggling as she carved their initials into the cherry tree under the moss." Spindle said, "He nervously asked her to be quick so they would not be seen. When she finished, she tugged his hand so he slipped off the branch and fell into a thistle puff. Then his cheeks turned the same color as her pink hair!"

Flora melted at the thought. A forbidden fairy romance! And Giltiri magic! It sounded like her friends' gifts. She leaned in to hear more.

"And it is forever to our shame that we didn't do enough the night the Witch Moth took her revenge." Spindle said, "We watched as Henry rushed out into the golden woods as the sun brimmed the horizon. He had decided once and for all to leave the human world behind and live with you and Luna in the cherry tree. The Empress had finally allowed their union. Henry looked so thrilled, his eyes aglow with the honeyed world of leaves stretched before him in a pathway to where his love was waiting for him... We should have known from the glistening dew drops strung on webs upon webs all around him that something wasn't right."

Flora's eyes filled with tears.

"All of Silkwood lost its magic that day," Bear said. "It was only recently that we regained our power to speak. Life is returning to the forest. Even some of the moths have started regaining their memories. They have waited for so long, unable to communicate other than to fly up into the stars in a fogged search for their light. We have hope that their day of freedom is coming soon."

"Why haven't you changed into moths yet?" Maple asked through a big yawn.

"We swore a pact that we would wait for the Moth Kingdom's return to power," Spindle said.

"We are the guardians of the forest, watching and protecting if the need should arise," Bear said. "It has not been safe for any small creature with wings since the Witch Moth stole the light."

"But let's not think of her now," said Geo. "Let's tuck in and get some sleep. He inched up onto the end of Thorn's bed and curled up into a ball.

The children pulled their fuzzy leaves up over them. They were so soft and warm, and though they'd been through so much, the spiders seemed miles away. It didn't take long for their eyelids to grow heavy.

"We haven't slept in two days," Thorn said. "I can't wait to fall asleep."

"That's true!" Ermine said, "So much has happened, I'd hardly thought of it. But we had to do the night shift, and then we walked all through the forest to get here. Now that we can finally rest, I'm sooo tired."

"It's probably a good thing, though," Flora said. "We need to sleep during the day and travel to the cherry tree at night."

"It's going to be weird sleeping during the day," Maple said with a yawn.

"I guess we'd better get used to it," Flora said, "Moths usually come out at night."

Flora awoke in the early morning. The tent was dark, save for a smattering of stars glowing through a hole in the silk. She felt something warm at her side. Bear kept watch next to her as she slept. He was much larger than the others, almost spanning all of her length. At their small size, he really was like a bear. She reached out and pet the fur near his head, not wanting to disturb any of his sharp spikes.

After several moments, she didn't think she could fall back to sleep, so she quietly crept to the hole in the tent to look out at the dark forest. Giant leaves and elephantine roots loomed above her. She sighed. She felt so small, so helpless. There were still children trapped in the mill. The Giltiri were still moths. Her poor parents! But she was as tiny as a caterpillar. She had to find a way to set everyone free, but she didn't know what she could do. Again, she blew into her hand to try to summon some light — nothing.

The truth was, in her heart, she wished she had wings like her friends. When this was all over, if it was ever over, Thorn and Maple and Ermine would still be moth fairies. And she would still be a girl. She felt so alone. She looked up through the patchwork of green to a small hole in the canopy where the starlight poured through. Dust swirled and glittered in its long, pale beam. She wished she could fly up to those motes and harness all their light.

"Can't sleep?" Thorn sleepily shuffled to her side. Geo lay asleep on his leaf bed, scrunched in a ball.

"Thorn, I don't know if we'll be able to find a way to…"

"Don't worry about that now. Let's just get to the cherry tree and see what we can find."

"I want to help, but I don't have my light anymore. Now I'm just… I'm just me. Hunched, frazzled, plain me."

Thorn made a face of bewilderment and shook his head. "Flora…you…you're not…" he swallowed. "Flora, from the moment I first saw you, you were the bravest girl I'd ever seen, hanging from a vine trying to save that little caterpillar from the owl."

Flora looked up at him, shocked. "That *was* you laughing at me from the window!"

Thorn looked sheepish, but he continued. "You're frazzled, yes. But you were…you." His eyes were wet, and his face was earnest. He took her hand. "I think…"

But he was interrupted by Bear.

"My dear little girl." Bear crawled over and stood on his haunches. His gravelly voice sounded like how spicy hot chocolate tasted. "I remember when you saved that caterpillar too… It's one of the reasons I was so eager to help you now." He winked at her.

"That was you?!"

Bear smiled. "Do you remember how you used to read the seasons by my sections?"

Flora grinned. "The number of orange sections on a Woolly Bear caterpillar's body tells you how many months of winter there will be," she explained to Thorn.

Bear's spines shivered. "It tickled a little, but I liked having such importance to you, though I am small."

"That's a nice talent to have," Thorn said, impressed.

"And it is not just the seasons that I can predict," Bear said. "I can read the stars and see the future. Did you know our kind can see twice as many colors? We see more than mere humans would ever give us credit for. And, Flora, the stars are calling *you*."

"Me?"

"Yes. I can see that your strand of silk plays a large part in the tapestry of the Giltiri story."

Flora bit her lip. "But I'm so small now… How could I?"

Bear laughed. "Think of the seasons: a power thought to only be harnessed by celestial orbs and the currents of storms. Large and monstrous things with secrets so hidden, none can unlock them."

"Except you," Flora whispered.

"A mere caterpillar. You can do it, little chenille. The power is within you."

Tingles spread from the base of Flora's spine to her fingertips. "I will try," she said.

"And she'll have help." Ermine said with one tired eye slit open.

"Yes, we'll be with you, too." Thorn said, determined.

Maple grumbled under her leaf. "Ugh! What time is it?"

"Once we're all awake," Thorn laughed.

Flora laughed with tears in her eyes. "The tapestry of life must have several strings. One for each of my friends. With all of you… I think I will weave light again."

As the sky slowly began to lighten, the forest erupted in birdsong, greeting the new day. The children cozied back down in their leaf beds, and despite the cacophony outside, Flora nuzzled into her flower pillow and fell right to sleep.

After a full day's sleep, the children lazily awoke to the evening sun setting the strands of the tent aglow. Flora felt like she could stay there, enveloped in that golden cocoon, forever. But they needed to move on. The caterpillars fed them outside their den at a mushroom table. They were each given a salad in an acorn cap. They licked their lips savoring every bit of their mint, oregano, and tiny muscari flowers tossed in huckleberry syrup. To drink, they were given rose petals with large dew drops inside.

"My antennae look enormous in this thing!" Maple said, looking at her reflection in her dewdrop. Thorn nudged her rose petal up a little so that it splashed her face.

"Thorn!"

"It's distorted, silly!" he said. "Though those things *are* really big."

Ermine punched his arm. "They're adorable!" she chided.

Flora looked at her reflection and stuck out her tongue. It looked twice as long in the dew drop.

The children almost forgot a whole legion of spiders was looking for them as they frolicked under the enormous flowers in the witching hour glow. Thorn darted from flower to flower, trying out his new wings, then flew fast and pushed Maple into a lush clump of creeping thyme. While he was distracted, Ermine pushed him in after her. Flora plugged her nose as if she were going to land in water and fell back into the purple flowers herself. Ermine sat down daintily on a rock nearby, not wanting to get wet with dew. The other three snuck up on her and doused her with wet flowers.

"You were asking for it, Ermine!" Thorn laughed.

Ermine screamed.

"It's not that bad!" Maple said.

But Ermine wasn't upset about getting a little wet. She looked past them in terror, pointing. "The spiders!"

23

PREDATORS

igweed!" Flora swore. In the distance, they could see spiders climbing through the branches of the forest lining the meadow. They looked like a menacing black goo creeping over the land. Flora wished she still had her magic. She felt so useless.

Bear let out a startling growl as he rushed toward the spiders and sprayed them with his spikes. A few made their mark in the front spiders' eyes, but the spiders kept coming closer. Geo swung down from a branch on a strand of silk and grabbed Bear before the hoard of spiders reached him. They swung up into the trees, narrowly escaping sharp mandibles.

Bear had given the children just enough time to get out of sight.

"Quick!" Thorn shouted, grabbing Maple's collar and Flora's hand. Ermine followed quickly. He pinned the girls to the bark of a root and shielded them with his camouflaged wings. Slowly, their clothes turned the color of his auburn hair and grew slats and streaks like gnarled wood. Flora looked down at her hands. Even her skin was changing! She knew it was just an illusion, but it really looked like her skin had become bark. She looked over at Maple. Her hair was a patch of lichen. Soon, they blended perfectly into the root.

The spiders made their way into their small clearing. They seemed to feel out every crevice with their darting legs and quickly found the mushroom where the children had had breakfast. They lingered there, tasting remnants of their food, then followed their scent to the hollow where the caterpillar tent was.

"What if they find the caterpillars?" Maple whispered.

"Hopefully they're too smart for that," Flora said.

"Shhhh! They'll hear you!" Ermine tapped them both to be quiet.

One of the spiders whirled in their direction. It slowly crawled to where the children were, pawing at the roots at the base of the tree. It brushed a hairy leg over their feet, and they all held their breath.

The other spiders eventually came back out of the caterpillar hollow, and the spider, whose nose was just a hair's width from the children, followed reluctantly. They all converged in the center of the clearing and huddled together for a few moments. One spider pointed toward the mill with a long foot. They all bobbed up and down in agreement, and, in a jangled mess of fur and appendages, the scouting party made its way back the way it had come.

But one spider stayed behind. The one that had brushed its foot over their feet.

"Come on," Thorn whispered. He slowly shifted over the root toward the base of some tall fiddlehead ferns. They would be good cover. As he shifted, his hair sprouted green fronds, and his clothes turned the earthy green of moss. He motioned for them all to follow, holding hands. Just as they moved away from the root, they looked back in time to see the spider pounce on the spot they had been in against the tree. "Whew!" Flora let out a breath. "That was close."

"Let's get out of here!" Ermine whispered.

"I'm pretty sure the spring is this way." Flora pointed. "If we can get to it, we can follow it to the cherry tree."

They kept close together, holding hands as they moved through the wood. Their clothes and skin shifted with Thorn, mimicking their surroundings. They stumbled through a patch of mushrooms, and Ermine suddenly looked ridiculous with a clump of tiny, long white enoki mushrooms popping out of her head. Maple stifled a giggle, only to sprout one large red mushroom with white spots from her own head, like a hat. Flora couldn't help but squeal; it was so adorable.

"Shhh!" Thorn turned to keep her quiet, then let out a snort. Flora had ruffly chanterelle gills flowing through her hair.

"You should see yourself!" She retorted.

He had grown a halo of rainbow fungi out of his head. He flashed her a crooked smile. "Ok, I think we're in the clear," he said.

Their mushroom crowns vanished, and they were themselves again.

"Do you think the caterpillars are okay?" Maple asked.

Ermine looked at Flora with a worried look, then smiled warmly at Maple. "I'm sure they're fine. They've lived in this forest for a long time. I'm sure they've dealt with spiders before."

"I hope we see them again," Maple sighed.

The children trekked through the giant meadow, not daring to fly or leave the shadows for fear of being seen by the spiders or the Witch Moth.

Soon, Flora heard the sound of water. "It's close!" she said, bounding toward the sound. They nearly fell off a small, muddy cliff as they stumbled out of the ferns into the open. Before them was the spring, now a river, rushing and raging over the geodes. Here and there, they could see crystal points jutting up out of the broken bits of stones. It looked like a river of fragmented moonlight. Flora's heart swelled. And best of all, the cherry tree had been shedding. Pink petals flowed past, dotted with a few full blossoms.

"It's like pink confetti!" Maple cried.

"Ok. To get to the tree, we just have to follow this upstream," Flora said. She tried to find a root to grab hold of to climb down to the water.

Then she heard something she hadn't even considered.

A sharp shriek rang overhead. The children looked up.

"Is that…" Thorn began.

"Yes," Flora said. "That's the barn owl."

"Well, as Flora says," Ermine said flatly, "…Ragwort."

There was no time to laugh at how funny it was to hear Ermine swear. The barn owl had spotted them. It turned and swooped, silent as a shadow, toward the riverbank. It was headed straight for them.

"HIDE!" Flora yelped out as she dove for the ferns. The children scrambled in behind her as sharp talons swept at their backs. The owl swooped up out of view as the children crouched in the dark of the foliage. Flora frantically tried to cover their entrance with any bit of debris and leaves she could find. They waited an agonizing few moments.

"Is it gone?" Maple panted.

Flora touched her finger to her lips to keep her quiet. She hoped the owl had given up but could not be sure. She knew they had incredible hearing.

Then their cozy greenery began to shake. The ground rumbled at their feet. The bird was pecking and clawing at the underbrush around them! Flora slipped down a chasm that opened up beneath her and grabbed Thorn's hand just in time as he reached out. Together, they clung to vines as they tried to gain their footing on solid ground.

Ermine shouted, "We have to get out of here!"

"How can we!? There's nowhere to go!" Flora covered her head with one arm as the owl's scraping claws rained dirt and debris over her head.

"This way!" Thorn let go of his vine and slid down the river bank. "We can try the river!"

"But it's going the wrong way! We'll be swept downstream!" But Flora had to admit that there was nothing they could do. The earth all around them was quaking to pieces. If they didn't escape by the river, they would be eaten or buried alive. She let go and slid down into the shimmering, warm water. Luckily, it wasn't too turbulent where they were. Thorn grabbed one of the cherry blossoms flowing past and pulled himself up into its cup. They could use the flowers as tiny boats! Flora whisked another flower to herself and got in. They looked like they were wearing fluffy pink tutus. She grabbed hold of a geode to stop herself from being pulled downstream and looked back up the bank.

"Where are the others?" She gasped.

Ermine tumbled out over the bank and plopped into the water. "We have to go. We have to go NOW!" she said as she grasped another flower, got in, and started splashing and swerving through the water into the deep part of the river.

"Where's maple?!" Flora yelled back over the sound of the rushing river.

As a cacophony of feathers fluttered up out of the ferns, they got their answer. Maple was caught. The owl grasped her pink collar in his beak. Her legs dangled at his neck. The bird cranked its head, turned its steely eyes toward them, then dove with its talons open.

"Deadnettle!" Flora let go of the crystal anchoring her to shore and followed Ermine downstream.

Thorn was beside her in a few moments, their flowers spinning them in a dizzying chase. The owl tried to snatch them out of the water, but missed.

"We have to save her!" Flora screamed.

"How can we?" Ermine cried. Tears spilled down her cheeks.

"Your string! Can you use it?"

"I tried already! I lassoed it around its foot, but my silk broke!"

"It's going to eat her, Ermine!"

The owl swooped again, barely missing Thorn. Its talons splashed the water, spraying them all with froth. But the water was too swift. The three plunged over rapids and were pulled through geode crevices. Flora's stomach lurched. She could barely hold on; her flower jerked around so much in the current.

She thought it couldn't get much worse, then she looked ahead and could see a drop coming. She yelped.

"Look out!" Thorn said as he careened over the edge of the large rapid and dropped out of sight. Ermine followed, facing backwards at Flora, and screamed, "No no no no!" as she bobbed up into the air and then plummeted into the mist beyond.

Flora held her breath and ducked down as far as she could into her cherry blossom. When the edge of the rapid came, her heart fell into her stomach as she was flung up, then there was a dizzying moment of the water falling out beneath her, her body suspended in air, and then she plunged down into the churning pool below. She bobbed back up and gasped, wet as a fish.

The owl flew up ahead of them to a large branch curving over the river. It had found the perfect spot. The water slowed beyond the rapid in a still, aqua pool. They would be under the owl in moments. All it had to do was dip a foot down and snatch them out of the water. Flora closed her eyes against the sea sickness and the terror of her unavoidable fate. Then the rushing stopped. Her blossom boat slowed. She was ready to be plucked...

"Look!" Thorn grabbed her arm, anchoring her.

Flora and Ermine looked up at the owl.

"No *way!*" Flora said.

The owl's cheeks were turning pink! His fierce stance relaxed, and his feathers seemed to soften. Maple was using her blush on him! They watched as it gently put Maple down on the branch. Maple reached out her hands and hugged it around its feathery neck. At first, the owl ruffled up in surprise, then it nuzzled into her. She whispered something to it, and it seemed to bow its head. Then it put out a wing, and Maple climbed up onto its back, close to its head.

The children stared at her, mouths agape.

"Well," she said, "what are you waiting for? He's going to give us a ride!"

"Maple's blush is the best thing *ever!*" Thorn whooped and jumped out of his cherry blossom into the water. He backstroked to the branch and made his way up onto the waiting bird.

Flora laid back in her flower and let it take its time floating to the branch. She was exhausted from the fright they'd had and still felt seasick.

Ermine looked up at the owl, then gave Flora a look as if to say, *Is this safe?* But then shrugged her shoulders. She was all grace and fluidity as she flew up onto the branch and landed on a pointed toe. She removed her sopping wet slippers and ripped polka-dot tights.

"Well, these are ruined," she said. She looked at them longingly, then dumped them into the river. Then she pulled out her ball of string and quickly made a rope ladder for Flora with magic.

Flora lumbered up the ladder, and Ermine put out a hand to help her get to the top. Flora half smiled and scrambled onto the branch herself, then plopped down in a huff. She couldn't believe they were actually going to ride on the back of the caterpillar's long-time enemy. She looked up at the owl with an uncertain pout.

The owl bowed to Flora. His bright black eyes blinked at her. He nudged her bare foot with his beak and shifted closer. Everyone else was already on his back, and he was waiting for her. He looked like he would never dream of hurting anyone. Flora felt just a little guilty for having stolen his meals in the past. But then she remembered how she had almost just been gobbled up, too, and laughed.

I don't feel too sorry, she thought, as she glared up at him. The owl put out a wing and brushed her body with a feather, tickling her. "All right, all right, I'm coming!" She resigned with a giggle.

The owl's outer feathers were slick and looked like flecks of ash and sparks on cedar smoke. But underneath, they were soft and white. Flora dug her hands deep into his downy layers and held tight. When he flapped his wings and soared out over the river, Flora thought she might be sick again, but soon they leveled out, and it was a thrill to see the river rush below them and the flowers on either side turn to a blur as they went past. Flora let herself breathe. She'd been so full of fright and flight, and then exhaustion, that she needed to take a moment to enjoy what was happening. Twilight twinkled all around them. The moon shone out of a constellation like an iridescent pearl on a strand of diamonds. The wind filled her hair with the vanilla scent of ponderosa pine.

"You guys! We're flying on an owl!" she said, in disbelief.

Maple let out a "Weeeeee!"

Thorn yelled, "Wahooooo!"

"Everyone, calm down, and make sure you're holding on tight!" Ermine said, sensibly.

The others' laughter echoed through the forest.

24

THE CHERRY TREE

oon, they were under the shattered pink light of the moon through cherry blossoms, like a canopy of delicate stained glass.

"It's beautiful!" Ermine cried.

"So. Much. PINK!" Maple yelled.

"Ok, we've reached the tree," Thorn said, "What now?"

"Have him land us at the base of the tree," Flora said.

Maple laid her cheek on top of the owl's head, and they made a slow, low arc over the meadow, then came to a wind-blown stop. The children jumped off the owl and said their thanks. Maple gave him one last hug, his cheeks turning pink again, and then kissed him on his beak. She waved goodbye, and he bobbed his head, then scampered through the air currents into the night.

"Well, that was lucky!" Maple beamed.

"How did you do it?" Ermine asked.

"I got so scared when he grabbed me that I passed out from the terror. Then I woke up dangling over you guys floating in the cherry blossoms in the river. I knew I was probably going to die, but you all looked *so cute* in those flowers that I couldn't help being happy that that was the last thing I was going to see! Then I started getting angry with myself. I'm always getting everyone to do everything for me. I'm always so afraid! I said to myself, 'Maple, it's about time you did something for everyone else!' I needed to try to save us. So I started blushing, thinking about how much I love you all. That was around the time the owl landed on the branch. Then, to my surprise, he put me down and

I looked up at him and saw his pink cheeks. I realized my blush had worked on him! So I asked him if he'd fly us to the cherry tree... and he put out his wing!"

Thorn shook his head in amazement. "Who would have thought something like a blush could save us?"

Maple giggled.

"Where do we go now?" Ermine asked.

"Let's circle the trunk and see what we can find," Flora said.

They climbed up over tangled roots, examining any nook and cranny they could find. But there wasn't any sign of magic.

"What exactly are we looking for?" Thorn asked.

"Anything to do with moths, I guess," Flora said. "When I foraged cocoons here, I saw moths going in and out of a spot near the middle, where all the branches fan out." She pointed.

"How do we get up there?" Ermine frowned. It was so high above them. "We should have kept the owl."

"What about these?" Thorn motioned up to where a trail of glowing mushrooms grew out of the moss on the bark-like steps. They dotted up the tree like a stairway. Thorn bounded from one to another, and the others followed. The mushrooms spiraled up the trunk and jutted out over the water that flowed out of the tree's roots. It was usually just a trickle, but now that they were tiny, it was a gushing waterfall, flowing into a whirling pool. A thick, wet fog floated up to them from the foam, making their hair moist and their steps slick.

"Be really careful; it's slippery," Ermine said. She grabbed Maple's hand and kept her close to the bark and not the edge of the rubbery flesh of the mushroom she was on.

Near the top the mushrooms ended and they had to scale the rough bark of the tree. They clung to whatever hanging moss they could find and struggled to find footholds.

"Now would be a good time to fly," Thorn said.

"Don't you dare!" Ermine said, "If you didn't do it right you'd fall right down into that churning pool. We need more practice."

Ermine flung her silk up to the top when they got close enough, and they used it to pull themselves up. The rough bark they had been climbing on gave way to smooth wood. A large circular platform had been cut to stand on at the top of the tree trunk. Large branches grew up around them like a crown.

Long strands of pink blossoms fell all around them like a giant tent. The branches seemed to pulse and move. As Flora looked closer, she realized they were filled with moths! A few broke free of their perches and fluttered around them, giant as eagles now that the children were tiny. Maple clung to Flora's sweater nervously. There were golden glints, long pink and green wing tails, delicate antennae, cute fuzzy bodies… Flora was so happy to see them again.

"What is this, a riddle?" Thorn was standing near an ornately carved inscription in one of the branches. The children gathered around, and Ermine read,

"The sound of a bell,
The eldest of all,
Shall lead to the door,
Of the Moth Kingdom hall."

"What does *that* mean?" Maple scrunched her face up.

"I don't see any bells anywhere," Ermine said.

Flora read the inscription carefully. "The sound of a bell. If it is a riddle, it probably means something different than what it says. That's the way Gran's riddles always were." She crossed her arms and squinted her eyes. "What's the sound of a bell?"

"A ring." Ermine said.

"A ring! Maybe it's not a sound at all. Is there any jewelry hidden in the branches? It could be a ring like you wear," Flora said.

Thorn smiled. He pointed to the wood they were standing on. Tree trunk rings circled the platform underneath them.

"Tree rings tell how old a tree is," Flora brightened. "Each year a tree adds a new ring!"

"I never knew that!" Maple said.

"They start out skinny and small and add a new layer every year. So..."

"The next line is 'The eldest of all'," Thorn said.

Ermine rushed to the center of the platform. "The smallest ring should be the oldest!"

The others made their way to the center of the tree. A large knot marked the center ring. Flora touched the edges of it.

"There's a crease here," she said. "See... there's a crack all the way around it."

"Maybe it's a trap door," Thorn tried jumping on the wood. Nothing happened.

"Maybe knock?" Flora got down and put her ear to the wood. She knocked on the center ring. The knot swung open like a door. Below was what looked like a long wormhole carved into the grain in the wood.

"Eek!" Maple squeaked. "Do we have to slide down that?"

"I think we must." Flora grabbed Ermine and Maple's hands. Maple grabbed Thorn's.

At whatever peril might befall them, they jumped into the hole.

The children spiraled down, down, down the chute and tumbled out into a hollow. It looked like the grand hall of a castle. There was a large opening at one end, hidden from the outside world by transparent water. It fell like two silvery curtains on either side of the opening. Moonlight made a faint ghost of a rainbow in the mist.

"We're on the other side of the waterfall!" Ermine exclaimed.

"It's breathtaking." Flora said.

A giant dandelion puff hung from the ceiling like a chandelier. Shiny tapestries of brocade embroidered with silk flowers and scenes of the forest were hung on the walls. Some of the delicate scrollwork looked to be made with metallic thread.

"Chinoiserie!" Ermine giggled. "Look at the detail!"

Two thrones sat at the back of the hollow, their seats soft with lichen and their backs jagged with quartz.

"This must be the throne room of the fairies!" Maple squealed as she danced across the room.

Flora walked over to the ledge and looked through the spaces between the ribbony waterfalls. The forest canopy was slowly being lit with glowing lights.

"What are they?" Thorn asked.

A fluffy silk moth with two pink circles on its wings fluttered out of the cherry blossoms and landed next to Flora. It was the Emperor Moth. Maple, Ermine, and Thorn gasped and retreated to the back of the room.

"The caterpillars have lit their tents to welcome their princess," the moth said.

"It's you!" Flora yelped, delighted.

"I'm sorry it took me so long to come to you!" the moth said, "I was luring the spiders in a different direction. But they will soon realize their mistake. We don't have very much time!"

"Who is she?" Ermine asked.

"Remember how I told you an Emperor Moth flew from my room to the cherry tree?" Flora said. "When I first came to the mill, I brought a caterpillar with me from home. It was crawling in my grandmother's bed when I lost her. It watched over me and made its cocoon in my window above where I slept."

"Oh! That's so sweet!" Maple said.

"When it finally awoke and made its way out of the cocoon, it had turned into this moth... and it told me to find the light. I didn't tell you my suspicion because I wasn't even really sure if I'd dreamt it or not! And I didn't know if I was right, but... Gran? Is that you?"

"Yes, it's me," the Emperor Moth said, smiling.

"Gran!" Flora hugged her large, fuzzy body, and Gran closed her wings around her. "Flora realized Gran's wings weren't pure white. They seemed washed out, like they had spent many years in the sun. "And you're a speckled Emperor Moth, right?" She said, with recognition in her eyes. "But will you turn back? I mean... not to be rude, but I've missed you so much..."

"I am a speckled Emperor Moth, my dear. But I'm afraid I am just a ghost of my former self. Madame Cribellum's magic was so strong, all I could do was turn myself into a caterpillar when she cursed me. I sort of twisted her spell. And then I was stuck until I could make a cocoon and escape. I'm sorry I didn't tell you everything when we saw each other last, my darling. There was no time."

"Oh Gran! Your note... It was awfully confusing. MOTHer looks just like mother."

"I sent you on a bit of a wild goose chase, didn't I? I really wasn't thinking very clearly in the moment. I didn't consider the double entendre. I just knew that Henry could help you, or at least perhaps some of his research could point you in the right direction. But you didn't know his name or that he was your father... I scribbled the word mother, thinking you would figure it out when you searched the mill."

Tears welled in Flora's eyes. Gran had suffered so much. She didn't want to tell her. "Gran... Henry and Luna are trapped in Madame Cribellum's amber necklace!"

"Yes, Flora. I found out what happened to them from the caterpillars today."

Flora nuzzled her head into Gran's fluffy white chest. "Why didn't you ever tell me about them? They're my parents! I had a right to know."

"I had to keep you safe, my little chenille." A tear streaked from her large moth eyes. "You were just a little girl, and I couldn't have you telling anyone about our secret. But we were discovered before I had a chance to tell you. I'm so sorry." She held Flora's face against her. "I still held out hope that your parents had escaped, or that at the very least the Witch Moth would be keeping Henry locked away in the mill. My magic was always too weak to find him. The Witch Moth is so powerful. The estate and its grounds were impenetrable to me."

Flora understood, but felt a creepy chill in her heart at the thought of her parents being trapped all this time while she was wondering where they might be. She sighed heavily.

Gran brought Floras face up into the moonlight with her mothy arms, and a glimmer of starlight glinted in Gran's eyes. Was she smiling?

"Don't worry, Flora. There is a light that is much stronger. One that I know can free all the moths."

"That's right!" Flora remembered. "When you spoke to me in my window, you said you'd found it!"

"Yes." Gran said, smiling. "I have."

Flora filled with excitement. Finally, she would know the answer to the Giltiri mystery. "Well? …Where is it?!"

"In you."

Flora cocked her head. "In me?"

"Remember in my story? How the Giltiri Emperor had a secret that could return the light?"

"Yes. What was the secret?"

"The light has been within you all along, Flora. I had a feeling your light would be powerful enough one day to break the spell. When our light went out, the last little glimmer was still hiding in you. You are the secret I hid when the light of my kingdom was stolen."

"And this journey, though difficult, has taught you how to use it. And now the time is coming where you will need to shine more than ever before. Because though there are many great powers in nature, you are nonpareil."

"Nonpareil." Flora rolled the word over on her tongue. It was the name of the little candies the chef had made — the word Gran had used all those nights ago. Nonpareil…*without equal*.

Flora shook her head. She was almost too embarrassed to admit it… "I've only used the light of other bright things, like the stars and the moon. Nothing as special as the Giltiri magic. But I… " She couldn't finish. She wanted to tell her that Madame Cribellum had stolen her light, and that they no longer had any hope, but at that moment, darkness crept across the forest like a shadowy veil. The lights in the caterpillars' tents went out one by one until there were no more.

"Look!" Thorn pointed to the shore below.

"The spiders are here!" Maple screamed.

"Flora! The Witch Moth!" Ermine yelled. Across the meadow, hordes of spiders were approaching. Carried on the spiders backs were the children from the mill, shrunk down and all tied up in spider silk like little mummies, only their faces showing. Madame Cribellum, or a retched version of her, was writhing at their front. Her torso and head were human, but on her bottom half were eight spindly legs oozing with purple puss at the joints. Her wings were crumpled at her sides. In place of her once-piercing violet eyes were four mirrored orbs.

"Flora, don't let the Witch Moth frighten you from being who you are meant to be." The Emperor Moth flew up into a cloud of gathering moths in the branches. "I know I told you to hide your light when you were a little girl, to not let anyone take it… but now is the time to break free, Flora. You will set all the moths free! You must shine!"

278

25

METAMORPHOSIS

lora!" Madame Cribellum screeched. "Come out, come out wherever you are! I've been looking for the source of the Giltiri magic for years! And you've led me right to it! A whole tree full of magic?" She laughed. "I knew I'd eventually run out of the dust on those disgusting wings. But now I don't have to worry. All I have to do is get rid of YOU!"

"She's lost her mind," Thorn said.

A tide of wings flew down from the cherry tree. Moths dove at Madame Cribellum's face, but she only laughed. "You cannot hurt me, you little fluffs!" She dragged her body up to the tree and ripped at the bark with her sharp nails. "I know you're in there!"

Hordes of spiders crawled up the tree after her.

Flora's heart lurched as she watched them scurry in a black mass up the bark toward the branches. Would they be able to scale through the waterfall and into the throne room?

Maple whimpered in terror. Thorn went over to her to comfort her. He held her rosy face in his hands, and her skin turned reflective. Her short hair began to flow like water. He placed her behind the waterfall curtain as the rest of her body shimmered into rivulets. "Hide here, Maple. You're too little to fight," he said. "Flora, where's the starry fabric?"

Flora pulled it out of her pocket. Thorn took it and did the same camouflage magic on it he did to Maple. It turned translucent and then disappeared altogether. He looked at Flora, raised his eyebrows, and smirked. He *could* make a cloak of invisibility.

"Take this," Thorn said to Maple. "You may need it if they get into the tree."

"I want to help!" she said. But then she took another look at the spiders writhing below and squished herself into the wall. "On second thought... Thank you, Thorn." She reached her hand out and felt where the fabric must be. She swiped twice, then felt it and grabbed.

"Be brave, Maple," Ermine said, and kissed her on the head. "Let's lead them away from here so they can't find her. Come on, this way!" Ermine motioned toward a door that held a stairwell. Thorn and Flora climbed the stairs after her as quickly as they could. Flora wondered where all the doors carved into the walls led. If they were to get out of this, she would have fun exploring the tree. But at the moment, her muscles felt like lead, and her blood seemed to run cold. She had no idea how they would get out of this.

They made their way up to another secret door made of bark and moss in one of the branches. They swung it open and found themselves high up in the tree. They looked down and saw the spiders congregating on the platform with the rings.

"They're after *me*," Flora gasped, trying to catch her breath. "You both should fly. We're not going to be able to outrun them, and you could get away with your wings." She had been the one charged to shine, and it was all her fault that they were going to be caught because her light was lost. She could see no reason why her friends should have to stay.

Ermine shook her head. "Like we'd ever leave you, Flora."

"We have to protect her," Thorn said. "If her light can save the Giltiri, then we can't let them get her. Climb up higher, Flora. We'll try to hold them back!"

Then, to their delight, Spindle, Geo, and Cinna came tumbling toward them on strands of silk whistling in the wind.

"Caterpillars!" Ermine cried. Spindle had two pine needles in her mouth and presented them to Ermine. To her small size, they were as big as knitting needles.

"We can make nets!" Spindle said.

"That's a great idea!" Ermine twirled one of the needles between her fingers. "Let's get to work."

Several more webworms catapulted into the branches, spewing silk, and Ermine quickly took up the ends. Together, she and the webworms began knitting.

It was as if starlight had melted down and shimmered into string. A lacy net of flower patterns and filigree began forming against the darkening sky. Ermine fluttered her wings and pirouetted through the air while using her magic. She flipped and twirled, spinning her threads. A fairy of moon beams made malleable. A sight to behold.

"She was meant for this!" Flora beamed.

"It's taking too long, though," Thorn said, looking down to where the spiders had noticed the net taking shape. He took a deep breath and nodded reservedly. "I can throw geodes at them! That'll distract them and give us more time." Thorn jumped onto one of the cherry tree vines and used it like a rope to swing down to the shore.

"Be careful!" Flora called.

"You too!"

Bear swooped down from the trees to join Thorn with a dozen or so spiky caterpillars, ready with their poisonous darts and horns. Even though the stones were now as big as boulders to his small frame, Thorn found a few smaller geodes. He tested one out by throwing it to the ground nearby. As the stone cracked, a splash of brilliant light-glitter spewed from its core. Thorn looked up at Flora with wide, excited eyes, then began throwing geodes at the spiders trying to make their way up the tree. Sparks and firecracker bursts exploded as the geodes made their mark.

Thorn whooped and jumped with glee.

Flora laughed, despite her terror. He had always wanted to throw geodes!

The spiders shirked back and made awful hissing sounds when they were hit with light. The masses tumbled over each other and fell like dominoes back down to the shore. Many of them stayed crumpled, never to rise again.

But some of the spiders were too smart. They flung themselves from the tree, attached to their threads, and abseiled toward Thorn. He flew back down to the ground and hid behind a boulder, camouflaged like stone.

Flora's heart sank. There were so many spiders, and Thorn wasn't doing a very good job of hiding.

Thorn kept throwing geodes as the spiders made their way toward him along the beach. The spiders got a sense of where the geodes were coming from and searched frantically through the shadows, trying to find him. Then slowly, one spider crept up behind Thorn and sniffed the air. It prodded the air with a furred limb close to his leg. Thorn realized he was being hunted and tried to scrunch up as small as he could, but the spider ever so gently swiped his wing. Thorn stirred. The spider realized what it had felt and pounced.

Thorn sprang up, trying to dart away, but the spider grabbed his leg before he could escape and pushed him down into the rubble. Thorn lay flat, frozen in fear. He was staring up into the underbelly of the beast. It reared up, ready to strike. Thorn squinted his eyes, trying to look away before death came…

Spines hurled into the spider's face as Bear's orange and black hairs exploded out of his body. He was swooping past on a strand of silk. The spider hissed and let Thorn go. Thorn darted, quick as an arrow, into the air.

"Nice shot, Bear!" Thorn called. He yanked one of the spikes from the spider's back to use as a dagger.

"You're not so bad yourself!" Bear said, shooting more spikes into the fleshy behind of another spider, "We seem to be scaring them off!"

But his swiftly moving body suddenly froze.

Madame Cribellum had retreated back down the tree and spotted Thorn and Bear fighting off the spiders. She yelled a curse, and Thorn froze too. She snatched them up with her legs and spun them in webbing. Thorn tried not to panic, because if he could stay calm, he had a way out. Madame Cribellum had spun them so quickly, she didn't notice that Thorn still had one of Bear's spikes in his hand. He kept his nerves and breathing as steady as he could and slowly began sawing away at the spider threads with what little motion he could muster.

But Thorn and Bear's efforts hadn't been for nothing. They had given Ermine and the webworms plenty of time to finish their work, and with the moths' help, they threw their net over Madame Cribellum. She writhed inside of it, dumping Thorn and Bear on the creek bed.

"We got her!" Geo cried.

Madame Cribellum wriggled and stretched, trying to free herself. The moths and caterpillars took up the ends of the net and held her down.

"Hold tight!" Spindle yelled.

Ermine giddily laughed at how well their plan had worked. She flew over Madame Cribellum's twitching body and stuck out her tongue. "See how you like being stuck in a web!" She sneered.

Flora thought of Ermine's legs, and all the fear and pain she'd endured in her years spinning and spinning for this retched woman.

The vindication Ermine must feel! she thought.

But then…

Madame Cribellum took a furious bite out of the silk and made a hole. The silk began unraveling, and the witch cackled in Ermine's stunned face. The sound echoed against the rocks and sent a chill down Flora's spine.

The tiny spiders were already saving their mistress. They crawled up over Ermine's web and ripped at it with their fangs.

The moths had no choice but to let go and fly up and away. Ermine tried to join them, but she wasn't used to her new wings yet, and her flying stuttered in her fear. Madame Cribellum yanked at the web and threw it into the spring. She grabbed Ermine by the legs and made short work of her. Soon she and the caterpillars were bundled up in webbing with all the other children on the shore.

Madame Cribellum dusted herself off and made her way back up the mossy, gnarled roots of the tree. She looked up at Flora with gleaming eyes and grinned with her hairy, furred mouth.

"Is that all you've got, Flora? A handful of worms and your weakling little friends?"

Flora needed to figure out how to get her light back, and fast. She tried to relax, but she couldn't. She reached down, down deep inside herself for any glimmer of light, but everything within her was utterly guttered. No spark, no gleam, no shimmering chards of anything in the dark pit of her stomach.

The spiders writhed up over the bark, making mushrooms and licorice ferns vibrate in their wake.

"Come now, Flora. We could always just go back to the mill! Lend me a little of the dust you have hidden away, and your friends could be free. I could just go back to being your mistress, and we could live our days in peace together."

Madame Cribellum truly *had* lost her mind if she thought that sounded enticing. And dust? Flora didn't have any dust. She didn't have any magic at all. And what little she might have left, she needed to hide. She couldn't let her take it!

Flora retreated higher up along the branches she clung to. She found a little hollow where the bark had rolled back. It looked safe, inviting. Like a bedspread. She imagined herself

crawling under the covers and falling to sleep, everything that
had happened just a wild dream.

But Madame Cribellum was real. She reached the platform
where the rings were and looked up at Flora with a sneer.

"Nothing is going to save you now, little princess. No wings,
no silk, no…"

A loud, hissing screech reverberated through the glen. The
barn owl was flying through the cherry tree branches! He'd seen
the commotion and wanted to find himself a juicy morsel. But he
clicked his beak and ruffled his feathers as he saw a little pink
and yellow fairy reaching out to him from the waterfall throne
room.

"Please! Come help us!" Maple cried. Her cheeks flushed
bright pink. The water illusion Thorn created had melted away.

Flora's heart sank, worried Maple would be seen, but it sang
at the same time. Maple was being so brave! The barn owl
swooped down to Maple and landed, splashing in the water
curtain. Maple gave the bird a hug and climbed up his wing.
With a mighty flap that sprayed spring water across the glen,
they charged into the air.

"Get her!" Maple yelled, slashing her arm out and pointing at
Madame Cribellum. The barn owl circled back and dove for
Madame Cribellum, delighted to have a spider snack.

Maple's yellow antennae fluttered against the rush of wind as
the bird flew. Her cherry cheeks were such a sight, they dazzled
many of the spiders, unbelievably going docile and giving her
wet, puppy dog eyes. Flora had never considered whether
spiders had cheeks, but many of theirs went bright pink!

The others quaked in fear, tumbling over each other as the
owl grew near. With a slash of talons, several spiders careened

off the platform and down to the pool below. The barn owl flew up through the branches, headed right for Madame Cribellum.

But Madame Cribellum was too quick. She pointed her spindly fingers at the owl, and with a gurgle, he passed out into a deep sleep and rammed into the bark of the tree. He toppled down the trunk, bumping through the cherry blossoms. Maple toppled with him, and they landed in a puddle of feathers, moss, and pink petals.

The spiders swarmed and grabbed them.

"No! Don't hurt him!" Maple cried.

They spun the barn owl's wings shut and carried Maple to the other children on the shore.

Flora was alone.

Madame Cribellum snarled as she crept up the tree toward her. Her spindly legs clicked against the bark as she made her way up over the little hollow Flora had found and peered down at her. Those mirrored eyes were pools of obsidian hate.

Flora thought her chest would burst out of fear. All of her hope was lost. Her grandmother couldn't be more wrong. She wasn't a flame for the moths to cling to…she was darkness. She was drab nothingness. And her friends had wasted their magic on her.

Flora clung to a fern to keep her balance; she was so hunched over from the weight of the lump on her back. It had been growing faster since entering Silkwood, and since the battle began, it had begun to throb. She winced with pain and looked up at Madame Cribellum through messy hair and tears.

Madame Cribellum's evil emanated toward her. She could feel it pulsating through the tree. She felt her legs quake with it, sending a shiver up her spine.

Madame Cribellum had to be using her magic on her because she had dark thoughts that she knew were not her own: jealousy, resentment, defeat.

She'd foolishly tried to shine her light, and everyone around her had stolen it.

If she had Maple's blush, she would be able to make Madame Cribellum sorry for her.

If she had Ermine's spinning, she could create a line of silk to escape.

And Thorn… if she had his power, she could disappear into the tree branch. *I wish I could just disappear forever!* she thought.

Tears spilled from her eyes. She wiped them with her sweater sleeve and looked down at the golden threads. It was not so long ago that she'd been searching for cocoons in this very tree. And now she was one of them.

"Why did I think I could make a cocoon?" She whispered. "I'm so stupid."

"That's right," Madame Cribellum said, gaining strength from Flora's weakness. "You *are* stupid."

"Don't listen to her, Flora!" Thorn shouted. He had been slowly cutting away at the cobwebs that held him with the spine he'd taken from Bear. Just a few more strands, and he would be free…

"Yes, Flora," Maple bravely shouted. "Think of the pink flower you gave me!"

Ermine joined in, "Think of the crystal you made from moth dust! You have so much light in you, Flora!"

"Think of all the beauty you give!"

"Think of your stars!"

"You have to shine, Flora!"

"Shine!"

The word echoed against the geode embankment and the tree, like ricochets of hope flying into the darkness. And they reached Flora. The encouragement and truth of her friends struck her and melted into her, pushing back the vibrating curtain of Madame Cribellum's spell.

Flora looked down at the silvery blue shimmers on the water, the reflection of the moon and stars. Her Gran once told her she was just as bright as those shimmers. But she wasn't always like the light parts of the water. She was like the deep, unknown parts as well—dark and strange—like a hidden gem.

What was the light without the darkness? Add some shadows and you have rays of light, you have sparkling dust motes. It was her darkness that made the light glow, made it shimmer. She wasn't a hot sweltering sun; she was a midnight sky with a twinkling star.

Her light wasn't lost… It was hidden somewhere deep inside her. She'd been shielding it, guarding it out of fear. She was like a gray stone with crystals inside. A thought came to Flora, clear and bright…

"I am like a geode," Flora spoke with a steady voice. She didn't need to hide her light anymore. And she wasn't afraid. "If you break me, I will shine!"

Madame Cribellum looked down at her with a wild, fanged grin. "You call that a shine? That pathetic little flame of yours? " Madame Cribellum laughed. "You can't shine. How could anything so ugly? You're just a little worm! Half moth…you might as well just be a caterpillar!"

"But caterpillars can make silk! And so can you, Madame Cribellum! What's so wrong with being a spider? Your webs are so shiny, like a rainbow! Why do you need us to weave for you? Why do you need our magic?"

Madame Cribellum blinked her mirrored eyes. Flora could see herself reflected in them over and over. They were not so different, were they? Madame Cribellum was as jealous of the moth wings as Flora was insecure about not having magic anymore. They'd both lost something dear to them. They were hurt and heartbroken. But in Madame Cribellum, it had festered for so long, she'd become this wretched thing. She'd hardened, so no ounce of beauty could be released from within. Flora suddenly saw who she could become if she didn't break the spell. Break it, like a geode. And instead of feeling ugly, for the first time, Flora saw someone beautiful reflected back at her. She saw her dark, flowing hair peppered with gold, her starry freckles, and her shining sapphire eyes. And she could see in her own face how she was able to feel sorry for Madame Cribellum. Mariposa. In the beginning, she had been beautiful. The sweet friend of a little boy, making webs and delighting in their friendship. She just couldn't see herself for who she truly was.

But in that broken, vulnerable moment, Flora could see her true self.

"Do you really think I could make something as beautiful as the moth fairies?" Madame Cribellum asked.

Flora clenched her fists and lifted her head as high as she could. "I really do."

"Then you are a fool!" Madame Cribellum lunged at Flora, but Flora didn't flinch. She staid her ground. Because she knew what must be done. She had spent enough time in the forest to know how the true magic of nature worked. Madame Cribellum was wrong about nature magic. It wasn't weak at all. The wind could be a small and delicate breeze, but it could also be a storm... and just as powerful in either state—because at its core was peace.

"No!" Thorn shouted. He had pulled free of his bindings and stumbled out of the spiders' grasp. He slashed the spine at their legs and fluttered his auburn wings in a mad rush toward Flora.

Madame Cribellum grabbed hold of Flora with her two front spider legs.

Thorn was so close, within a few feet. He pulled the orange spine in his hand back, ready to plunge it into Madame Cribellum's back, when she reached up with a hairy back leg and swatted him into a branch. The spine spun out of his hand, landing at Flora's feet. Thorn slumped down to the tree's platform. "The spine, Flora! Use it!" Thorn rasped.

Flora looked at Thorn with sorrow in her eyes and shook her head.

"Why? Please!" Thorn cried.

Flora had to be broken, and this was the only way she knew to do it. She looked up at the spider who could not let go of her hate, and chose to let go of her own.

Thorn watched as Madame Cribellum's fangs made their mark in Flora's chest.

Flora's heart seemed to crack open as the pain of Madame Cribellum's venom spread. Her blood felt like ice crystals shattering through her veins. She fell into a small hollow in the tree bark and was caught by an old wisp of web. She slowly, painfully, pulled her limbs inside her sweater and stared unblinking up at the sky as her body went numb.

There were no star flowers that could save her now. There was no light that she could hold onto and use to make her own.

The swirling moths landed in the cherry tree boughs. The whole world seemed to go still.

"She's dead!" Madame Cribellum sneered. She crawled down from the tree to the children, her wounds oozing over the bark of the tree. She laughed maniacally and threw six arms up to the sky. "Your princess and your light are gone!"

Flora closed her eyes and let the darkness seep over her like a velvet shroud.

26

LIGHT

he children were crying. Maple sobbed. But the rest of Silkwood was dead silent, as if it felt the loss of its promised princess as deeply as her friends. Clouds crept over the moon, plunging the meadow into darkness. Then the Emperor Moth's voice spoke out from the dark branches of the cherry tree.

"When a caterpillar goes into her cocoon, she is completely unmade. She returns to dust. But our dust is born of magic. Hidden inside our silken threads, the power of metamorphosis takes place. For the caterpillar must die to have a new life… She must be broken to shine."

There was a loud ripping sound, and slowly, a faint light shone from the hollow where Flora lay.

"Look!" Maple cried.

Flora was glowing.

"What?!" Madame Cribellum cranked her neck to see. "NO!"

Flora opened her eyes and pulled herself up from the bark. In the darkness, she faced the shadow that kept her from her light —the fear that made her too paralyzed to shine. And she embraced it. She became its opposite, its counterpart. She wasn't too small, she wasn't too weak…she was one of the Giltiri. The stone that held her light in, her fears, her heartbreak—it had

broken. Her sweater was ripped at the back, and she let it fall
away…

She could feel them, In her heart she had known all along… The silk her grandmother had given her was magic, and she'd whispered her own into it as well. Flora looked over her shoulder. There was golden fuzz on her neck and shoulders, covered in a diamond brilliance of dust. And in place of her hunch, the things Flora had always wanted were there. She felt the glee of it all form in her chest, and it burst out into her limbs in radiating sparks. She. Had. WINGS!

They had been inside of her, growing, itching to get out, and her sweater was their cocoon.

They shimmered with rippled lines of silver and gold… just like the sparkles on the water. And each upper wing had a small bright spot in the squiggles, like a star. She was amazed at how they were already a part of her, as if she'd always had them. She could easily move her shoulder muscles, and they flapped open for all to see.

When she did, everyone in the glade gasped at a shock of iridescent blue light. She was an underwing moth! Her hind wings were a midnight black with white scalloped edges, and to Flora's delight, each wing had a brilliant blue band, that, when brought together, made a crescent moon. They matched her sapphire eyes! Underneath, her wings were pale moonlight blue with bands of black crescents. She was enfolded in their glow. Her wings were so beautiful, she could barely breathe at the sight of them. She looked like a cerulean night sky.

Then Flora felt a strange sensation on her scalp. In her mess of thick brown hair, she now had two feathery strands of silvery antennae. She pulled them down to look at them. They glimmered, limned in starlight. Flora smiled, eyes wide, and let them pop back up. She had a new sense she'd never felt before. It was the power to sense light, to harness it, to extract it. She could feel the glow of all the living things in the forest around her, in the fireflies illuminating the branches, in the stars, and in the shining hearts of her friends. She was connected to them with invisible strands of light.

Of course she needed her friends. They didn't steal light from her. They shared it, refracted it like crystals, and her light was stronger with them. She reflected their light, like the moon does the sun. Flora giggled, and light as anything, she lifted her glittering wings and shot into the air.

Light burst from Flora into the meadow, much brighter and more powerful than any prism. It felt like a bolt of lightning shooting through a web of metal. Flora felt the fire course through her. With magic so full and deep, she could see twice as many colors, just like Bear had said she would.

The spiders scattered.

The power of Flora's metamorphosis sung through the forest. Golden tendrils dusted the children, setting them free. And as their webbing fell away, they saw that they had returned to their true forms. They stood blinking on the shore, examining their own wings.

Ermine grabbed Maple in a hug, smiling with so much relief and happiness. Then she held Maple back and said, "Hey! Are you using your blush on me?"

"No!" Maple laughed. "That's just you!"

Flora was so happy to see all the children in their true form. Little Cloud, with hair already turning silver, was a Clouded Silver with white wings with silvery specks. Large Atlas had the giant wings of the Atlas Moth with huge flashing triangles. Orange-haired Burnet had black and orange wings with long black tails trailing behind him: the wings of the Long-Tailed Burnet. Isabella, who had told everyone that she knew snow was coming when they were still leaves turning, was, of course, the

Woolly Bear's moth—the Isabella Tiger. Flora loved seeing how each child had been an echo of their wings before they turned.

But then her smile faded. She balled her hands into fists, and she shifted her gaze at Madame Cribellum. Madame Cribellum shirked back, frightened.

Flora hovered over the wretched woman, her head held high. Her magic hadn't drained at all. In the spider's mirrored eyes, Flora saw her own eyes glowed brilliant sapphire like her wings. Her hair swirled up as if it were underwater. Light beams shot out of her fingers. She looked like the goddess of some mythological tale. She almost frightened herself. She yanked the amber necklace from Madame Cribellum's neck. "I'll take this, thank you," she said.

"Please! Please! I'll leave. I'll never come back!" Madame Cribellum fell back into the spring water, pleading for her life. She splashed through the froth near the waterfall.

The spring water leapt up at Madame Cribellum, bubbling around her with a mind of its own. She screamed as jagged crystals clustered at her waist and grew up over her body and then her face. She tried batting them away, and tried using her magic to force them off, but they were too strong.

The crystals grew and grew until they sealed around Madame Cribellum into a shining sphere. As the water settled, the outside of the crystals formed a round rock shell.

The Witch Moth was trapped inside a geode.

The children cheered.

Flora's light slowly dissipated, and she gradually came down to the shore where her friends practically attacked her in a hug.

"Flora! You did it," they cried, as they all fell into each other like a giant sigh of relief, wings intermingling.

"Do you think Madame Cribellum will be stuck in there forever?" Maple asked.

"Gosh, I hope so!" Thorn said.

Flora looked at the geode with knitted eyebrows. "The magic had a mind of its own. She'd hardened like a geode in her heart… so the magic put her in a prison of her own making. I don't know what I would have done if it hadn't done it for me."

"She certainly needed to be confined," Ermine said.

"Maybe it'll let her go when she's had enough time to think about what she's done." Maple said.

Flora supposed time would tell.

Down from the cherry blossoms, the Giltiri flew. Gathering in the glade, they joined in a circle, transforming back into their true forms. Some were teeny and golden, some large and mottled with wild patterns, some soft and muted. Stripes, spots, and checks, they were a kaleidoscope of color. They grabbed their children, who could now remember their parents. And even though years had passed, it was as if no time had touched the children. They were the same age as when they had been stolen. The fog of Madame Cribellum's spell had been lifted.

The Emperor Moth flew down from the stars, and before it landed, it grew into a sparkling old woman with frizzy hair and a white silk dress. She no longer had a hunch, but was strong and regal. Her pink glasses now mirrored the large pink circles on her wings.

"Gran!" Flora cried, "You look radiant!"

Gran whisked Flora up into her arms. Flora's breath hitched. She'd waited months for this moment. She'd cried herself to sleep night after night, dreaming of being in those freckled arms again. And here she finally was, wrapped up in her bright, luminous glow. Flora brushed her cheek against her soft chest and let out a sob. "I missed you so much!"

"I was with you all along, my little chenille! I knew you could do it. But I suppose I can't call you a caterpillar anymore, can I? You have wings now!"

"Aren't they beautiful? They're just like the shimmers on the water! She spun in a circle to show her.

Then Flora lowered her eyes and lifted the amber necklace. She got a closer look at what was inside. The amber smelled of sugary myrrh. Too sweet a smell for the awful thing it held. She couldn't hold back her tears.

"I guess the magic didn't work on Henry and Luna," she said, "...my Mother and Father."

"I wouldn't be too sure," Gran said with a wink. She plucked the amber necklace from Flora's hands and flung it into the spring.

"Gran! What are you doing?"

The spring vibrated softly. A dim light from under the surface grew stronger and stronger. White foam dispersed to form a circle of aqua water. Then, two figures rose up out of the water, suspended in sparkles.

"A strong magic was unleashed when you turned into a moth," Gran said. "It is the very essence of miracles. Of metamorphosis. Life from death. We have our light again, Flora. Nothing is impossible!"

The two figures lit up, and all could see they were Luna and Henry, restored. Luna's wings were delicate and translucent. They were a pale green, almost aqua. Their long pink tails trailed beneath her like ribbons. And somehow, Henry now had wings too! Flora knew he didn't have them before; she had just been looking at him in the amber, and he had none. His upper wings looked like a black and white animal print, like a leopard. His hind wings were orange with black spots. Henry and Luna embraced in the air, just as they had been in the necklace, then slowly awakened. Henry looked down at her and shook his head in awe. "We're free!" He kissed her gently on the forehead. Then she grabbed his face and kissed him passionately. The crowd cheered as Henry's face blushed. They landed on the shore to a cheering audience.

Luna brushed a finger on Henry's wing and said, "Look what I gave you!"

He opened his wings and examined them. "The Garden Tiger Moth!"

"Because we met in the garden, and you love animals so much," she laughed.

He hugged her.

Then Luna looked at the other Giltiri watching, and her eyes rested on Flora. "Is she?" she asked Gran.

Gran nodded.

"My baby!" Luna cried. She rushed to her Flora and
wrapped her in a tangled hug of soft green wings. "I knew from
those eyes!"

Henry followed and wrapped them both up in his arms. "My
darling girls!"

Flora didn't know what to think. Parents! Her childhood had
been filled with love, so it wasn't the same feeling she had when

she finally hugged her Gran. She didn't know Henry and Luna, so she hadn't missed them. But there was a snagged thread in her heart that seemed to soften and fall into place as her mother took her in her arms. She couldn't wait to get to know them.

"Yours are the most beautiful wings I have ever seen!" Flora said, blushing.

"Not as beautiful as yours are." Luna took Flora's hands and kissed her forehead. "They are the wings of the Blue Underwing. They are also known as the Nonpareil Moth. It means *without equal.*"

Of course! Gran must have known somehow. Flora had so many questions about the Giltiri. But for now, she just wanted to take every moment as it came.

Flora opened her wings to look at their flash of iridescent blue. "I'd always dreamed of wearing a dress like the moonlight ripples on the water," she said. "But I never dreamed they could be a part of me!"

"You're better than a reflection of light," Gran said. "You *are* light."

"But wait!" Flora said, "My name doesn't match my wings like the others. Shouldn't it be Blue, or Nonpareil, or something like that?"

"Flora was my mother's name," Henry said. "You're not just a moth. You're a Nuthatch, too!"

Flora sucked in a breath. The woman on the ceiling of the entrance of Nuthatch Estate was the Goddess of Spring… Flora! And then something occurred to her. Nuthatch Estate belonged to her now! The conservatory, the books, the bird topiaries, all those rooms… The cream puffs! Even the mill. It was all hers to do with what she wished someday. At that moment, she wanted to burn the mill to the ground… but thought better of mentioning that to her new father. She only smirked.

"Your full name is Flora Catocala Nuthatch!" Henry exclaimed.

"Your father wanted to use the Latin for underwing moths" Luna wrapped her arms up under Henry's and looked up at him with adoring eyes. "He loves knowing the scientific names of things."

Flora had a new name! She clasped her hands in delight. "Catocala! What does it mean?"

"Catocala means 'beauty underneath'." Henry said.

"Beauty underneath," Flora repeated. It was just like how Thorn had described the underwing moths. And it was fitting for Flora too. She had found her light and beauty hidden inside. In the form of grace for Madame Cribellum, confidence in herself, and the bravery of trusting her friends. It had all been inside of her, waiting to sparkle. "Like a geode!" she said.

27

THE GILTIRI

iltiri magic had filled the forest again. The sky turned a moody charcoal as the moon settled in the nook of the low sky. Lanterns made of glow worms inside flowers were strung in a glen of soft moss and sparkling dew. A grand feast was prepared of sautéed mushrooms, fiddlehead flatbread, nettle salad, sugared violets, and star flower wine. The smells drifted through the ferns and curled in Flora's nose. She realized how hungry she was! Finally, she would get to taste the food of her people... Gran's delicacies!

All of the moth fairies came in elaborate silk wear they had retrieved from their old haunts. Their magical couture entranced Flora. There were tiny crystal beads threaded with silver and gold, flowers and vines made from moon-glow ribbon, jewel beetle buttons, hummingbird feather crowns, and all of their glorious wings splayed for the dances. They put the Parisians to shame!

Gran gave Flora a gossamer lace dress to wear that looked like it had been threaded with starlight. And under the skirts, a petticoat of the palest, iridescent blue. "To match your wings, love," she said.

It was almost as if no time had passed; the spell of Madame Cribellum was erased so completely. Silkwood was aglow again.

Flora met so many new friends that night. She met Maple, Ermine, and Thorn's parents, whom they could now remember.

Then, to Flora's extreme surprise, Gran introduced Flora to an elderly Giltiri man with long white hair and kaleidoscopic

wings. Gran held his arm close and nearly squealed when she told her, "Flora, this is your grandfather, Ripheus!"

"Whaaat?! I never expected to have a grandpa!" Flora held out her hand to shake his. Ripheus seemed to be where Flora got her fiery spirit from, because instead of shaking her hand, he grabbed Flora and spun her around. "My little love!"

"You have Sunset Moth wings!" Flora gasped. They were striking black like her underwings and really did look like a fiery multicolored sunset with bright orange, aqua, and pink.

"Do you like them?" He flashed a proud grin and turned for her to see them in all their glory. "Fit for a king, eh?"

"Don't encourage him," Gran said, rolling her eyes.

Ripheus grabbed Gran's hand and kissed it. She giggled as he spun her out into the glen to dance.

Henry and Luna were so thrilled at having found their daughter that hey almost forgot to notice each other during dinner. But eventually their eyes locked, and they embraced in a dance with the other Giltiri. They were finally awake, and together, and nothing would ever keep them apart.

The fairies danced and danced in the glen, smitten through with glowy magic, and where their feet touched the ground... a fairy ring of mushrooms grew.

After she'd kissed and hugged her family to her heart's content, Flora took a stroll along the perimeter of the glen, admiring the Giltiri in a dazed awe. She needed some time to herself to formulate her thoughts about everything that had happened. And it would feel good to spend a little time alone in her forest again. She found a silken stairway strung between the thick slabs of bark up a pine tree and half climbed, half fluttered her way up into its sweet-smelling branches. She found a suspension bridge made of silk that spanned between the pine needles. It was cleverly disguised as a cobweb. She didn't know how she'd never noticed the network of tents and bridges in the trees before, and wondered if there was magic involved. She stopped in the center of the bridge to absorb her new world. She gazed up at the stars and wondered if they had foretold all that had happened.

So many years ago, her father had taken her mother's cocoon, and such a wild story had unfolded because of that tiny act. What would this world be like if it hadn't happened? She wouldn't exist. How strange it was that sometimes bad things had to happen in order for the good to shine through.

She sighed heavily, leaned out over the ropy edge of the bridge, and looked down into the glowing forest. The bridge wobbled, and she clung tight, trying to catch her balance.

"Quackgrass!" She said as her feet lost their footing and she tipped over.

"Careful!" The branches jangled, and Flora looked up to find Thorn hidden among the pine needles, his body the color of hunter green. He fluttered down onto the bridge and sauntered toward her as she held on for her life, his hands in his pockets. His body shifted back to normal as he walked toward her.

"How can you be so nonchalant?" Flora asked. "Help!"

"You have wings, silly."

Flora blinked. "Oh yeah!" She lifted her brand-new wings and fluttered haphazardly up into the air. He caught her hand and pulled her down next to him.

She sat down in a harumph. "Had you been there long?"

Thorn grinned. "I may have been keeping an eye on you." He plopped down next to her and dangled his legs over the edge. "It took me a long time to get used to my wings. I figured you might need a little help."

"You've only had them for a couple of days!" Flora laughed at him.

"No, we got our memories back... We all remember being Giltiri now. I'd had wings for a few years before Madame Cribellum took us."

"Oh! That's right... I hadn't thought of that. I guess I'm the only one that's new here." Flora put her arms around herself and shivered. There were so many changes she would have to get used to. It was dizzying.

"Look. If you vibrate your wings really fast, it warms you up." His wings buzzed behind him. Their jagged edges blurred and became difficult to see, almost invisible.

Flora tried to move hers as fast as she could, but they only flapped in a stilted rhythm. "How are you doing that?"

"You have to sort of empty your mind and let it happen. Sometimes when you're really relaxed or thrilled about something, it'll just start happening."

Flora bit her lip, and her eyebrows twisted in concentration.

Thorn's cheeks dimpled as he looked at her with amusement. "That looks like the opposite of emptying your mind."

Flora rolled her eyes.

Thorn laughed. "Your antennae just rolled with your eyes." He pulled the edge of one of them down lightly, and it popped back up. The sensation sent a ripple down her spine. She looked up at him with bright eyes. He tilted his head and smiled at her.

Her wings began vibrating on their own.

"That's it! You're doing it."

Flora sucked in a breath. She hoped the warmth from her vibrating wings would explain her blush.

"How did you do it?" Thorn asked, quiet as the whispering wind through the pines. "I thought you were dead for sure. I thought… I'd lost the most precious thing I'd ever known."

Flora stilled and looked up at the glittering sky. She said, "In the end, I realized that nothing can take your light. Nothing can steal it. You can't use it up, and it can't ever run out. And once you let go of your fear… let yourself enter the darkness with the knowledge that not even death can snuff it out… Then you are

free to shine." She looked at Thorn. They both had tears in their eyes.

"Flora," Bear's gravelly voice came from the edge of the bridge. "We're waiting for you in the glen."

"Oh! I must have lost track of time. I'm coming," Flora said. She looked up to find that the caterpillar now wore a knight's uniform with a shining jewel beetle helmet and a breastplate carved with moons and stars. When he saw Flora looking, he said, "A gift from your grandmother."

Thorn got up quickly and flew into the air. "I'm supposed to be there already. I'll see you down there, Flora." He winked at her and shot down into the darkness of the trees.

"What's going on?" Flora asked.

"A ceremony. Here, I'll escort you," he said with a bow, then put out three arms to her. Flora giggled.

Bear walk/crawled her down the end of the bridge, then attached one end of silk to the branch of the tree and held the smooth thread out to her. She held on as he abseiled with her down to the ground.

Flora walked back to the glen to find a long aisle of star flower pollen laid down its center. It twinkled like the Milky Way. All the Giltiri gathered on either side. Flora was confused as she was led by Bear to one end. She looked up and saw that at the other end, her Grandparents stood on a large rainbow fungus jutting out of a tree like a stage. They looked down at her, smiling. Her grandfather Ripheus wore a gold crown, and Gran wore a circlet of diamonds on her head. Flora realized it was Gran's ring! All this time, Gran had worn her crown on her finger.

The most delicious sound began playing. The sound of a harp, no doubt with strings made of silk. Flora recognized the tune as one Gran used to hum. Then Gran beckoned Flora forward.

"Go on," Bear said from beside her.

She walked down the aisle in a daze with Bear large and lumbering at her side. As she looked at the crowd around her, the faces of the Giltiri smiled back at her. When she reached the rainbow fungus, she saw that Henry and Luna stood off to the side, Luna wearing a silver crown with a tiny crescent moon resting on her forehead. Ermine, Maple, and Thorn stood near the front of the crowd.

"Fly up to them, Flora," Luna said.

Flora flew up to her grandparents. Gran held a necklace in her hands.

"Flora, you have shown great bravery in the heart of trial. Your light has led us all back home. As a reminder for all of your sacrifice, accept this gift from the Giltiri."

The necklace was strung with half a small geode. Faint rainbow crystals shone from its inside. Ripheus held Flora's hair back, and Gran strung the necklace around her neck. Gran spoke in a loud voice to the crowd,

"Though we flew through the shadows, and were diminished to dust, we have found our light!"

The crowd cheered.

Flora kissed and thanked her grandmother, then she spoke to the crowd.

"I couldn't have done it without my friends! Ermine, Maple, and Thorn, you should be up here too! Please…"

Thorn flew up swiftly, with a big grin on his face, and Ermine dragged a shy Maple up behind her. The crowd cheered loudly and then died down when Flora put her hands up to calm them.

"These friends helped me through every trial. Ermine protected me. Maple loved me. Thorn encouraged me. My light could not shine without theirs. I've learned now that we burn brightest when we reflect one another."

The crowd cheered again, and some of the friends and couples in the crowd nudged each other or held each other close, agreeing with her words.

The children all huddled together, arm in arm, and Flora shed tears of the same metallic starlight she had the night she made her sweater. She wiped her eyes and used the light to put sprinkles of light in their hair, like crowns. The children all held hands and looked out to the crowd that was cheering again.

"You need one, too, Flora!" Maple said.

"Here, let me," Luna said. She rubbed her fingers together, and a bright string of light formed between them. It was like a piece of silk, but it began hardening when she swirled it into an art nouveau circlet of vines. When she put the curled ends together, they held their shape.

"What kind of silk is that?" Ermine asked on her tiptoes.

Luna raised an eyebrow and smiled. "Moonlight."

Flora couldn't wait to learn more about Giltiri magic. She could already picture herself creating some bright silk, Ermine spinning it, and Maple giving it some of her blush to make the wearer feel at peace. Or Thorn could turn it into a cloak of invisibility! They would have so much fun.

Flora's heart leapt as her parents put the circlet of moonlight on her head together. A crown of light! All of her dreams had come true, and more. She squeezed their hands, then grabbed her friends, and they flew, giggling, into the night sky, looking like a handful of stars.

They tried diving and swirling in the clouds without any fear of spider webs ensnaring them.

Maple grabbed the other girls' hands mid-flight. "I can't believe it! We're free!" She squealed.

"And we can fly again!" shouted Ermine, in a voice more excited than the reserved girl had ever been.

Thorn sidled up to Flora as they soared over the forest, and he put his hand out for her. She smiled back at him and put her hand in his.

"Your wings are as bright as you are," he said, and kissed her on the cheek.

The moths had finally found their light.

316

EPILOGUE

f you are looking to thread starlight into one of your gowns, embellish forest fronds onto a new hat, or have slippers that shimmer like a babbling brook, there is a special place for you to peruse. There is a fabric shop in a tiny town near the forest's edge. It has the most luxurious, smooth silk covered with delicate designs. There are four shop owners who dress as beautifully as their fabric.

The head weaver wears thick white furs, black dotted Swiss gowns, and intricate braids in her hair. The bookkeeper wears brown herringbone and tweed suits with a pheasant-feathered hat. The fashion designer is a profusion of pink, with silk roses dotting her dresses and sometimes a touch of yellow to match her wavy bob. The embroiderer wears shimmery lace with secret blue petticoats hidden beneath her skirts... to match her sapphire eyes. The four seem so happy together; it is almost as unbelievable as their wares. People come from far and wide to buy their fabric and are always delighted by how wonderful their new cloak, carpet, or dress makes them feel.

"Like magic!" they say.

And it is.

ACKNOWLEDGMENTS

There were seasons where I felt like this book would never see the light. But there was a spark in me that felt it must be written, and that pull led me on synchronous adventures that I will always treasure. There were moments both magical and strange—like finding a ring of mushrooms in my garden the day I wrote about one, or discovering my sofa had become infested with moths when I'd procrastinated. I had an extraordinary time writing this book, and I'd like to thank the inspirations and companions who joined me along the way.

While my baby Oliver went through eighteen casts and surgeries to cure his clubfoot, I would hold him close and imagine his cast was a cocoon, knitting his little tendons and bones into the right shape. I wrote about Flora's sweater cocoon during that time, inspired by the magic of hope.

My friend Juliana took me to a river full of geodes and caught fireflies with me for the first time. That experience sparked the beginnings of this story. We've spoken on the phone almost every day for the last twenty years. I can't imagine life without her candor, advice, and encouragement.

My friend Sharon was the cutest thing I'd ever seen when we met in school, and she turned out to also be the smartest and bravest woman. She has taught me to treat everyone with kindness, and to not take anyone for granted.

When my friend Blaze and I first met, we were both mothers of young boys, artists, and had long-lost books. We decided to dust them off together. What ensued has been a collaborative friendship I could only have dreamed of. I am ever inspired by her illustrations, and my own have been honed by her artistic eye.

My unique friendship with my sister Lucy led to much of what inspired this story. Lucy means light, and she has certainly been a light to me when mine has been stolen.

My sister Spiro took me on an adventure in New Zealand, where we went to a lantern festival, glow worm caves, a forest of tent caterpillars, hot springs, Hobbiton… and everything said *yes* to what I had in my heart for this story. It culminated in learning about how moths in Māori culture are considered spirit messengers, and their celestial parent is a star.

All of the moths in my story are real! There really is American folklore about the Woolly Bear Caterpillar's segments (though it is only a myth), and the superstition of the Witch Moth being a harbinger of death came from Central American and tropical regions. I am indebted to lepidopterists and moth enthusiasts the world over for painting, photographing, and describing species.

The Clifden Nonpareil moth was first recorded at Cliveden Estate in England in the 1700s. Images of the house and grounds inspired some of my descriptions of Nuthatch Estate.

Leizu, the empress of China, discovered silk five thousand years ago. Legend says that she unraveled a cocoon when it fell into her teacup. I've always loved this story, and it fueled my imagination for Flora's cocoon foraging and caterpillar fascination.

The city of Lyons, France, is known as the world's "silk capital." Its history and connection to luxury designers inspired me to include some French influences in my story.

One of the people who taught me to look at the natural world with wonder is my father. Thank you, Dad, for telling me silly stories to distract me on hikes, pointing out all the birds, and making sure I have everything on the packing list!

I think everyone goes through a formative phase where they think nobody understands them and they have no friends. I want to thank my mom for not asking me to assimilate when that phase hit me hard. She's always told me I'm the brightest (she tells us all that), and while we roll our eyes, it's nice to know there's someone in the world who believes it is true.

My husband Beau was the first person to suggest I might like writing, and he would be the last person to ever tell me to stop. Thank you for telling me to never give up, for having faith in all my grandiose ideas, and ever being the calm in the storm.

To my three boys, Finn, Oliver, and Harry: You're just as much rapscallions as you are darlings to me. With twinkles in your eyes and ready smirks… I can't imagine a very interesting life without you. In a way, Flora is a bit of a sister to you; she took up so much of my brain during your childhood. I hope one day you'll appreciate why your mother was so obsessed with moths.

ABOUT THE AUTHOR

Bridget Beth Collins lives in Seattle with her husband and three boys. She grew up playing barefoot in the wild forests, gray sand beaches, and frothy gardens of the Pacific Northwest. She follows whatever creative whim strikes her fancy and shares it as Flora Forager online. Some of her favorite things are spicy herbal tea, meandering walks with her dog, getting crushes on flowers, and imagining herself in a magical world.

You can find paintings, flower art prints, and more at Floraforager.com

Books:

The Art of Flora Forager
Flora Forager ABC
The Fairy Journals
Flora Forager: A Seasonal Journal Collected From Nature
Metamorphosis: A Flora Forager Journal

Made in the USA
Monee, IL
24 September 2024

66463657R00184